MAC'S CABIN

C.J. Petit

C.J. Petit

TABLE OF CONTENTS

PROLOGUE

Boulder, Colorado
April 30, 1874

Bob Phillips rolled his empty freight wagon into the company yard as the early evening shadows stretched across the extensive grounds announced the end of another day. After he parked the wagon next to three similar heavy wagons, Bob stepped down and looked at the team of horses that still needed to be unharnessed and brought into the freight company's large barn and thought he should just walk away and let them stand there. But tomorrow was payday and he cursed under his breath as he began to undo the heavy leather harness.

He had this debate every day for almost a year now. He wanted to go back to his old life – the good life – but he'd put it off for some weak excuse or another, because he knew what he faced if he returned to that life. They were looking for him, and when they found him, he wouldn't live another minute.

He was sore and dog-tired when he left the yard and plodded along the boardwalk heading for his apartment, and as he passed Carrington's Saloon, he paused and looked through the window, thinking that maybe stopping for a beer wouldn't be a bad idea.

Bob was still thinking about it when his eyes drifted to a nearby table where four men were playing poker and he felt the tug of the old life calling again, until he noticed the hat perched on the dealer's head. He'd only seen one hat like that before in his life; an off-white Stetson with a plaid band around the base of the crown. He was frozen in place, staring at the hat when the last card in the hand was dealt and the brim of the hat tilted upward, revealing the cold eyes and familiar face of Wild Willie Patterson. Then their eyes met, and for a moment, Willie's eyes scrunched as his mind stripped away the full beard of the man staring in the window at him, then flew open in recognition.

Willie threw down his cards and shouted, "It's that back-stabbing bastard!"

Bob bolted from the front of the saloon and sprinted down the boardwalk, knocking aside a woman carrying her groceries.

His aches forgotten, Bob ran for his life, taking a right at the first cross street available and racing down 6th Street in an attempt to lose Wild Willie. He then turned into an alley between the back of the saloon and an apartment building, glancing behind with wild eyes hoping he'd made good his escape. He then entered the back door of the apartment building and waited in the mud room, breathing heavily and staring at the door, expecting Willie or one of the others to bust in any second.

Wild Willie, along with his three fellow poker players, had exploded out of the saloon and raced down the same boardwalk and took the same turn onto 6th Street, having not seen the escaping Ed Richardson anywhere in front of them. They glanced down the first alley, then continued down the street, splitting up to check every alley and store where he could have gone, but not finding him anywhere.

When they rejoined in front of a haberdashery shop two minutes later, each man was as frustrated and as angry as the other.

"Where'd that son of a bitch go?" Willie asked rhetorically as he scanned the Bob-less street.

"I didn't see him, boss. What was he wearin'?" asked Cookie Priester.

Willie shook his head and replied, "I ain't so sure. He had a beard and it took me a second to figure out who he was. When I seen that ricochet scar, though, I knew it was him. I know he wasn't packin' iron, though. He had a green, knitted wool hat on, too. After that, I just don't know."

MAC'S CABIN

"Do we keep on searchin', boss?" asked Jimmy Page.

Willie thought about it for a minute then answered, "Not right now. He's hidin' somewhere. Tomorrow we do a little investigatin' and see if we can find out where he's holed up."

Vern Porter, who was holding three jacks when they had been interrupted, asked, "Are we gonna head back and finish that hand, Willie?"

Willie, who was about to fold his worthless hand, replied, "Nah, too many cards were showin'. I'll deal a fresh hand."

Vern felt cheated but didn't say anything as the four men then walked back up 6th Street and turned left to return to their card game, still scanning the streets for their erstwhile partner.

———

Bob waited in the entrance of the apartment building for another ten minutes before opening the door and sticking his head out to make sure no one was watching. When he felt it was safe, he turned left and continued down the alley and then followed another alley to the back of his apartment building.

As he climbed the stairs to his apartment, he knew he had to leave Boulder quickly. Willie wasn't about to let him live. Wild Willie Patterson and his boys would hunt him down like a wounded deer.

He entered the apartment and heard, "I'll have dinner ready shortly, Bob."

Bob mumbled, "Okay." and took a seat on the couch in the small apartment. He glanced over at Molly and thought about taking her when he ran tomorrow.

He was still brooding when the door practically crashed open and Molly's eleven-year-old son, Tom blew into the room, leaving the door open.

"Close the damned door!" Bob snapped.

Tom came to a sudden stop, then turned and closed the door, muttering, "Sorry."

Tom then returned to the other side of the apartment where his mother was cooking and with a proud look on his face, said, "Mama, I got paid by Mr. Wilkerson today."

He then reached into his pants pocket and pulled out three crumpled one-dollar bills and two quarters, handing them to his mother.

"Thank you, Tom. I'm very proud of you. You keep this for yourself. You worked hard to earn it," she said as she gave him back a quarter.

Tom took the coin, slid it back into his pocket and said, "Thank you, Mama. It wasn't so hard. All I do is deliver groceries."

Molly stirred the stew and replied, "I wish you'd be in school instead, Tom."

"Aw, Mama, I'm okay. I wasn't learnin' nothin' anymore anyway."

Molly sighed and said, "I'm sure you could learn to speak proper English if you stayed in school, Tom."

"Mama, if I talked all proper like that, I'd get beat up."

Bob listened to the conversation and wanted to scream at them to shut up. He had real troubles that had nothing to do with proper English or carrying groceries.

After Molly had ladled the stew into the bowls and set biscuits and coffee on the table, Bob began eating and Molly would glance at Bob occasionally but not saying anything, knowing he was in a particularly foul mood.

When she began eating, Bob said, "I got a job that's gonna take me to Fort Collins for a little while. I'll leave you twenty dollars for expenses while I'm gone."

Molly just nodded. Maybe this would be the time when Bob didn't return. She was just so tired of his behavior, but she was trapped. He was her husband now and they couldn't get by on the fourteen dollars a month that Tom was making carrying groceries and stocking shelves. Their rent for the small apartment was twelve dollars.

———

Bob Phillips told his boss early the next morning that he was quitting and was paid his wages. He had to wait until the bank opened to empty the bank account, giving him almost three hundred dollars. When he had packed his travel bag last night, he had included his trusty Colt New Army pistol and gunbelt. He was glad he hadn't sold his horse and rig when he had first arrived in Boulder last year and was soon mounted on his gelding and heading south for Fort Collins.

CHAPTER 1

May 7, 1874
Fort Collins, Colorado

Mac Jones turned his horse to the hitching post outside of the land office, stepped down and tied his horse at the hitching rail. He patted his gelding's neck and hopped up onto the boardwalk and then entered the small office.

Once inside, he stepped up to the counter, spotted a bespectacled, small man sitting at a desk writing on a printed form, so he waited until the clerk finished writing whatever he was writing rather than interrupt the man in his work.

The clerk had heard him enter and after almost a minute of silence, finally glanced up and saw Mac standing quietly behind the counter.

"Can I help you, mister?" he asked.

"I'll just wait until you're finished. You seemed busy and I didn't want to interrupt you."

The clerk smiled and replied, "Now, that's a first. I'll be done in just a moment."

While he waited, Mac studied the large map of Larimer County on the wall, tracing different locations with his fingers and finally stopping at the junction of the north and south forks of the Cache La Poudre River. He then tapped the spot with his index finger and returned to the counter.

The clerk finished writing his certification of completion of a homestead and slid the paper into a box for filing later before he stood and walked to the counter.

"Well, sir, you've earned my attention, and I do appreciate your consideration. Now, how may I help you?"

"I've been working out at the Circle T ranch for the past year and I'm looking to find my own place, but not for a ranch. I want someplace that's a bit out of the way, and I was wondering if you have anything around the junction of the north and south forks of the Cache La Poudre River?"

The clerk's eyebrows rose, and he replied, "There are some staked out, but it's pretty wild country up there. On the other hand, there's great hunting and the trout practically jump into a frying pan just by asking. It'll be kind of hard to homestead, though, because the ground is sandy and there isn't a lot of open ground."

"I know the ground. I've been up there a couple of times and it was exactly what I was looking for, so I figured I'd give it a go."

"Well, if you wanted to homestead that land, it'll be hard, but you could do it if you want to put in the work."

Mac replied, "Now, if I understand the rules about homesteading, I can pay $1.25 an acre and only have to stay on it for six months before I can claim title to the land, is that right?"

"Yes, sir. Two hundred dollars for a hundred and sixty acres, and six months later, assuming you lived on it and planted a crop, the property would be yours."

"Another rule is that if I served in the War Between the States, that time counts toward the six months. Is that right?"

The clerk smiled and replied, "Again, you are quite correct. Do you have your mustering out papers?"

Mac pulled out a folded envelope from his pocket, removed the contents, and handed the stained sheet of paper to the clerk.

"It's not in the best shape anymore," he apologized as the clerk read the form.

After a full minute, the clerk slid it back to Mac and then held out his hand.

Mac shook his hand and the clerk said, "That's a very impressive piece of paper, Mr. Jones. You saw quite a bit of action and took a few hits, too. But how did an Iowa boy get all the way to Fort Collins, Colorado?"

Mac shrugged and replied, "It's a long story, but basically, after the war, I headed west and worked my way across the plains and here I am."

Mac then looked at the name plate on the clerk's desk and said, "Mr. Hopkins, I'll tell you exactly what I want. I don't want one quarter section. I'd like a full section of land between the two forks of the river, and at least one of the section's borders on one of the two forks. How can I make that happen?"

Elias Hopkins scratched his head absent-mindedly and after thirty seconds answered, "Well, there is one way of doing this, depending on how much you'd be willing to pay, of course. Now, with your length of service, the time restriction for one quarter section would be gone just by filing and building a ten by twelve dwelling and planting a crop. So, you could literally build a hut and dig up some dirt and I'd grant your homestead. Did you know that because they wrote that law and said ten by twelve, but didn't bother adding 'feet', some unscrupulous types are building a ten-inch by twelve-inch box and calling it a dwelling?"

Mack laughed at the idea but let Mr. Hopkins continue.

"Now, if you'd like to get all four quarter sections, you could pay the eight hundred dollars for the six-hundred and forty acres, plus the homestead fee, of course. Then, you could build a larger cabin in the center of the four quarter sections so there was a ten by twelve-foot dwelling on each quarter section. It would mean a twenty by twenty-four-foot cabin, though. Then, you'd have to till some land on each quarter section before the inspection. After that, it would be yours."

Mac was a bit confused and asked, "One large cabin could be built in the center of the full section and qualify as four dwellings?"

"Exactly. I grant that it might be a bit odd, but compared to many of the others I've seen, it's practically normal."

Mac then took a minute to think about the suggestion. He hadn't planned on building anything that large, but it wouldn't be that much harder than a smaller cabin knowing how many of those tall lodgepole pines were up there.

"Okay, Mr. Hopkins, let's do that. What do you have available?"

Elias Hopkins walked around the counter and approached the same large map that Mac had just inspected and pointed exactly where he had just tapped his finger a minute earlier.

"This is a full section about a quarter of a mile past the junction of the two forks. It's already staked out, so you won't have any problems finding the center. Just to let you know, though, there is a feeder creek that runs almost directly through the center of that location and empties into the north fork. Outside of that, it's probably the best place up there. You do have to worry about flooding, though. The Cache La Poudre runs deep after the snow melts in the mountains and can flood the lower sections of that property. It's running pretty fast right now, in fact."

Mac asked, "Do I have anything else to worry about up there?"

"Just the usual bears and mountain lions. Oh, and I do have to warn you about Black Eagle."

"I've heard about his little band of Arapahoe renegades. That's not even his real name. He was born Swimming Beaver but when he broke out of the reservation, he changed it to Black Eagle because it was the opposite of White Chicken, which is his opinion of all of us pale faces."

Elias laughed and said, "All of his group have changed their names to something dark and fierce. I don't know where they are right now, but they do operate in that area, too."

"Well, Mr. Hopkins, let's get the paperwork started," Mack said as he popped his palm on the counter.

It took almost a half an hour to get the preliminary papers done and Mac had to dig into his cash reserves to cover the eight hundred- and thirty-five-dollar cost for the land and the homestead fees.

As they finished the paperwork, Mac signed one last form and asked, "By the way, are there any other people up that way?"

Mr. Hopkins replied, "No, sir. You'd be the first."

Mac slid the last sheet over to him and replied, "That sounds even better."

They shook hands and Mac left the land office poorer in cash but pleased with his decision.

His next stop was to get a wagon and some mules before heading to LaPorte. He thought he would need more firepower once he was up in the wilderness and thought it might be wise to stop at the large gun shop, unsure if there was one as well-stocked in LaPorte.

He mounted and rode the two blocks to a store bearing a large sign reading Pete Hinton, Gunsmith, a shop he knew well.

Over the years, Mac had progressed from his old army-issued Springfield muzzle loader to a Winchester '66 Yellowboy and now a Winchester '73 carbine. He still had the Yellowboy and kept it in excellent condition, so he wouldn't need another repeater. He still had a Colt New Army pistol, too, but decided to buy one of the new cartridge pistols, preferably one that used the same .44 rimfire cartridge as the Winchesters.

He entered the shop, inhaling the intoxicating aroma of gun cleaning fluid as he approached the counter.

MAC'S CABIN

"Morning, Mac. What can I do for you?" asked Pete Hinson as he left his workbench, wiping his oil covered hands on a rag.

"Pete, I just bought some land up where the Cache splits and I wanted to pick up some more .44 ammunition and probably a cartridge pistol, too."

Pete replied, "You're gonna need more than that if you're planning on staying up there, Mac. You got a shotgun?"

Mac was almost embarrassed to admit that he didn't and shook his head.

Pete sighed and said, "That's something you absolutely need, and then, no offense, but I wouldn't go shooting any of those big bears up there with your Winchester. It'll just make them mad. I've got a used Sharps in excellent condition that I can let you have for a good price. It's a Model 1867 carbine and uses the .52-70 cartridge. It'll even stop a grizzly cold in his tracks."

"Okay, Pete. You sold me. Add the Sharps and the shotgun to the list. Now, do you have any of the .44 caliber chambered Colts?"

Pete shook his head and replied, "Nope. I'm out of stock of the .44s, but I do have a couple of .45 Colt if you're interested. If you're stuck on the .44 rimfire, though, I have four Smith & Wesson Model 3s that use that cartridge."

Mac was unsure of the Smith & Wesson, considering them almost toy guns. He was a Colt man and thought about those .45s for a minute before saying, "Okay, Pete. Let me see a Smith & Wesson and one of the Colt .45s."

Pete brought two boxes out and set them on the counter, before pulling the .45 caliber Colt Peacemaker from its box and handing it to Mac.

Mac hefted the pistol and found it not much different in feel from his New Army model, just a little lighter. Pete showed him how to load the pistol and after it was empty, Mac dry-fired the revolver before setting it down on the counter.

Pete then demonstrated reloading the Smith & Wesson and Mac's eyes lit up as the gunsmith simply cracked the pistol open like a Remington derringer, dropped in six .44 cartridges and then popped them all out at once with the extractor. After closing the pistol, he handed it back to Mac who put it through the same evaluation he used on the Colt.

When he finished, he said, "Well, Pete, I hate to break tradition, but give me two of the Smith & Wessons. I'll need eight boxes of the .44s, three boxes of the .52-70s for the Sharps and four boxes of birdshot and four of #4 buckshot for the twelve-gauge."

Pete smiled as he began bringing the ammunition to the counter and stacking them up before asking, "Do you want a scabbard for the Sharps, too?"

Mac rolled his eyes and said, "Yeah, I suppose."

After he paid for the large order, Mac asked him to hold it there while he bought his wagon and mules. He was impressed that he was able to get out of the gun shop with only having spent $97.35, but was pleased with his purchases, knowing Pete was right about the big-bore Sharps and the shotgun.

When he returned from the wagon builder, he was driving a heavy teamster wagon with wider wheels and a spare axle under the bed. And, instead of mules, he had four large draft horses in the harness, having met and succumbed to another good salesman at J.L Carlisle's Wagon and Carriage. The costs for the day were mounting and he hadn't even made it to LaPorte yet. But again, he was pleased with the strength of the wagon and the power of the draft horses that could keep the heavy wagon moving no matter what the load.

After loading all his new weapons into the bed of the wagon and tying his horse behind, Mac decided to make a stop at the hardware store and then the large dry goods store in Fort Collins, knowing they had a wider selection of goods than their counterparts in LaPorte.

MAC'S CABIN

First, he stopped at the hardware store and began with the basics for setting up his camp, starting with a large tent, and something he found next to the tent that made him smile – a portable canvas bathtub. Then he added a large tarp and some smaller tarps, two large coils of heavy rope and a large reel of cord, four sawhorses, and some two by fours and some wide boards just for temporary builds. He bought a heavy block and tackle for moving the logs before moving on to the tools: a one-man crosscut saw, two double bladed axes and some spare handles, a pickaxe, two spades, two hatchets, three different sized augurs and dowel borers, a hammer, a sledge, a heavy maul and a dozen wedges, two planes, hinges for doors and windows, screws, a barrel of nails, and then some empty pails and four bags of mortar. He finished the order with a sharpening wheel to keep all of those tools in working condition. After loading the big order onto the expansive wagon's bed, he drove the wagon to the dry goods store to finish the day's shopping.

There, he bought a standard order of food that would last him two weeks, more shirts and pants, some heavy work boots and two pairs of work gloves. Then, he spotted something that he didn't need, but he wanted. He bought a fishing pole, a large spool of fishing line and a card with assorted fly hooks, a net, and even a pair of wading boots. He wanted to see just how accurate Mr. Hopkins' statement about the trout jumping into the frying pan really was. He knew that deer and other game was plentiful in his new home, but fresh trout every now and then would be a pleasant change.

His last stop in Fort Collins was at the café where he had a good, hot lunch, which took him to almost one o'clock before he rolled the new wagon out of Fort Collins to begin the drive to LaPorte.

It was only twelve miles to LaPorte, but another fifteen to his land, and all of it was uphill, especially the fifteen after LaPorte. Mac figured three hours to LaPorte and four to his building site.

———

Back in Boulder, after Tom had left for the day, Molly left the apartment and walked to the freight office. She needed to know if Bob was going to return this time or if he was really gone for good. He'd been gone a week and she wanted to know.

Thirty minutes later, an unsurprised, but despondent Molly Phillips entered the apartment and flopped onto the couch. Bob had lied to her. When she had asked the foreman of the freight company about Bob, he had told her that Bob had quit, and had not been sent to Fort Collins as he had claimed.

Molly realized that he had abandoned her and Tom as he had threatened to do several times in the past year. He had even been gone a full day twice but had returned each time. Now, he wouldn't be coming back.

All she had was the twenty dollars that he had left her and the money from Tom that she had been setting aside. She didn't have access to the bank account, either, although she doubted if it was still there.

She was on her own again, and this time, she was still married and couldn't even find another husband to support her and Tom. It was even worse than when Chester had died.

Molly just stared at the blank wall twelve feet away for fifteen minutes and then slowly lowered her face into her hands and began to cry.

———

Bob Phillips had arrived in Fort Collins and spent a few days more or less in hiding. He had enough money, but ever since that stage holdup, he had considered it his getaway money and even though he had used some of it, he still wanted to keep it with him in case he had to run again. *What kind of blasted luck had him run into Wild Willie in Boulder?*

He had found a job at J.L Carlisle's Wagon and Carriage and taken a room at Johnson's Boarding House for the time being until he decided what to do.

While he was at work that day, he had seen Mac enter and negotiate for a new freight wagon and a team of draft horses and had heard bits and pieces of the negotiations. The man was building a cabin all by himself north of LaPorte, and he had money enough to buy the wagon and the expensive draft horses, too. Bob filed it away for future reference. But for now, he'd stay here until he was sure it was safe. The job wasn't much, but it was safe and away from Wild Willie and his P boys.

When he had been running with Wild Willie, he was the odd man out, the only one with a last name that didn't start with a 'P'. It was close, though. He used his real name, Ed Richardson, when he was in the gang and had often joked about being a 'P' with a large appendage, but now, his former acquaintances were the last people on the planet he wanted to see.

When they had robbed the Denver to Boulder stage a little over a year ago and made off with almost four hundred dollars in loot, they had been identified by several witnesses, and Cookie Priester's pinto made it easy for the law to catch up with them.

They thought they had gotten away clean, but the pinto changed that when they stopped in the small town of Preston. All four of the 'P' boys were in the saloon having a beer while Ed had gone to the dry goods store to buy some more ammunition. When he was returning with the two boxes of cartridges, he spotted a lone lawman looking at Cookie's pinto, then cocking the hammers of his shotgun and slowly walking to the saloon. Instead of pointing his cocked revolver at the back of the sheriff to assist his gang brothers, Ed had trotted over to the horses as the sounds of a confrontation began inside the building, emptied their stolen money from Wild Willie's saddlebags, climbed up on his gelding and walked the horse out of town, then rode more quickly once he was clear.

He had continued on without stopping to Boulder and hadn't shaved for a month as he laid low.

But he had made the mistake in believing that Wild Willie and the others would hang, but they had never even made it to a jail cell. They had put up their hands letting the sheriff lead them out of the saloon, and as they entered the jail, Cookie Priester had feigned a trip and fall, distracting the sheriff, who was quickly set upon by the other three. They had beaten the sheriff to death to avoid any noisy gunshots, returned to their horses and made a clean getaway, heading in the opposite direction that Ed had taken, ironically abandoning Ed Richardson, who they thought was still in the dry goods store. They didn't discover the missing loot until they were fifteen miles out of town, and couldn't go back, not with a dead sheriff behind them.

When Ed had arrived in Boulder, he adopted the Bob Phillips persona, grew a full beard, and then married Molly Saunders, who was recently widowed. He needed to blend in, and married men were less suspicious than single men, and besides there was that other advantage. He was a lusty man and needed regular satisfaction. She even came equipped with a kid, making him a family man, which made him laugh at the idea. But he didn't like the boy, barely tolerating the kid to have his mother warm his bed. He had even taken on a job as a freighter and had settled into a routine, but much hated, boring life that was safe from discovery by the law or Wild Willie. At least it was safe until he looked into that window at Carrigan's Saloon.

Now, he was working and hiding in Fort Collins. He decided he'd look around for another widow, only this one without a kid. He was getting lonely and he didn't want to keep visiting Mother Evelyn's bordello.

———

As the draft horses pulled the wagon easily up the steady incline toward LaPorte, Mac reached behind the driver's seat of his wagon and removed one of the Smith & Wessons and loaded it with cartridges. He had almost forgotten to buy a gunbelt with cartridge loops before he left the shop, but Pete had reminded him of that omission. The man may be a good gunsmith, but he was a better salesman, probably better than the one at the wagon builder's, but not as costly.

He changed gunbelts after filling the cartridge loops with ammunition, then wrapped the old belt around his old, trusty Colt New Army and its holster and put it into the bag with the new guns.

After he was comfortably wearing his new revolver and gunbelt, he took out the shotgun, loaded it with buckshot and slipped it back into the bag before removing the Sharps. As the carbine version, it was shorter and lighter than the rifle or musket, but he appreciated the power of the .52-70 cartridge. He really didn't hope to have to find out how effective it was against grizzlies, but he sure would like the range for bringing down an antelope.

He knew LaPorte may not have had as many well-stocked shops as Fort Collins, but it did have an all-important lumber mill, which would save him a lot of work. Even then, it would be weeks of twelve to fourteen-hour days of back-breaking labor to construct his new home.

For seven years now, he had envisioned his cabin in the woods — his remote refuge from the past. It would be his sanctuary, and he had to build it by himself as his penance.

———

Mac arrived at LaPorte earlier than he expected and pulled the wagon up to the diner first, so he could get something to eat before continuing on, knowing he wouldn't want to cook anything after he arrived. He'd want to find the building site and do some critical exploring.

He hopped down from the wagon and trotted up the steps to the diner and walked inside, finding an empty table near the window so he could keep an eye on his wagon and horse.

Thirty minutes later, Mac paid for his dinner, walked out to the wagon and stepped into the driver's seat and snapped the reins, guiding the big draft horses away from the diner and left LaPorte as the setting sun blazed in his eyes, almost wishing he wore a hat with a brim.

He drove the team across a roadless track keeping the Cache La Poudre River to his left, and before sunset turned out the lights, found a suitable camping site six miles out of town and angled the heavy wagon toward the location. He didn't need a campfire, so he just parked the wagon near a creek and stepped down. After taking the draft horses out of harness and bringing them to the stream and then ground hitching them in some fresh grass, he unsaddled his gelding and let him drink and graze.

The wagon's bed was stuffed and covered with the large tarp, so he unraveled his bedroll near the wagon, kicked off his boots, took off his new gunbelt and slid into the bedroll. He kept the gunbelt near his right hand as he laid on his back watching the stars beginning to flicker in the night sky.

It had been such a long, convoluted journey that had led him to lying beside a wagon containing the tools of his new life, staring into the cooling Colorado night, and wondering if the land and cabin were the end of that trail. If they weren't, he had no idea what he would do.

Mac's eyes popped open when he felt something wet and squishy smack into his forehead. He automatically swiped at it and soon wished he hadn't. He looked around at the offending bird and slid out of the bedroll, then, still in his stockinged feet, he carefully wound his way to the nearby creek and washed his hands and face of the bird bomb. He hoped it wasn't a harbinger of the rest of his day.

He didn't have a big breakfast, just coffee, jerky and hardtack biscuit. It took him longer to harness the team and saddle his horse, but an hour after that inauspicious start to the day, he was in the driver's seat and heading northwest, continuing his climb to his new property.

Under normal conditions, the remaining ten-mile wagon drive would take two hours, but this route was far from normal, and by the time Mac reached the split in the river, it was already after ten o'clock, but the scenery had been getting more and more spectacular as he rose into the wide pass. He finally reached his destination when he saw the split where the river's two forks joined before the water made its mad dash down to LaPorte. He spent another twenty minutes finding a ford across the northern fork of the Cache La Poudre before driving the team and wagon through the fifty-foot wide fast-running northern fork of the river. He kept an eye on the depth of the water as it splashed against the wagon's wheels as they rolled along the rocky bed. He had taken the precaution of moving anything that couldn't afford to get wet to the top of his full load and was grateful for the wide wheels of the freight wagon and the power of the four draft horses as it crossed through the rocky-bottomed waterway.

The river was only a little over three feet deep at the ford, the wagon leaving the river just five minutes after entering and the wagon's bed had remained reasonably dry during the transit, despite the torrent caused by melting snow. Once across, Mac tried to find the marker that was supposed to be there marking the southeast corner of his property, but didn't see it anywhere, suspecting it had been swept away in the spring flooding. It wasn't the critical marker anyway, but he knew he was on his land and turned northwest again, heading for the center marker where he would have to build his large cabin.

The huge forest that covered his land had a finger of trees that jutted out along the northern fork of the river, so he steered the wagon around the tree line, and after a couple of hundred yards of stone-covered ground, he reached normal earth and entered the forest, crossing through the mix of lodgepole and ponderosa pines as he worked his way toward the center of his full section, wondering just how close to the center that creek was and how big it was.

Mac found the creek five minutes later and finally brought the heavily laden wagon to a stop and stepped down to find the marker. He kept the creek to his right as he walked scanning for the upright stick and still not finding it, the sheer number of tall pines making it difficult. So, he shifted further away from the ten-foot wide creek and a minute later, spotted the marker dead ahead.

When he found it, he looked right and saw the creek still nearby. With that twenty by twenty-four-foot cabin requirement, the distance between the center marker and the creek was critical. So, he stepped off starting at the marker and heading for the creek, estimating a yard for each step. He never even made it to step three, before he found himself standing on the creek's bank. That meant that the creek crossed just seven or eight feet from the center of the section.

He turned back to get the wagon and his horse as he began thinking of ways around the problem. If the creek had just been another five or six feet away, it would pose no great obstacle, but seven feet? That was a serious issue, but it was a challenge he vowed to conquer, adding the increased difficulty to the cost of his penance.

He reached the wagon, climbed aboard and flicked the reins to get the full wagon moving. The thick muscles of the four draft horses bulged as the animals strained to overcome the inertia of the heavy wagon, getting it rolling slowly forward seconds later. But it was a short run to the marker and Mac soon pulled back on the reins, set the handbrake, and stepped down.

After unsaddling and leading his gelding to a welcome nearby clearing of almost four acres of grass, he unharnessed the horses and led them to the clearing and ground-hitched them all with long ropes, so they could graze and even make it to the creek that continued along the edge of the clearing.

The first thing he did upon returning was to make himself a quick lunch that mimicked his breakfast, only without the coffee. He took one of his new tin cups and walked to the creek, and scooped up some of the clear, icy water to wash down the jerky and hardtack and made the mistake of treating it like normal water. He took a big swallow and when the ice-cold water hit his throat, he almost gagged in surprise. He had tasted ice that didn't seem this cold!

He put the cup on one of the many rocks near the creek and let it sit in the sun and warm a bit as he scanned the trees near the creek as a possible solution to his cabin-creek dilemma. He first thought of building two long cabins on each side of the creek to satisfy the residency requirement, but he couldn't claim to live in both of them at the same time, so he returned to an above the water idea.

MAC'S CABIN

As he examined the trees, strange ideas began to pop into his head, and grew even stranger as he expanded on them. Everything would depend on where those trees were.

He took the cup of water and tasted it first and marveled at its purity. All he could taste was wet and cold. It was very satisfying, too, as he drained the cup and returned to the wagon.

Before he did anything about his cabin design, though, he had to set up a permanent camp until the cabin was complete. He didn't want it too close to the site for the cabin as he'd be falling trees at that spot, so he set it up two-hundred feet from the center marker, or about halfway to the clearing where the horses were grazing.

It took three hours to set up the tent, dig a proper fire pit, and then move his food, weapons and supplies inside. Then, he spread out two of the small tarps and set all of his tools on top and folded the tarps over to keep them dry.

His final step was setting up the portable canvas bathtub outside near the tent. He was alone, after all and he doubted if the birds or deer would care if he was naked.

With his campsite all set, Mac needed to see about the trees and how they could be used to aid in his construction. He walked to the center marker and crouched down and looked at each corner of where he envisioned his cabin.

As he sat on his heels, his eyes spotted something in the creek that brought a smile to his face. He watched the trout fighting its way against the current, it's sleek body furiously working to defeat the onrushing water. Maybe Mr. Hopkins was right about the fish after all.

He then stood and walked to his supplies and pulled out the reel of cord and a yardstick. He began putting knots in the cord every three feet until he'd done fifty of the knots. He then cut the cord and set the reel down.

Next, he took off his boots and put on the waders, knowing he'd be crossing the stream at least twice and didn't fancy walking in that icy

21

water. With his legs deep inside the rubber boots, he grabbed a hammer and a handful of nails from the keg he had bought in Fort Collins.

"Okay," he said to himself, "I need a twenty by twenty-four-foot cabin, and it's got to be over that creek, that might get wider when that snow first begins to melt."

Then, he measured twelve feet from the center marker and looked to his left and found a lodgepole pine three more feet away. He walked up to the pine and tapped a nail into the trunk about four feet off the ground, then turned and walked to the creek, stepped into the water and crossed carefully, stringing the cord out behind him and counting as each knot passed through his fingers. The creek was just short of nine feet, and he found another lodgepole pine twelve feet on the other bank, tapped another nail into the tree four feet high, then began to walk parallel to the creek toward another lodgepole pine. It was almost twenty-seven feet away and after he reached the pine, he set the cord down momentarily and pulled out a small cord he had cut earlier, tied it around a nearby rock and hung it from the knotted cord. When it was plumb, he marked the tree with his finger and tapped in a nail, attached the knotted cord and removed his plumb cord. The cord was only about three feet off the ground at this end. So that meant the ground had dropped almost a foot in just twenty-seven feet. He then crossed the creek again and looked for his last pine for his tree-cabin. It had to be in just one spot, or close enough not to matter, and when he found it, it wasn't a lodgepole pine, but a much bigger Ponderosa pine.

When he checked the plumb on the cord crossing the creek, he was pleased to see that there was almost no difference in height between the two trees on this end.

He tapped the nail into the Ponderosa pine and then ran the cord to the original lodgepole pine and tied it off.

Now, he had the dimensions of his cabin: thirty-six feet, by twenty-seven feet. That was more than enough to meet the homestead requirements. He ran the math and realized his original small cabin was going to be almost a thousand square feet!

MAC'S CABIN

It also meant that the logs he would have to use for the base of his cabin would be that much longer and require much more support to hold up that weight. Not only that, he'd have to make full use of his ropes, block and tackle and his draft horses to move such huge logs. He also began to rethink the idea of a log cabin altogether. The base for the cabin would have to use some of those beautifully tall and straight lodgepole pines, but the weight of a log cabin built on top of the platform would be excessive. Mac decided then to make use of that lumber mill in LaPorte to build a frame house atop his log underpinnings. That meant that almost all of the strenuous labor would be in constructing the base. He'd make a barn out of logs near the clearing, though.

He removed his waders, put on his normal boots, then sat on a rock and took a stick in his hand and began to sketch out a design for the cabin, including some of his odd ideas, which would take advantage of building it above a creek.

He then calculated how many boards and what sizes he would need to finish the job and knew it would take several trips to deliver that much wood to the site. Maybe he'd have them load his wagon and hire some teamsters to transport the extra wagon loads of sized boards and columns he would need.

But the next few days would be his to prepare the foundation for his cabin. Once the platform foundation was ready, he'd return to LaPorte for the lumber.

As he lay in his bedroll in his tent that night, he began envisioning his cabin, adding doors, windows, a fireplace, and two porches; one in the front on the south side of the creek, and a smaller one in back on the river side. He took his plans past the cabin and added things like a bridge across the creek, a large corral near the barn, and a large smokehouse to keep him in meat.

But underlying all the plans and designs was the recognition of the original purpose for his cabin deep in the woods; it was to be his refuge and the labor in its construction was to be his penance for his sin.

———

The sun was barely above the horizon the next morning when he began his project. He had already eaten a big breakfast, knowing he would need the energy for the day's work.

He changed into the new work boots, grabbed one of the two-bladed axes and the one-man crosscut saw from the tarp and headed for the Ponderosa wearing a pair of new work gloves. Knowing how sweaty he would be in just an hour, so he didn't wear a shirt. He did, however, have his Yellowboy with him, leaning on a nearby lodgepole pine.

Because Mac had grown up on a farm, he was skilled in a wide variety of areas, one of which was felling trees. It was just a case of simple physics. Take away the support from the side of the tree facing the direction you needed it to fall and that's where it had to go.

So, he began to chop into the Ponderosa's trunk at the four-foot level to give him some margin for error when he needed to level the stump. He was making his cuts, so the tree would fall away from the creek.

Wood chips flew as the gash in the big pine's side grew into a wedge. Mac continued to swing as the sharp blade bit into the trunk until he had passed the halfway point. He stepped back, wiped the wood chips and sweat from his face and chest, then took a few deep breaths.

It had been a while since he'd done this kind of work and he discovered just how much he'd missed it. He set the axe against the same lodgepole pine with his Winchester '66 and picked up the crosscut saw. He'd be using different muscles this time, but it would be just as hard.

After only a dozen pulls on the large saw, he heard his first crack as the Ponderosa began to lean slightly. He glanced up at the tall tree and then made two more cuts and saw the bark beginning to pull away from the saw's steel surface. He made one more quick cut, slid the saw from the tree and quickly began stepping backwards as the pine began its descent, slowly at first until it rushed to the ground, its branches snapping off as they collided with nearby trees until it collapsed onto the ground and bounced once.

Mac walked back to the exposed stump and looked down at the rings and estimated the tree was more than twice as old as the country, having begun its life before George Washington began his, but it wasn't a time for philosophical meanderings. He needed to cut down three more trees this morning.

The lodgepoles were easier to bring down as they were more than a foot thinner in diameter than the three-foot thick Ponderosa and didn't have the thick bark of the bigger tree. But for him, the profusion of lodgepole pines was a real blessing. They were all tall, straight and gently tapered with high branches, making ideal cabin material. None of the trees in the old forest were shorter than fifty feet tall, and some were double that height.

As he cut down the three lodgepole pines that would serve as his corner supports for his floor over the creek, he made sure he kept the cuts above the cord nails, which was what he needed to level the stumps.

His last task of the day was to level the four stumps, using the crosscut saw to leave nice, flat surfaces that allowed for the change in elevation, so the floor would be reasonably level. He'd cut them six inches above the nails, which would make the platform higher off the ground.

He had worked straight through lunch and when he was finished for the day, he was more than satisfied with his progress. Granted, he had four trees he needed to clear away, but the four stumps were just what he needed to build a cabin that was four and a half feet off the ground on one end and three and a half feet on the other and would be safe from any flooding. It would be more than large enough to satisfy the ten by twelve-foot dwelling requirement on all four quarter sections, too, although he suspected that Mr. Hopkins back in Fort Collins would just take his word for it.

Mac washed in the icy waters of the creek and was cooking an early dinner to make up for his missed lunch. He had fried up some bacon and then tossed in a can of beans then let them simmer while he drank some coffee and admired his day's work, knowing that the next few days would be even more difficult, and would require some horsepower. He was suddenly grateful for the salesmanship of the wagon builder. Those big draft horses would do a much better job than mules.

As he sat and ate, he began scanning the rocky ground for flat rocks for his fireplace, finding them everywhere. and knew he'd be able to build a large hearth in his new cabin. He walked over to the creek and pried a nice flagstone from the shoreline and washed it clear of the mud from its bottom surface. When he set it aside, he noticed a bright rock on the floor of the creek, just beside the hole he had created. He reached down and plucked up a gold nugget that must have weighed almost two ounces.

He shrugged and put it in his pocket. Placer gold could be found in a lot of the streams and rivers in north central Colorado, so he wasn't surprised when he spotted it. To him, the gold would be a plague, not a gift as it would bring hordes of greedy, desperate men to his piece of paradise. No one would know about the gold if he could help it.

He brought the flat rock to the spot where he'd be building his fireplace and set it down and returned to his Ponderosa stump seat.

He was still designing the fireplace in his head when he heard the horses beginning to snort and whinny in panic, attracting his immediate attention. So, he hopped to his feet, grabbed his Winchester and ran to the clearing, and saw all five animals with the whites of their eyes showing as they stared toward the other end of the clearing and pawed the ground.

Mac cocked his repeater's hammer and walked slowly into the clearing, scanning the other side for the cause of the horse's distress.

He just reached the edge of the open ground when he spotted the black bear more than halfway across the clearing walking toward the horses. He didn't think the bear would attack the horses. He was

26

probably just curious, but a bear was much more valuable to him than it was a threat to the horses. He wished he had taken the Sharps, but it was too late now, but it wasn't a grizzly or even a brown bear, so maybe the Winchester would do the job, even at this range.

As he raised the carbine to his shoulder, the bear must have gotten a whiff of human and suddenly looked right at him, and rose to its feet, just as he squeezed the trigger.

The Winchester barked and the cloud of gunsmoke exploded from its muzzle as the .44 caliber round crossed the hundred and eleven yards to the bear and drilled into his chest, knocking him to the ground, but not killing him. He was rolling in the dirt when Mac's ran toward the injured bear, levering in a fresh cartridge. The bear was in pain and rising to his feet in anger, when Mac's second shot at a much closer range finished the job and the bear roared once before dropping to the ground.

Mac trotted across the clearing to the dead bear and kept his muzzle pointed at him until he was close enough to be satisfied that he was dead. Once he was sure, he returned to this campsite to get a rope, so he could drag the carcass back to his camp using a draft horse. Once he was there, he'd carve up the meat and get the fat for some invaluable bear grease.

Twenty minutes later, he was squatting as he dissected the bear, separating the meat from the fat as he carved. He tossed the fat into a pail for rendering into bear grease later, but the meat would be appreciated, too. There was so much fat that he filled a second pail, too.

When he finished, he placed all the meat onto one of his remaining two unused small tarps, and knew he'd have to build a quick, temporary smokehouse to make full use of the meat.

After he had removed all the fat and meat from the bear, he just buried the remaining carcass on the other side of the creek, knowing that it would still be found by the night critters.

When he returned, he trimmed some of the branches from the fallen trees and after making a wider, shallower fire pit, he built some racks overhead. He took out one of the steaks for breakfast but began hanging the other chunks of bear meat over the parallel branches.

Then, he created a tent out of the last small tarp using more branches for support and built a fire underneath the meat-covered branches, ensuring that the flames stayed low. He had found a dead oak just before the clearing and had cut some of the branches from the fallen tree and returned them to his camp for just this purpose. He began tossing the oak branches onto the fire, closed the tarp over the front and watched as heavy smoke began leaking out of the top.

It wasn't perfect, and would take a lot longer, but he'd have some smoked bear meat that would last a lot longer than fresh meat.

He then took a few minutes to think about the other requirement for homesteading: cultivating a crop. It was something he had done for the first eighteen years of his life, working the soil, so it should be the easier of the two requirements.

Speaking of soil, he thought as he scooped up some of the dirt near the bear carcass to inspect its value. It was sandy and not very good for most crops, but carrots, potatoes, turnips (not that he'd go there), tomatoes, peppers and lettuce all would grow well here. He could even plant strawberries, which he loved as a boy. He had plenty of water that he could divert for irrigation, too.

———

His first full day in his new home was almost over, and Mac sat near on the Ponderosa stump, having just returned from tossing some more oak wood on the smoky fire. He listened to the rushing water behind him and just listened to the enveloping night. It was never really close to being silent here. Maybe around Christmas when the snow was deep it would be, but not now. Not with the creatures that hunted at night – the owls, coyotes, and even the mountain lions. He could hear some of them digging at the bear remains across the stream and guessed they were coyotes. He could have just left it out to make it easier for them, but he figured he had to work to get it for them, and they should work to get their share.

He had cooked down the bear fat in his pot on his cooking fire pit earlier and when it had melted down, he had almost a gallon of bear grease, and had moved it all to one pail. It was a useful thing to have around. He had to wash out the other pails and the pot when he finished, but it was a small price to pay for the grease.

It was getting chilly already and he was still wearing his light jacket, so he left the stump to return to his tent, stopping by the smoke fire to add some thicker branches. He would have preferred an apple wood or hickory, but oak was pretty good and was grateful for finding it. There was still plenty left from that one fallen tree, too.

He was pretty tired when he slipped into his bedroll, and even though it was early, he slipped into sleep.

CHAPTER 2

The second thing Mac did after waking was to restart the smoke fire and toss in some more oak. It was still pretty warm inside the temporary smoker and he figured a few more hours would do it.

He walked down to the stream, washed quickly and then filled his coffeepot and filled a pot for warming some water so he could shave. He didn't mind shaving in cold water, but this water was beyond cold and he thought he'd be pressing his luck. He toyed with the idea of trying out the portable bathtub but put it aside until later.

After breakfast, he began his serious work on the foundation, and this was going to be critical.

After dressing for work, he returned to the clearing and moved the horses to a different location so they could continue to graze and brought one of the draft horses back with him and set him into a harness before tying him off.

He then attacked the Ponderosa first. He needed to cut some supporting logs to keep the weight of the split logs and the cabin itself from sagging or breaking the split log platform. It took him four hours to measure, cut and put the support logs in place.

Then he made a new knotted cord with fifteen three-foot knots and measured the thirty feet along one of the fallen lodgepole pines, made a cut through the trunk, and began to cut the branches on the long, thick pole.

Now, came the split logs for the platform. He took one of the axes and began cutting a split down the length of the trunk. When he was finished, he placed his first wedge into the cut and smacked it into the trunk with the maul, then inserted the remaining wedges in the cut and pounded them into the trunk, then worked his way back, having to make several cycles before he was rewarded with the loud crack as the log began to split.

After almost an hour of muscle-ripping work, the trunk was lying in halves at his feet, Mac knew that this was going to be a lot of work, but it was necessary work; for the cabin and for his penance.

He needed three, so after another three hours, had his support logs cut.

His final job that day was to use the draft horses to pull the logs into place over the stumps. It wasn't that difficult, but the center split log was annoying as the log kept knocking over the cut trunk supports. He eventually used the block and tackle to lift one end of the log and place it on one of the moveable support trunks, then move the block and tackle to the other end and lift that end and slide it sideways onto the Ponderosa supporting log.

He was completely exhausted when he finally returned the draft horses to their clearing with his thanks, then dragged himself to his tent and laid on his bedroll. He didn't bother waking for dinner as he just fell asleep as he was.

———

Over the next two weeks Mac continued to build his foundation, which began to look like the raft he had envisioned, as he began sliding more split logs across the tops of the three longer split logs that crossed the creek and served as a base.

There were two oddities in the platform when he had all the logs in place, the most obvious being the extended split logs for the front and back porches. The second was only visible when standing on the platform itself. There were two very different holes cut through the logs.

The first was above the creek, where Mac had chopped away the inside edges of two neighboring logs, leaving an eighteen-inch hole directly above the water five feet below. Then, on the shallow end of the cabin, three of the logs had been cut short and were supported by a rock wall on four sides with a rock base. The rocks had all been mortared like a fireplace, but in the bottom corner of the enclosure was a mortar-surrounded hole with a pine plug. Mac had noticed that the canvas bathtub, while useful, wasn't a long-term solution, so, as he was building his fireplace on the opposite side of the cabin, he came up with the idea for the built-in rock tub, which he could use after the canvas bathtub became too leaky to use.

The smaller, round hole had come to him early. He had running water right under the cabin, so he decided that rather than digging an outhouse and having to make the trip in the dead of winter, he'd be able to use his indoor, self-cleaning privy. He'd have to wall it off because of the cold air coming in through the hole, of course, but it was still going to be very convenient.

Now, he was ready to return to LaPorte to get his lumber for his building and for the furniture he would need. He'd buy a cookstove, too, but knew it would take more than one trip and he'd have to assemble it when he got it into the cabin.

He was getting low on food, too, so he'd need more supplies and the lumber. It was time to return to LaPorte.

———

Molly was lost. She counted the money she had and came up with forty-seven dollars, most of it the money that Tom had been giving her from his job. She had to make a decision soon. The rent was due at the end of the month and if she paid the rent there wouldn't be enough to pay for the stage from Boulder to Fort Collins. Did she stay, or did she go to Fort Collins? If she did leave, what good would it do? He had abandoned them and wouldn't want to see them again anyway. But he was still her husband and she had no future at all unless he divorced her or took her and Tom back.

When Tom came home an hour later, she told him that they'd stay in Boulder for as long as they could but may have to go to Fort Collins.

———

Mac had just finished his breakfast and took his empty plate to the stream, squatted on the shore and plunged it into the water, swishing it around and using his fingers to clear off the surface. As he did, he spotted another shimmering gold nugget just past the tip of his left boot. He pried it out of the sand and guessed it was a little bigger than the first one, so he just stood, pushed it into his pocket and returned to the tent to put the plate, fork and knife away.

He might not need the gold, but he'd need a good-sized chunk of cash for today's trip. He needed to visit his bank.

He had carried his cash in a money belt that had rarely left his waist since leaving Burlington, Iowa seven years ago after selling the family farm. It had gotten thinner during that first year away, but not by much, but grew steadily, and occasionally rapidly after that, especially during those two years as a bounty hunter. But the majority of the cash he had in the money belt was still from the sale of the farm and his mustering out money. Even after the war, Iowa farmland fetched high prices, especially when it was so close to a town. With the nice house and barn, he had gotten over five thousand dollars for the family farm, but it was down to forty-eight hundred when he had become a deputy sheriff and by the time he had finished his two-year career as a bounty hunter, it had swelled to well over seven thousand dollars. When he left the Circle T ranch outside of Fort Collins two months ago, he had almost seven thousand five hundred dollars wrapped around his waist under his shirt. Even after buying the land, and buying all his supplies, wagon and horses, and weapons, he still had over six thousand dollars.

Now that he had his home, he had found a cleft rock on the other side of the stream and left the cash and mustering out paper in the money belt, then folded it in some spare canvas before sliding it into the split and covering it with another rock to keep it dry and hidden.

He was driving his empty wagon across the creek, evaluating his work as he passed the odd platform structure, and when he reached the other side, stopped, hopped down, went to his bank, and took five hundred dollars before replacing the money belt and its covering rock before boarding the wagon and heading toward LaPorte.

Mac's drive into LaPorte was much faster than it would be going back because it was all downhill and the wagon was empty.

When he arrived in LaPorte, he stopped at the lumber mill and talked to them about what he needed and asked if they could deliver it to his cabin site. They told him it was no problem and after calculating how much he would need for his projects they told him they'd send six wagons tomorrow. He even included cedar shingles for the roof. They had a special, even larger double wagon for the long beams he would need, too.

He was glad he had decided to stop at the lumber mill first and realized that the cabin would be done a lot sooner now, which meant he'd need to stop at the hardware and dry goods store and pick up what he needed.

At the hardware store, he picked up a lot of hinges and latches and screws for the doors and windows, in addition to the tools for working the wood; planes, augurs, a dowel borer, hand saws, and a canister of glue. He bought two hand pumps and the necessary pipes to drop down to the creek, three cases of quart-sized Mason jars, and a small crate of empty canisters and four more pails. After he loaded the large order into the wagon bed, he rolled over to the dry goods store and added some more cookware, including a Dutch oven, a wider variety of food, including eggs, which he hadn't bought earlier. He bought a dozen bars of white soap, some tooth brushes and tooth powder, a stack of towels, which were handy for a lot more than just drying off after a bath in the canvas tub, and as a final item, he added a nickel's worth of mixed penny candy.

His last stop before leaving LaPorte was at the feed and grain store. He bought two large sacks of oats and then seeds for his gardens, which he would be planting soon. Once they were in the ground and the cabin was done, he'd be able to ride to Fort Collins and tell Mr. Hopkins that he had satisfied his homestead requirements already, hoping it would be within six or eight weeks.

It was a happy Mac Jones that flicked the reins to his wagon heading back to his camp site.

———

Bob had been unhappy since he'd been in Fort Collins, watching his money supply drop despite the job. It was because he was spending more money at Mother Evelyn's than he expected. He may miss having Molly around for that reason, but he wasn't about to go get her.

Then, Bob's luck changed. He was eating dinner at the boarding house when the landlady introduced a new guest. Mrs. Mildred Richards, a recent widow who decided she no longer wished to cook or clean her empty farmhouse and decided to live in the city. To Bob, that meant money, too.

She wasn't as pretty as Molly, but she had more meat on her bones and Bob preferred more softness anyway. He decided he'd introduce himself to Mildred later.

———

Mac reached his campsite by three-thirty and spent another two hours unharnessing the team and unloading his supplies and new tools. He was glad he had bought the penny candy, though, and popped a peppermint into his mouth as he continued to set things aside.

With the lumber coming tomorrow, he needed to think about how he would build the house. He sucked on his candy as he drew his plans in the dirt with a stick. It wasn't exact, but he could do that later on paper. He had the basic outline in his head, and the biggest problem would be the roof. He'd ordered one long beam and three support beams to keep it from sagging.

He had some of the smoked bear meat and one of the seemingly endless supply of potatoes in the hundred-pound sack, a giant spud that could have passed for a watermelon. He had also bought a big crock of butter, which he had missed over the past two weeks. He had also picked up some milk, storing both perishables in a quick creation, which made full use of that icy creek. Mac had dug a long hole in the creek bed, lined it with rocks, and used bigger rocks to block the current. He then stuck one of his pails in the front of the hole and used it for his butter while the large milk can occupied the other half of the hole, the swirling water keeping it fresh and cold.

After dinner and the cleanup, Mac climbed onto his raft foundation and stepped across the rounded logs making sure he didn't twist an ankle. They would be the support for his boarded floor. He wandered over to is privy hole and looked down to the swift current five feet below and grinned. He had already decided to add some logs across the bottom of the house to block the wind from crossing under the floor and helping to keep the house warmer, but that would be after he built the barn. If he didn't put those logs under the raft to block the wind, sitting on that indoor seat with the breeze racing past would be almost painful.

He then stepped out onto the front porch logs that stuck out from the others and was glad he had that idea, too.

His last two steps were the large stone bathtub and the fireplace. He still would have to add some flat rocks in front of the fireplace but other than that, the basic design was done. He would have two pumps; one emptying into the stone bathtub and the other at the other end of the house for the kitchen. Both would drop right into the creek, so they'd be easy to add.

After he hopped down, he returned to his tent to do some serious sketching and final designing on the house, which would begin seriously after the arrival of all the lumber tomorrow.

―――――

The next morning, when Bob Phillips reported to work, his boss told him and two other men that they'd be taking three of the new wagons to the lumber mill in LaPorte and loading them with boards and following three other wagonloads up into the Cache La Poudre split for a customer. The lumber mill would be providing lunch for them, and they should be back by six o'clock.

It was a good deal for the wagon builder as he'd get a good rental fee for the wagons and he was getting more money for the use of his four men than he was paying them.

So, Bob and the other two men assigned to the job drove the new wagons out of the builder's yard and after making the drive to LaPorte, loaded up the wagons with the mountains of boards, then set off north of LaPorte, the bizarre double wagon of lumber and long beams and yet another wagonload of lumber. Bob wondered who would be building something up in that wilderness with so much lumber. There must be two hundred dollars' worth of wood in the four wagons and the double wagon.

———

While he was waiting for the wagonload of lumber, Mac used the time to finish his plans for his house. The more he drew, the more extensive it became. He knew the first job, the flooring wouldn't be that hard, but he needed a smooth surface to stand on before he tackled the roof, which would not only be difficult, but it could be dangerous.

He had just finished a late lunch when he heard the crack of whips and the shouts of the drivers as they drove their teams across his ford six hundred yards away. He quickly cleaned up and walked to where he expected to have them deposit their loads.

Soon, the lead driver came into view and Mac waved to let him know he'd reached his destination. The man waved back and then the other wagons became visible after they passed the tree line.

Mac saw the long roof beam and wondered how he'd get the monster up there but knew that was the biggest challenge and was already working on a solution as the wagons drew to a stop.

"Howdy!" the lead driver shouted as he stepped down.

Mac walked up and said, "Howdy, I'm Mac. I see you have a bunch of wood to keep me busy for a while."

C.J. Petit

"Bill Henderson," he said as they shook hands and glanced at the platform, "that's a mighty peculiar piece of work you've got over there."

Mac laughed and had to agree with him and as the other men gathered around, he explained why he had to build it in that spot and why it was so large. But they had work to do, and began to unload his order, which took a lot less time than loading it had taken.

As they worked Bob noted the large campsite and the four draft horses in the distance. He recognized the man from a few weeks ago when he bought the big wagon and those draft horses and began to feel that nagging urge to deprive someone else of his wealth.

He was helping with one of the shorter support beams and asked Mac, who was on the other end, "Why are you buildin' way out here, mister?"

"If you looked around you, you wouldn't ask that question." he replied, but Bob didn't understand the answer.

"I'm Bob Phillips. You must be pretty well off to buy this much stuff." Bob said.

Mac replied, "I grew up a dirt farmer and went off to war when I was eighteen. I wanted a place to call my own ever since. I figure I can grow my own food up here and sell enough to keep me going."

"What can you grow up here?" Bob asked as he and Mac grabbed another of the three support columns.

"Potatoes, carrots, onion, tomatoes, lettuce, strawberries and all sorts of other things that like sandy soil."

"You hunt any?" he asked.

"When I need to. I got a black bear a couple of weeks ago, but I've seen a lot of deer, some antelope and the trout in the river and that creek seem downright friendly."

Then Bob scanned the work Mac had done so far and asked, "You do this all by your lonesome, or do you got a partner?"

"No partner. I did it by myself and I'll finish it by myself. It's like a sort of penance."

Bob was unfamiliar with the word, but made a quick assessment that Mac wasn't right in the head. *Who lives out in the middle of nowhere?* But he stored away the information for later use that he lived alone and seemed to have a decent supply of ready cash.

The loads stacked on the ground, Mac waved as the men climbed aboard the wagons, turned the teams and soon exited the campsite to return to LaPorte, and for some, like Bob Phillips, to Fort Collins.

After they were gone, Mac thought about the conversation with Bob Phillips. It had been a probing conversation, obviously trying to see if he had any money, but it was the man himself that had him searching his memory. The other men were all regular, honest working types, but Bob was different. More than that, he recognized him from somewhere, but couldn't make the connection. He was sure of one thing, though. He'd keep a Winchester close and, when possible, wear his gunbelt. He expected to see Bob Phillips again.

But that was for later. Right now, he'd start working out the method for getting those columns in place.

————

Early the next morning, Mac was busy laying down his floor using one-inch thick and eight-inch wide boards. Initially, he just hammered nails into the spots where the boards contacted the rounded edge of the log supports underneath to get them where he wanted them. It was a very fast job, compared to the previous jobs. All he needed to do was to trim them to length. He even made the floors for the big front porch and the smaller back porch. When he reached the indoor privy hole, he left a larger open square that he'd cover later with a proper seat.

He had the floor laid down by two o'clock that afternoon, which meant that tomorrow, he'd do the roof columns. The three center support columns were all twelve feet tall, and the long roof joist was thirty-six feet. All were eight inches square, so the weight alone precluded any kind of lifting, but that's where the memories of how barn raising worked came to his rescue.

He had a lot of big hinges in his collection of iron, and some angle irons as well. He had bought them for doors and footing supports, and now, they'd help him put up his main joist for his roof. But that was for tomorrow. His day was done, so he decided he'd celebrate the floor by doing a little fishing.

He dropped down from the floor and walked to the tent, took out his unused fishing pole, some line and a couple of fly hooks. Then, he donned his waders and crossed the creek and walked another few hundred yards to the much wider north fork of the river and tried his luck, tossing his line upstream and just floating it downstream.

Forty minutes later, he was almost giddy as he returned to his camp with three large cutthroat trout. He had released three other, smaller fish, and didn't doubt that more were out there that were even larger than the ones he had caught.

After gutting the fish, he fried the meat in bear grease with some salt and pepper and had a delightful dinner with another baked potato and butter and a large, cold glass of milk to wash it all down. A fresh cup of coffee at sunset which he enjoyed while dangling his long legs off the front porch capped off a very productive day.

―――――

Back in Boulder, Wild Willie and the boys had found out that their old partner, Ed Richardson, was now Bob Phillips and had worked as a freighter and even had a wife and kid, which caused a lot of amusement. Imagine Ed Richardson with a kid!

He had run, as they expected, and they assumed that he had taken the wife and kid with him, so they didn't bother trying to find her.

Besides, even if he ran leaving her here, he wouldn't have told her anything.

But it meant that they were closer to finding him now that they knew what name he was using, and Ed/Bob owed them for abandoning them and the money that he stole, ignoring the fact that they had abandoned him when they believed he was still in the dry goods store.

CHAPTER 3

Mac was ready for the big experiment. He had positioned the three support columns in the center of the floor. Then, he had stood each column in turn and when it was where he wanted it had attached one of the heavy hinges to each base on the side facing the river and carefully laid each column on its side, letting the heavy hinge keep it in place. His biggest concern had been the last column, which hung over the edge of the floor by ten feet and had placed a cut log in the spot to give it support.

Using one of the draft horses, he slid the long center joist over the three supports until it was in position and then screwed in some hinges on each side loosely but with long screws, joining the roof joist to the support columns. He was ready to see if this was going to be a total disaster and really wished he had kept the men here for a few more hours to do this, but it was too late now.

He attached a rope to the clearing side of the roof joist and tossed it over a thick branch high above his head before attaching the end around the horse's harness. Then he began walking the horse slowly, watched the rope go taut and then the contraption began to move. The long joist began to rise as it was being lifted by the rope and the three support columns that were anchored to their locations by the big hinges. It was the scariest part of the construction and he expected one of the floor hinges to break free or the roof joist to rip out of those loose hinges holding it onto the support beams.

But it continued to rise and just before it was level, he stopped the horse and heard the beautiful sound of the support columns slamming into the floor.

He quickly undid the rope from the draft horse, patted him on the neck and trotted quickly to the floor and began screwing the angle irons into place. After an hour each support column base had three angle irons holding them in place and Mac thought his right forearm would never work again. After it had recovered, he removed the three support hinges and replaced them with angle irons. The support columns were now anchored solidly to the floor, but he needed to secure the long roof joist to the columns six feet above his head.

He leaned a crude, homemade ladder against each beam and attached angle irons to the tops of the support columns and the roof joist before climbing back down. He'd add some flat angle irons to the sides of the roof joist tomorrow, but the hardest and most dangerous part of the framing was done.

———

Over the next week, Mac did the much more agreeable job of framing the outer walls and laying on the roof itself. After the terrifying job of raising the main joist, they were positively pleasant. Once the framing was complete and the roof was completed, he began putting up the outer walls.

As he worked, he kept an eye on his lumber supply and as he neared completion of the outer walls, he was pleased to note that he hadn't used even a third of the boards yet, which opened up many opportunities.

He hadn't planned on making inner walls, but with that much wood remaining, even allowing for the construction of furniture and the barn for the critters, there should be more than enough to at least line the inner walls and maybe make a wall for the stone tub, too. Why, he had no idea. Maybe it was just a throwback to when he was young and felt the need for privacy, something he never experienced in the army.

After another week, the place was looking very much like a real house more than a cabin. He wanted to have glass in at least two of the six windows, and that would require another run to LaPorte. He'd need to see about the cook stove, too.

So, early in the morning on Tuesday, June 12th, MacKenzie Lee Jones drove his heavy wagon out of his home, arriving in LaPorte at nine o'clock.

He entered Armstrong's Dry Goods and greeted the owner, Z.T. Armstrong.

"Good morning, Z.T., I need to buy some big things for the house and you'll probably have to order some of them."

"What do you need, Mac?" he asked.

"Well, the biggest item is a cook stove and the flue, and I'll need some mattresses, pillows, and all sorts of other things for setting up my cabin."

"Well, Mac, I may be losin' some business and irritatin' the missus, but this may be your lucky day. Jake Abernathy is sellin' his house and is tryin' to sell what's inside it first, figurin' he'll get more out of sellin' it that way. It's over on Second Street. There's a sign out front."

Mac replied, "I appreciate it, Z.T. I'll still be back for a lot of other stuff, though."

"See you in a while, Mac."

Mac left the store and drove to Second Street, saw the sign and entered the still full house, and introduced himself to Jake Abernathy. After inspecting the house, Mac made him an offer for everything that Jake happily accepted, not wanting to spend time dickering with women over a serving spoon or a hand mirror, or with men over a gun rack or a hand mirror.

Mac counted out the cash and Jake helped him carry the items he already had put in crates out to his wagon. They filled the wagon with chairs, tables, dressers and small things like lamps and rugs and mirrors. Mac said he'd be back for more, including the cook stove and the heat stove tomorrow.

He still drove back to Armstrong's to buy the linen, two mattresses and four pillows, not even noticing that he already had some waiting in Jake Abernathy's bedrooms.

When he entered, Z.T. asked, "How'd it go, Mac?"

"Well, Z.T., I think Jolene's not going to be too pleased with me because I bought all of it, lock, stock and barrel. Tell her I'm sorry for doing that, but I did need to fill up my cabin."

With the gift of timing seemingly inherent in all wives, Jolene Armstrong walked out of the back office where she had been doing the books, and asked, "Did I hear that right, Mr. Jones? You cleaned out Jake's house?"

Mac grimaced slightly and said apologetically, "Yes, ma'am."

After staring at Mac just long enough to make him uncomfortable, another wifely gift, she smiled and said, "I'm glad it worked out for you, Mac. I only had my eye on that setee he had in the parlor anyway."

"Well, Jolene, if you can talk Z.T. into helping me unload it, when Jake and I put it on my wagon on the next trip, I'll drive right over here, and we'll put it right in your parlor. In fact, there's quite a bit of stuff that I don't have any need for and you'd be doing me a favor for taking some of it off my hands, so I don't have to cart it all the way up to my cabin."

Jolene's eyes lit up as Z.T. groaned in the background when she asked, "Like what, in particular?"

"Well, there's the entire dining room, the setee and a sideboard, and some paintings for starters."

Jolene's smile grew as Z.T.'s anticipated honey-do list grew, and his back began to ache already.

She said, "Well, when you find things that you don't want, just stop by. I'm sure Z.T. can find buyers for anything that you don't need, and I don't want, either."

With Jolene's use of the word 'buyers' reached his ears, Z.T.'s back suddenly felt better. Maybe this wasn't going to be all bad after all.

Mac said, "Well, I would appreciate your doing that, Jolene. And, Z.T., you keep all the profits from the sale. You did me a great favor by telling me about Jake selling his things."

Now *that* was music to Z.T.'s ears.

"Mighty big thanks, Mac," said Z.T., "I'll be glad to help."

After Mac bought the unnecessary bedding, as well as some more food, he and Z.T. loaded his supplies onto the overflowing wagon. He stepped up into the driver's seat, flicked the reins, and waved to the Armstrongs before starting his return home.

———

Mac couldn't believe his luck as he drove back to his house. He wouldn't have to build his own furniture and that meant he'd have a lot of leftover wood, so the barn could be bigger, and he'd be able to make a bigger smokehouse, too.

He just needed to calculate how many more trips it would take to move an entire house of stuff to his cabin, even after dropping off a lot of it with the Armstrongs. Then, he'd need to store some of the things he wanted, but didn't need right away, too.

By the time he had moved everything into his house that day, it was well into the night, but he had plenty of lamps to put the darkness in its place.

———

As it turned out, it took five trips, even after unloading a third of it with the Armstrongs. Jolene had been downright gleeful as he and Z.T. had unloaded the items. His last trip, in addition to the last remaining items from Jake Abernathy's place, he also picked up his order of six glass windows, and twelve gallons of dark green paint, but a week and a half later, Mac had a more than fully furnished house, complete with a cook stove, a heat stove, dressers, two beds, complete with mattresses, quilts and pillows. He even had china dinnerware, glassware and flatware. He still had to add the windows, doors, build some counters, install the pumps and build the interior walls before he finally painted the place, but it was almost there.

The cook stove had almost turned into a disaster when the ramp he had built to move the heavier pieces from the wagon to the house almost cracked under the combined weight of the stove part and his added mass. He hadn't realized just how much more he weighed after almost two months of heavy labor for twelve hours a day, seven days a week. His usual one-eighty had ballooned to two-ten, and none of it was fat.

He was almost overwhelmed with how this had all turned out and was even luckier that the rains had only been sporadic, and the tall pines kept most of the rain off the wood.

By the last day of June, his house was complete. He had added interior walls, creating two bedrooms in addition to putting up walls around the bathtub and the privy. He built a kitchen counter with lots of open shelves, both above and below the counter, and installed a cast iron sink and his two pumps. His last finishing touch took longer than some of his bigger projects and began when he sliced a disk off of the fallen oak log's trunk. He cut the huge disk to shape, then planed and smoothed it as much as he could, and finally put hinges on the back. As he installed the seat for his indoor privy, he found himself giggling constantly as he screwed it in place, still hearing the rushing water just five feet below him.

He was in the first bedroom, which he regarded as his bedroom, and had stripped down for a bath in the stone bathtub. He had water heating on the cookstove and the heat stove in preparation as he walked naked to the bathroom and began pumping water into the tub. It took longer than he expected, and then he knew he'd have to wait a while for the water to almost be boiling to counteract the icy water that was in the stone tub. If it had been made of normal rocks, the tub would have been horrible on the skin, but he had used river rocks for the construction and used hundreds of smooth, smaller river rocks to cover the bottom, making it surprisingly comfortable. He had even angled one end of the three-foot deep tub, so he could lean back slightly.

After his bath, he unplugged the tub and left the tub as the water drained through a long hose into the creek.

He opened the top drawer of his dresser and pulled out fresh clothes and set them aside for the morning. When he first had opened the dressers, he had been surprised to find that they were full of clothes, but almost all of them didn't fit, which was a good thing, because they were all women's clothes. He had moved most of them to the second bedroom, anticipating their future use as rags. He still had the bottom two drawers filled with women's clothes, though.

It had been an incredible two months, and now he was settled where he wanted to be. He still had to build his barn and make those log walls below the house to keep out the wind, and make a smokehouse, too. He had decided he'd add a small extension from the front door, like a mud room, which would also serve as an entrance to a cold room he'd have to build under the cabin.

He even had time to plant four gardens for his seeds, knowing he'd have to figure out how to prevent rabbits from enjoying the bounty. With the exception of the potatoes, the other gardens weren't very big now, just enough to satisfy the homesteading requirements, but he'd expand them when he had the time.

With the house complete, his gardens planted, Mac felt a ride to see Mr. Hopkins in Fort Collins was due. By this time tomorrow, he should be the owner of a full section of paradise.

————

In Boulder, Wild Willie was still unhappy with losing Ed Richardson's trail, but figured Ed couldn't have gone far. He was guessing he had flown the coop to head to Fort Collins, the closest decent-sized town to Boulder. Ed hated small towns. He could have gone to Denver, but he was known in Denver, as they all were, so Willie was almost certain that Ed had gone to Fort Collins.

But money was running low, and they needed to do a job soon. They weren't about to get jobs, though. Work was for suckers.

The heist that he was planning was to knock off the Boulder to Fort Collins stage. The first Tuesday of each month, the printer in Boulder shipped a box of new banknotes to the Fort Collins National Bank. The guard pretended to be a businessman traveling on the stagecoach, but the leather travel bag he carried contained stacks of new bank notes, almost all of them one and five-dollar bills, but usually two each of tens and twenties.

They'd knock off the stage on the 7th of July and then continue on to Fort Collins and see if they could find their good old buddy Ed Richardson.

———

Molly hated herself. The landlord had come that afternoon while Tom was at work for the rent and said that he hadn't seen Bob around lately and, in not very subtle terms, said he'd help her with the rent for certain favors. He offered her five dollars and told her he'd pay her five dollars each week, which would more than cover the rent, but he would drop by to 'collect' when it pleased him.

She was going to refuse but had finally let him have his way with her. After he had gone, and she had made the bed, so Tom wouldn't know, then sat down and cried. She had become a whore.

She had recovered by the time Tom returned, then had packed their bags and told Tom that tomorrow, they would take the stage to Fort Collins and confront Bob Phillips. If she was a whore here, she could be one just as well in Fort Collins.

———

Bob Phillips was getting really tired of his boss at the wagon maker. The man was having him do a lot of menial work that any snot-nosed kid could do.

But the good news was that he and Mildred Richards were getting quite close. He had told her that he had lost his wife, too, which he thought was a brilliant play on words. She had been sympathetic, and

49

he had found out that she had over three thousand dollars in her bank account from the sale of the farm.

Everyone else in the boarding house wished the couple well as both had experienced the sorrow over the loss of a beloved spouse.

———

It was the first day of July and Molly and Tom were on the morning stage heading for Fort Collins. Tom noticed how quiet his mother was and he thought it was because of Mr. Phillips, which was partly correct. Molly simply couldn't believe she had sunk to that low of a level to keep a roof over their heads.

She had all of twenty-six dollars and change in her purse, and no idea what would happen to them in Fort Collins.

———

Mac didn't bother harnessing the team to go and visit Mr. Hopkins. He'd just take his gelding, Pete. He hadn't ridden Pete much the past couple of months, only using the wagon for his trips into LaPorte. He rode him twice riding the perimeter of his property, exploring the square mile for anything interesting. He'd found a lot of indications of game, including the omni-present white-tailed deer, some antelope, bears, including some large prints that he guessed belonged to a grizzly, more cougar prints than he expected, and one group of prints that did disturb him; moccasin-clad footprints. It wasn't a large band – maybe five or six – which meant it was probably Black Eagle and his not-so-merry men. But they had been old tracks, so they were probably gone. Nonetheless, he made it a point to be fully armed when possible.

He had moved all his guns into the house, of course. He had built three more gunracks in addition to the one from Jake Abernathy's house, and when he was outside, he kept one of the Winchesters nearby. He had finally used the Sharps as a tool and not a target rifle, when he had taken an antelope from three hundred yards just four days earlier.

He still had the tent up and had moved all his tools inside, along with some of the excess things he had from the Abernathy purchase. He had some of the larger items under the house itself, too.

But today, he'd ride Pete to Fort Collins, so it would be a much faster trip than with the wagon. He'd probably do some shopping while he was there for the things that he couldn't find in LaPorte. He still had over a hundred dollars in cash from the lumber trip, so he wouldn't have to raid his bank. He was thinking of buying some fire crackers in Fort Collins to celebrate Independence Day on Saturday in style, too.

Mac set out at nine o'clock that Wednesday morning, expecting to be in Fort Collins a little after noon.

———

Mac passed through LaPorte before ten o'clock and pressed on to Fort Collins, thinking, as he always did now, of his property and what was next on his agenda.

The morning sun was harsh on his eyes as he rode, and he wondered if he wouldn't be wise to wear a hat like everyone else. Ever since he'd mustered out and removed that blue cap, he'd never worn a hat except to keep out the cold, and that hat was a fur-lined cap with ear flaps that may not have looked as manly as a Stetson, but it sure was warmer. But that blue infantry cap had served no purpose at all except to make each man look just like the man next to him, so the colonels and generals didn't see men. They saw toy soldiers they could maneuver on a toy panoramic battlefield, and just shrug when a whole row of toys soldiers was mangled by the other player's grapeshot firing toy cannon.

No, he wouldn't wear a hat just to look like everyone else.

That war had scarred him deeply and when he had finally been allowed to return to Iowa, his father had opened those wounds and poured salt into them. But he didn't blame his father, it was his fault and he was still seeking a forgiveness that only he could grant to himself.

He finally broke the thread of thought from possibly buying a brimmed hat, to the war and then to his return to the farm, and let his mind get back to the subject of building the barn for the horses. He still had a lot of lumber left, but he'd build the walls with logs like a normal log cabin, but the roof, doors and stalls would be boards. He might even add a loft for hay.

He was in his normal planning mode as he passed the halfway mark to Fort Collins.

———

Molly and Tom stepped down at the Overland Stage depot in Fort Collins and Molly asked the manager if he knew Bob Phillips.

He didn't, so she decided to go to the café to get something to eat. She and Tom were walking to the café when Bob Phillips drove by with a new wagon and saw her and that brat and was horrified. *What was she doing here!*

He halted the wagon and hopped off and jogged over to Molly, who finally noticed him and prepared to let him have a verbal assault.

But Bob stopped her intended attack when he said, "What are you doin' here? You ain't even my wife, you know."

Molly was totally stunned and said, "What do you mean, I'm not your wife? I was there at the marriage ceremony."

"Yeah, I know. But Bob Phillips ain't my real name. I made it up, so that marriage license ain't worth the paper it's wrote on."

Molly was thrown into a daze and asked quietly, "Then what's your real name?"

"Ed Richardson. So, you may as well get out of Fort Collins. I got some bad hombres after me. It's why I run like I did. Here's twenty dollars. Go buy a stage ticket back to Boulder, but don't bother me no more!"

He did an about face and trotted back to his wagon, released the hand brake and cracked the reins. The horses responded, and the wagon drove away leading a shocked Molly standing in the street with her travel bag and a twenty-dollar bill in her hand. *What had just happened?*

It took another two minutes before Molly said, "Let's go get something to eat while I decide what to do, Tom."

Tom nodded, then they walked down the street to the café for lunch.

Molly imagined many bad things at the end of their trip to Fort Collins, but this hadn't been one of them.

———

Forty minutes later, Mac trotted Pete up to the land office for his meeting with Mr. Hopkins.

He dismounted, tied Pete off, and entered the small office, again finding Elias Hopkins sitting behind his desk, writing.

As he had the last time he was in the building, Mac just waited for the clerk to finish his work while he studied the map again, now being able to visualize the property that the map represented.

He was so immersed in studying the map that it wasn't until Mr. Hopkins cleared his throat behind him that he jerked in surprise, then turned with a grin, saying, "Sorry, I was woolgathering."

"So, I noticed. What can I do for you today, Mister...?"

"Jones, Mac Jones."

"Ah, yes. Mr. Jones, the four quarter sections up at the river divide. Don't tell me that you've finished your cabin and planted your crops in just eight weeks?" he asked with eyebrows raised.

Mac kept his grin and replied, "Yes, sir, I have. And, I have to admit, it's a lot better and even bigger than I had expected. You've got to see it to believe it."

"Tell me about it," Mr. Hopkins said as he leaned against his counter.

Mac then began vividly describing his new house, including the odd, over the creek construction and how he was able to furnish it so quickly. His hands were flying as he detailed step-by-step how it all came together as Mister Hopkins grinned.

———

After their lunch, Molly checked them into the hotel and went to their room.

Once inside, Molly said, "Tom, we can't keep eating at the café. Let's go over to the dry goods store and get some tins of food and other things we can use in the room while I decide what I can do while we're here."

"Okay, Mama."

As they crossed the street to the store, Molly was ashamed to think what she'd have to do. She knew no one here and had only one way to make money. Then she realized she couldn't stay here either, not with Bob Phillips, or Ed Richardson here.

———

Elias Hopkins still had a smile on his face when Mac finished his monologue when he explained his gardens, including potatoes, onions, peppers, carrots, tomatoes and even strawberries.

"Well, Mr. Jones, I've got to admit, that's an impressive amount of work for just two months. Most of my homesteaders take that long to build a small cabin, and they usually have help."

"I was working over twelve hours a day, every day since I arrived, Mr. Hopkins, and I was fortunate enough not to have any disasters."

"I'm going to mark your homesteading requirements as complete, Mr. Jones, but it sounds so interesting, if you don't mind, I'd like to come and visit sometime if I have a reason to go to LaPorte."

"You can stop by whenever you'd like. I'm kind of proud of the place, and I won't mind doing some bragging."

Mr. Hopkins laughed, then took a few minutes to fill out the forms, handing one copy to Mac.

They shook hands and Mac left the office with the deed to a full section of land that was his in perpetuity.

He mounted Pete and headed for Miller's Dry Goods. He had a hankering for, of all things, oatmeal.

When he reached the store, he stepped down, tossed Pete's reins over the hitchrail and stepped inside.

"Howdy, Mac. Haven't seen you in a while. How's that homesteadin' goin?" asked Joe Miller when Mac entered.

"It's almost done. I built my cabin north of the Cache River split, and just picked up the deed a few minutes ago."

"Well, congratulations, Mac. What do you need today?"

"I'll just go and pick it up."

Mac walked to the last aisle and after picking up the large tin of oatmeal and some brown sugar, he remembered that his fly hooks were getting low as some of the trout had made off with a few and headed for that aisle.

Tom was standing in front of the fishing rods and marveling at the beauty of the long pole with a reel on the end, too.

Molly was holding four tins as she stood next to Tom, wishing she could do something nice for him, but knew it wasn't possible.

Tom knew it as well, but still felt the tug of the fishing rod and imagined fighting a big trout as it struggled to get free of the hook.

Mac reached over and took a card of the fly hooks and looked at the boy staring at the unattainable fishing rod and remembered how he had wanted one when he was a boy; not a homemade branch with a string tied on the end, but a real fishing rod. He had never had one until he had bought his own a few weeks ago.

He glanced at the woman standing next to him and noted her worn dress and assumed she was his mother and judging by the look on her face, she wanted desperately to fulfill her son's wishes but couldn't afford to.

"That's a mighty nice piece of fishing gear there, ain't it?" Mac drawled.

Tom popped out of his imaginary fishing exploits, looked at Mac and replied, "It sure is pretty."

Molly also turned when Mac spoke.

"Yup, it sure is. Useful, too. I just built me a cabin up where the Cache La Poudre splits, and the trout out there are so friendly, all I need to do is walk out in the mornin' with my frypan and two of 'em just hop right in."

Tom laughed and asked, "So, you don't need a fishin' pole at all?"

Mac shook his head, then replied, "You'd think that, wouldn't ya? But you see, I told them trout that we have to follow the rules and there'd be no more jumpin' into frypans. I bought me a rod just like that one there, a big spool of fishin' line and some of these fly hooks, and whenever I'm in the mood for eatin' trout, I go out to my back porch, and throw my line into the creek that runs under my cabin and take the first two trout that are in the front of the long line of fish beggin' to be the lucky ones to make it to my frypan."

Tom continued to laugh and then asked, "You got a creek under your cabin?"

"Yes, sir. Seems that our government made these rules for homesteadin' that made me build my cabin right in the middle of my property and there was this wide creek runnin' right through where they said I had to build it. So, I cut down four trees and build it right on those stumps."

Tom tilted his head and asked, "Really?"

"Yup."

"How big are the fish that you catch?"

Molly momentarily forgot her troubles, was smiling and on the verge of grinning as she listened to the repartee.

Mac closed one eye and looked at Tom with the other as he scrunched his face and answered, "Now, that's a might hard question to answer, my young friend, 'cause when I tell ya, you won't be believin' me about my cabin with the creek underneath. But I suppose it would be impolite not to answer, so I'll tell you what happened to me about a week ago when I was out on the north fork of the river doin' my laundry. Now, I'm hunkered down on the rocks, poundin' my britches clean when I hear this loud roar and I jump up and see this big ol' brown bear standin' in the water on his back feet with his claws up in the air. Now, I'm scared so much, I don't move a whisker and suddenly, there's this big splash and this whale-sized brown trout flies out of the river and swallows that bear whole."

Tom's face was entranced yet covered with hilarity as Mac continued.

"Well, sir, that trout goes to swimmin' upstream and I could see that bear fightin' and wigglin' inside that giant fish's tummy when suddenly, the fish pops out of the water again, opens his big mouth and with an enormous belch, spits that nasty wet bear back into the river. The bear goes runnin' off whinin' like a scared puppy, and the trout looks at me, and as the lord as my witness, says, 'I thought he was chocolate'."

Both Tom and Molly burst into laughter while Mac just waited, not finished with the story.

It was Molly who sensed that more was to come and asked, "And?"

Mac smiled then said, "I was so shook up by then, that a talking fish wasn't even a surprise anymore, so I said to the fish, 'I didn't know that trout ate chocolate', and he says, 'Of course, we do. How do you think we become brown trout?'."

Molly and Tom renewed their laughter, with Molly having to wipe tears from her eyes.

When they had almost stopped, Mac finally finished the yarn by saying, "And just before he goes swimmin' away, the big fish says, 'Don't even ask me what rainbow trout eat.'"

Both Molly and Tom were still laughing when Mac selected one of the fishing poles and reels, a spool of line, two cards of fly hooks, a net and a set of smaller waders.

Then he looked at Tom and said, "Now, I'm gonna buy these here fishin' things cause I'm a forgetful kinda feller. I sometimes forget that I already have all of 'em at my cabin already. And then, after I pay for 'em, I might have one of my forgettin' attacks again and leave 'em at the counter for some other feller to have so he can have fun catchin' those trout, too. But these here wadin' boots are kinda small for grown men to wear, unless he's a short feller. I think they'd be just about right for a boy ready to be a man. Don't you think so?"

Tom couldn't believe what he was hearing and asked, "Mister, do you mean it? You're gonna give all the fishin' stuff to me?"

Mac scratched his head and replied, "Nope. I wouldn't do that, 'cause your mama would probably start sayin' things like 'we can't take 'em' or 'it's not right' or some other mama-talk. I'm just sayin' that if I left 'em at the counter, it'd be kinda silly for them to go to waste or let some other feller who don't even cotton to fishin' to pick 'em up, that's all."

Tom grinned and glanced back at his mother who was still smiling, which was a good thing.

Mac then turned and carried the fishing gear and his oatmeal and brown sugar to the counter. He paid for the order and then remembered what he planned on doing Saturday and said, "Hold on for a minute, Joe. I need some firecrackers, too. Do you have any?"

"Sure. They're out front, right by the window."

"Add five dollars to the bill and I'll go and get some. I'll be right back. Oh, and can you put one of the fly hook cards, the oatmeal and brown sugar in a separate bag?"

"I'll do that," then added, "that's a lot of fireworks, Mac."

Mac shouted back over his shoulder, "I intend to celebrate in style, Joe."

Mac trotted over to the front window and began loading up on different firecrackers, until he had a full armload, then walked back to the counter.

Mac separated the firecrackers into a big pile which included all of the bigger fireworks, and a smaller pile of firecrackers, then added two boxes of matches, one for each pile. Joe took the hint and bagged them that way.

After Mac paid the bill, he glanced over at Tom, winked and set the smaller bag of fireworks onto the fishing pile and then gathered his oatmeal bag and his fireworks bag and left the store.

He was sliding his bags into his saddlebags when Molly quickly approached, and Mac looked over at her.

"Why did you do that?" she asked.

Mac leaned on Pete and replied, "For the simple reason that I recalled what it was like when I was a boy and wanted a real fishing pole more than anything else in the world, but my father couldn't afford to buy me one. I looked over at your son and saw the gleam in his eye and knew that I could make that dream come true. It was a very selfish thing to do, really."

Molly smiled and said, "Thank you very much, then. And I don't believe it was selfish at all. I notice that you lost your drawl, though."

"It's not a tall tale without the drawl," Mac replied, "and it had to be a brown trout to make the story work, but there aren't any in the river. There are cutthroat trout, though."

"Do you really have a cabin over a creek, or is that part of the tall tale?"

"No, I really do. I'm very proud of it, too. It was difficult at times because I was working alone, and I still have a lot to do, but it's livable and I'm satisfied with the work."

"My name is Molly Phillips. It was my son, Tom, that you made happy."

"It's nice to meet you, ma'am. I'm Mac, Mac Jones."

Tom came walking out of the store with his arms full of boy things and a giant grin on his face.

"Thanks a lot, sir. I can't believe it yet."

Mac smiled and said, "Well, you just be careful with those firecrackers. Have your father around when you set them off. I don't want to hear that I caused you any harm by letting you have them."

Tom wanted to say that he didn't have a father, but was worried he might lose the firecrackers, so he just said, "Okay."

"Well, it's been a real pleasure meeting you, ma'am, and you, too, Tom, but I've got to get going. It's a long, uphill ride to my cabin. And,

Tom, you watch out for that bear-eating trout when you're out there fishin'."

Mac grinned at the boy, then mounted Pete, waved and turned him north as Molly and Tom watched him ride off.

Tom said, "I like Mr. Jones, Mama."

Molly didn't reply but just sighed and walked with Tom back to their rooms. She already had a very strange idea in her head, and it involved Mr. Jones.

———

Mac left Fort Collins and kicked Pete up to a medium trot, anxious to return to his house. But as he rode, he couldn't help but think about his encounter with Mrs. Phillips and her son. They seemed like such nice people, yet judging by her dress, she didn't have much. He began to wonder if there was a better use for all of the women's clothes in the dressers, but then thought he'd be sticking his nose in where it shouldn't belong. He probably went overboard in buying so many things for Tom, too. He hoped that the boy's father didn't take umbrage for a stranger providing for his son.

Then there was the name – Phillips. It rang a bell somewhere and he couldn't connect it with anyone. It would drive him crazy if he thought about it, but he thought if he let it go, it would suddenly pop into his mind.

He stopped in LaPorte on the way back for some lunch before pressing on to his house, following his tracks rather than even glancing at the river. If he kept this up, he'd have a regular road in a year or so, the broad wheels on the freight wagon making wide ruts that he intentionally didn't follow each time, so the trail would be flattened.

By the time he had unsaddled Pete and carried his things back to his house, it was mid-afternoon, and he thought there was enough time to start working on a proper corral before he made the barn. He'd split logs to make rails and others for the posts, but he'd use the trunks of some of the lodgepole pines as fence posts to expand the corral all the way from the clearing to the back of the barn, which he had already planned on building halfway between the cabin and the clearing. It would be a roomy corral, with grass, water and the protection from the wind afforded by the trees.

So, after Mac had put away his oatmeal and brown sugar, then left the firecrackers in the tent, he donned his work boots and work gloves, grabbed one of his axes and the saw, then headed for the woods between the clearing and the creek, still wearing his gunbelt, and carrying the Yellowboy.

By the time the sun was low in the sky he had felled four of the lodgepole pines for splitting tomorrow.

He was getting so used to the physical strain of cutting and hauling that he didn't even realize just how hard it was anymore. When he worked with the axe and saw, or the maul and wedges, he never wore a shirt, so he wouldn't have to do laundry as often, and as he worked it would be obvious to any observer that MacKenzie Jones, at the age of thirty-one, was now in the best physical condition of his life.

———

After they returned to their hotel room, Molly left Tom to admire his new fishing gear while she walked back to the dry goods store and stepped up to the counter.

"Excuse me, but that gentleman who bought the fishing gear for my son, do you know where I could send him a thank you note?"

"Well, ma'am, that might be kinda hard. Mac used to work at the Circle T ranch northwest of town, but he bought himself a whole section of land up north of LaPorte, where the Cache La Poudre River splits into two forks. He just told me he finished his cabin, too."

"He seems like a nice man."

"Mac's just about the nicest feller I know. I'm gonna miss havin' him around, too."

"His wife is a very lucky woman," Molly said.

"Oh, Mac's not married. He's up there by his lonesome."

"Well, thank you, sir," Molly said.

"You're welcome, ma'am."

Molly left the store, thinking how absolutely insane tomorrow would be. She just didn't see any other option other than the one she had already been reduced to in Boulder. She just hoped that Mr. Jones really was a good man.

CHAPTER 4

After his first breakfast of oatmeal with coffee, Mac readied himself for the job of rail splitting. He'd keep the rail lengths reasonable at twelve feet, so he should be able to get sixteen rails out of each of the four pines he had dropped yesterday. He would use his knotted cord to keep the cuts reasonably the same length. They didn't have to be as accurately cut as the boards for the house had to be, but he wanted them to look good.

So, Mac Jones left his house at eight o'clock, made two trips to the downed trees with his axe, saw, maul and wedges to start work on his corral.

———

The coach was leaving at nine o'clock, so after breakfast at the café, Molly Phillips and Tom boarded the Fort Collins to LaPorte stagecoach.

As the coach rolled along, it was Tom, who had reluctantly given up his fishing pole to the driver for storage on the roof, who said, "Mama, why are we going to LaPorte?"

Molly answered, "Tom, we are going to see Mr. Jones and see if we can stay at his cabin."

Tom grinned and said, "Good. Do you think he'll take me fishin'?"

Molly smiled at her son and replied, "I'm sure he will, Tom."

———

Mac was working like a demon on the logs, having already split two of the twelve-foot long logs into four thick rails. He began dragging and aligning the rails along the path that he had in his head for the corral to get a more accurate idea of how many rails he would need. He already had ninety-six feet of rails along the ground and hadn't even reached the clearing yet. He wanted at least fifty feet into the clearing, so he finally came up with around a hundred rails.

He had a pail of water on one of the stumps with a tin cup inside, and by noon, he had drained the pail dry, and decided to take a break for lunch. His rail total was already thirty-six, so only a measly sixty-four to go before he started on the posts.

———

After arriving in LaPorte, Molly and Tom had lunch at the diner, before beginning their journey. She had no idea how far it was to the cabin, and assumed it wasn't more than ten miles.

So, after they finished eating, Molly grabbed the two travel bags, and Tom took his fishing gear and his fireworks, then they walked out of town keeping the river on their left, but soon found the wagon tracks leading them to Mr. Jones' cabin and followed that path.

Even if it was only ten miles, Molly hadn't counted on the constant upward slope. Neither she nor Tom was very strong, and the baggage began weighing heavily on them after three miles. Finally, Molly suggested that they leave some things behind a nearby rock and come back and get them later.

They each had a single travel bag after stowing their other things behind the boulder and pressed on. When they got thirsty, they'd swing by the river and get some water to drink in the small pools that would form alongside the faster moving current.

It seemed like days as they plodded up the steady incline as the Cache La Poudre River roared alongside.

———

After lunch, Mac attacked the lodgepole logs again, getting even more into the rhythm of the job. Before he cut the first log, he had made his first cut at twenty feet, so the thick end of the trunk could be

65

used for the barn and the thinner end for the rails. It still gave him three twelve-foot logs, or a dozen rails for each tree, so he had to take down four more trees to give him enough rails.

It was past five o'clock when he finally called an end to the day when he finished splitting his sixtieth rail. He was covered in wood chips, and sweating profusely when he left the worksite, and the thought of a bath sounded pretty good as he began moving his tools to his tent.

———

Molly and Tom were exhausted after the fifteen-mile walk up the steady incline when they came to the river's ford. Molly's legs had been cramping for the past two miles and she just didn't think she could go on any further.

They both stared at the swiftly flowing water and Molly asked, *"How can we cross that?"*

Tom suddenly smiled, pulled his wading boots that he had draped over his shoulder, and replied, "I'll just put on the wading boots that Mr. Jones gave me, Mama, and I'll cross the river and tell him to come and get you."

Molly was hesitant as she looked at the fifty-foot wide river racing past and said, "Maybe we should just shout for him."

"Mama, he's too far away and the river makes too much noise. I can make it. It's only three feet deep."

She didn't want Tom to be swept away, but she didn't see any other option, so she said, "Okay, but be very careful, Tom. Please don't fall. If you feel like you can't make it, turn back."

"I won't fall, Mama!" Tom shouted with the enthusiasm only a boy could have over the prospect of crossing a rapid current.

She watched as Tom pulled off his leather boots and then climbed inside the long, rubberized boots, pulling the suspenders over his small shoulders. He smiled at his mother and was proud that he could help for a change and stepped into the water.

Tom slowly stepped into the deeper water, getting a feel for the riverbed and the current as he walked carefully across. The deeper the water became, the harder it was for him to stand, and he began to lean more and more into the current. He didn't understand the power of the water flowing past his legs. He wasn't halfway across and began to have a problem as soon as he lifted one foot off the bottom of the river, so he began shuffling his feet more slowly.

Molly was horrified a she watched him fighting the current and shouted, "Be careful, Tom!"

Tom waved but was beginning to think this was a bad idea himself. He only weighed eighty pounds and he could feel his footing beginning to slip, despite his sliding steps.

Then she shouted again, "Come back, Tom! I want you to come back now!"

———

Mac thought he was losing his mind when he thought he heard a woman shout in the distance as he walked back to the cabin. Then, he heard a second shout and knew he wasn't imagining things.

He began to run at a decent pace toward the sound of the shout which was near the river's ford a couple of hundred yards away. He just cleared the tree line when he heard the woman scream and saw a boy flailing in the swift current as he was swept downstream.

Mac didn't bother to even look at the woman as he broke into a sprint heading for the river ahead of the struggling boy.

Tom was fighting for his life as the water tugged at him and rolled him one way and then ripped him right back in the other direction. The shock of the cold water added to his abject terror of what would soon drag him under the surface, his waders filling with the frigid water.

Molly was preparing to run into the river, despite her inability to swim, when she saw Mac sprinting across her vision in a dead run toward the river's edge, then suddenly stretch out and fly across the water before knifing into the boiling river.

He emerged again twenty feet further downstream and in five powerful strokes grabbed Tom by his suspenders and stood in the four-foot deep water.

The water had closed over Tom's head and he had simply given up, succumbing to the inevitable, when he felt a hard pull on one of his suspenders and was suddenly yanked back into the life-giving air. He gasped as he was being dragged by powerful strides, and then began hacking up the water that he had inhaled.

Mac walked through the icy, raging water, his work boots giving him a solid grip on the riverbed as he took hold of Tom's second suspender loop and pulled him toward the shore eighteen feet away.

When he reached the shore, he rolled Tom onto his stomach, then began pounding his back as he shouted, "Tom, are you all right?"

Tom responded by regurgitating a gush of water as Mac continued to thump his back.

After another thirty seconds of spitting and spluttering, Tom squeaked, "I think I'm okay."

Mac knelt upright, looked upriver and shouted, "He's all right, Mrs. Phillips. You stay there, and I'll be back in a little while."

Molly felt an incredible surge of relief and waved her thanks to Mac, before sitting on her travel bag and crying over the release of the fear for the near loss of her son.

Mac rolled Tom onto his back and scooped him into his arms and carried him easily across the stony ground. He noticed that Mrs. Phillips was sitting on a travel bag with another nearby and wondered what had precipitated their leaving Fort Collins.

Tom's eyes were still closed as Mac reached the cabin, climbed the steps to the front porch and carried him inside.

He carried him into the first bedroom, set him gently on the floor and then said, "Tom, are you awake?"

Tom's eyes fluttered for a second then he looked at Mac and asked, "Mr. Jones?"

Mac smiled and replied, "There aren't too many other people around here, Tom. Now, did you want to get undressed or did you want me to help you?"

"I can do it, but my other clothes are all in my travel bag."

"I'll go get them and your mother in a minute. After you take off your wet clothes, just dry yourself off and then get into the bed and crawl under the blankets and quilts. You'll feel better soon enough. Okay?"

"Okay."

Mac pulled Tom to his feet, made sure he wasn't going to fall, then walked to the bathing room and took two towels from the stack and set them near Tom, who was struggling to get out of his waders.

Mac helped him out of the tall boots then, let Tom handle the rest of his disrobing as he took the waders into the bathing room and dumped the water out of the waders before hanging them over the edge.

"Just leave your wet clothes right there, Tom. I'll get them later," Mac said as he re-entered the main room.

After he was sure that Tom was under the covers and breathing normally, he left the house, trotted to the clearing where the horses stood watching his approach, unhitched Pete, then jumped onto his back and rode him bareback out of the clearing, heading back to the crossing.

Molly didn't know whether she should be ashamed more for letting Tom talk her into trying to cross the river or by not being able to help, and felt more useless and worthless than before she had left Boulder.

She soon spotted Mac Jones riding his black horse from behind the trees on the other side of the river. He was still shirtless and wet, and she felt an embarrassing rush as she looked at him.

Mac rode to the crossing, let Pete step across the river until he reached the other side, then slid off his gelding and said, "Tom's okay, Mrs. Phillips. I had him undress and get under the blankets and quilts to get warm again. I'll get you across and then come back for the other things. Okay?"

Molly tried not to stare at his chest, but couldn't help herself but finally said, "We had to leave some things back a few miles behind a boulder."

Mac smiled and said, "I was kind of surprised that he didn't have his fishing pole. I'll go and retrieve them in a little while. You'll probably want to see Tom right now."

"Yes, thank you. How am I going to get across?" she asked.

"It may not conform with propriety, but I'll have you sit on my horse, you can carry a travel bag in each hand, and then I'll mount behind you and hold onto you until we're across. I'll take you to my cabin where Tom is, then I'll return and get your other things. If that's not acceptable, and I'd understand if it wasn't, I can go and harness my team to the wagon and bring you across properly. I just didn't believe you'd want me to waste another half an hour before you could see Tom."

"You're right. I'd rather go across right now. Could you help me onto your horse, please?"

"Did you want to ride side saddle or straddle his back?" Mac asked.

"I'll ride side saddle, if that's all right."

70

"That's fine," he replied as he placed his hands on her waist as she put hers on his bare, powerful shoulders and felt a much more powerful flash of heat as her skin met his, another proof of her many flaws.

Mac lifted her easily and guessed that she only weighed about a hundred and ten pounds, which for a woman almost five and a half feet tall, was too thin. Mrs. Phillips hadn't been eating enough.

He set her on Pete's back and handed her the reins, saying, "Hold onto these while I get the travel bags."

After she had the reins securely in her hands, Mac took two steps and snatched up the travel bags and wondered if they had walked the entire distance from Fort Collins or had just walked from LaPorte, which would still be one heck of a long walk uphill, especially for two thin people carrying baggage.

He handed Molly one travel bag, took the reins, and then handed her the second before swinging in behind her.

"Now, Mrs. Phillips, I want to let you know that I'm not trying to take advantage of the situation, but I don't want to risk having you fall into the river, so please forgive my indiscretions."

"I understand, Mr. Jones," she replied as she felt another, longer rush as his right arm slipped around her waist and held her firmly in his grasp.

He nudged Pete into the water and the gelding began stepping carefully across the stony bottom, the current not having nearly the effect on his relatively thin legs and greater mass.

Molly didn't notice the crossing at all as she only felt Mac's arm around her waist. Even in the light afternoon breeze, she could smell his husky masculine scent that threatened to overwhelm her and felt ashamed of herself. *Had she no shame? Her son had almost died just minutes before, and here she was getting excited because a man had his arm around her.*

They reached the opposite bank in just a minute, but it seemed so much shorter and yet so much longer to Molly as she suddenly missed Mac's grip around her waist when he slid onto the ground.

She handed him the travel bags and put out her arms, welcoming his hands around her waist again and knowing that she was a shameless hussy for enjoying it.

He took both travel bags and let Pete just walk behind him. If he raced off somewhere, Mac could use one of the draft horses to track him down, but he suspected correctly that Pete had no intention of running off.

Once they were underway, Mac finally asked the big question, "So, Mrs. Phillips, what made you take such a difficult journey to look for me?"

Molly kept her eyes ahead and replied, "The man I thought was my husband told me yesterday that he had lied when he married me, that his name wasn't Bob Phillips at all, and that the marriage certificate wasn't worth anything. Then he told us to go away, but we didn't have any money or anyplace to go. I don't know anyone in this area, and you were so nice yesterday, I was wondering if you could help us."

Mac digested all of the information and said, "I'll tell you what, ma'am. Why don't you and Tom stay with me until we can work out the particulars of what you need. Okay?"

Molly nodded and said, "Thank you, Mr. Jones. I really am grateful for your help. I've never done anything like this before and I'm ashamed to have to put such a burden on you."

Mac smiled at Molly and replied, "I can pretty much guess that no one has ever done anything like this before, but don't be ashamed about it. You didn't have a lot of choices."

Molly said, "You don't even seem surprised by all this."

"Trust me, ma'am, I am still surprised, but we'll make something work."

When Mac used that phrase, the image of the landlord and what she had done two days before flashed in her mind. She was disgusted with herself because she knew that she'd have to sell herself again. At least Mr. Jones wasn't revolting like the landlord or Bob Phillips.

They walked the rest of the way in silence, and when they passed the tree line, Molly beheld the most incredible sight she'd ever witnessed. It was really a good-sized house that looked like it had been built on a raft with a creek flowing underneath. It was even painted a dark green, so it almost blended in with the forest.

It stopped her in her tracks as she stared at the engineering wonder.

"That's not a cabin," she finally said in amazement.

"I suppose not. It was going to be one, but I had to improvise. I still call it a cabin, though."

As they approached the house, Molly began to see all of the cut trees and wood chips all over the place, then she saw the steps leading up to a porch on the opposite side of the creek that ran under the house.

"You have to cross the creek to get into the house?" she asked.

"No, that's the back of the house. I'll be building a bridge back here soon anyway. The front of the house has the entrance on this side. It's also where the bedrooms are."

Molly shook her head when he said bedrooms but didn't comment as they cleared the house and she saw the large front porch with wide steps and the back of the fireplace.

When they walked up the solid steps, and crossed over the equally sturdy porch, Mac put down the travel bags and opened the front door, letting Molly enter.

Then he said, "Tom is probably already sleeping in the first bedroom. His wet clothes are on the floor. I'm going to go and saddle

73

my horse and ride down to get your other things. Feel free to make yourself at home."

He then turned and trotted back down the porch steps and led his horse toward a large tent.

When Molly walked inside, she gasped at the high sloped ceilings, the huge front room with a cookstove, a sink, cabinets and couldn't believe her eyes when she saw a full set of china. It even had a sofa, two easy chairs, a large kitchen table and four chairs!

She began to turn slowly as in a trance, drinking in the incredible construction. There were no studs visible on the walls, but she did see a small room near the kitchen and wondered what it was.

First, she needed to check on Tom, and turned down the wide hallway and opened it softly and found Tom sleeping under heavy quilts as she again found herself in disbelief. The room had a big bed, a dresser, a side table, two lamps and even a mirror! This was getting too much to swallow.

Then she checked the second bedroom and found it furnished in the same manner. She felt like a voyeur as she walked into the room and pulled open the top drawer of the dresser and finding neatly folded shirts, britches, and men's underpants.

Then she opened the bottom drawer and was taken aback to find dresses and other woman's apparel. Finding the women's clothes scared Molly. *What happened to his wife?* The man at the dry goods store said he wasn't married. Maybe he just had a woman staying with him, but she wasn't here anymore, and all of her clothes were. It gave Molly a sick, creepy feeling.

After closing the drawer, she left his bedroom and crossed to the room across the hall and opened that door. She didn't think she could be surprised any more than she had been, but she was much more shocked to see a privy seat. The idea disgusted her as she walked to the carved oak seat, grimaced and looked down.

When her eyes told her that there was a creek flowing five feet away, she began to laugh. This was a very strange cabin. She turned, closed the door and found another door to what appeared to be a closet and wouldn't have been surprised to see if he had a woman stored inside, but found something almost as surprising when she saw shelves of soap, both white and flowery scented, shampoo, toothbrushes, tooth powder, and even hairbrushes and hand mirrors.

She quickly closed the door and had a mixed reaction as she returned to the well-furnished main room/kitchen. She began looking at the shelves finding flatware, glasses, pots and pans and even a Dutch oven. The cook stove was well cared for and had a stack of firewood and kindling in boxes nearby.

She found a large, well-stocked pantry near the back door and stood examining the tins and jars amazed at the variety of the selection. She closed the door and turned around.

There was one more interior door across from the pantry, and Molly hesitatingly walked to the door, closed her eyes until they were slits, swung it open and gasped.

She walked trancelike into the room and looked down at what appeared to be a huge bathtub made of stone. She guessed that's what it was when she saw the drain in the bottom with a plug. But there were river rocks on the bottom, too.

As she turned to leave, she saw a large shelf with over a dozen towels.

After closing the door to the bathing room, she walked out the back door onto the porch and saw the creek racing past and marveled at what she had just explored. *Who was this strange man who chose to live out here, and what had happened to his woman?* She returned to the cabin's main room to cook some dinner, knowing that he'd be back soon. He seemed to be so nice, but she had been made a fool by Bob Phillips and there were so many strange things here that she couldn't begin to understand. She had a few hundred questions to ask when Mr. Jones returned.

———

Mac had almost as many as he rode along his wagon trail, looking to his left for the boulder that Mrs. Phillips had said she had used for cover for their things.

Aside from whatever reason she had for leaving Fort Collins, there was the even bigger question about what he could do for them. He knew as soon as he had seen those travel bags that they had nowhere else to go. He couldn't imagine how desperate she must have been to make that walk at least from LaPorte to come to his cabin not even knowing him at all. For all she knew, he could be some murderer hiding from the law.

But he'd have to wait until he returned and talked to her before he could come up with any kind of plan. What he did admit to himself was that he had thoroughly enjoyed talking to her yesterday and wouldn't mind having her and Tom stay.

He found their boulder a few minutes later and smiled as he picked up the fishing rod and other gear along with another travel bag. There wasn't any food, either, so they must be pretty hungry, and he hoped that Mrs. Phillips at least cooked something for herself and Tom while he was gone.

He put what he could in his saddlebags, and arranged everything else around Pete, finally hanging the travel bag over his saddle horn before mounting and heading back for his cabin.

———

Molly was still thirsty from the long walk and pumped a large glass of water. She was still troubled by the women's clothes and soaps as she took a large swallow of the clear water and almost dropped the glass as she felt the icy water rush down her throat. She gagged, set the water down and held her neck. The water was colder than the water they drank on the walk to the cabin, and that was pretty cold. She left the water and began to prepare something to eat.

The longer she stayed in the cabin the more questions she had. Everywhere she looked, she found things that one wouldn't expect to find in a cabin fifteen miles from anywhere else. There were even woven rugs on the floor, for Pete's sake.

———

Mac unsaddled Pete and returned him to his clearing with the draft horses before walking back to his cabin, knowing one thing for sure; he'd be moving his things into the tent again. Just when he was getting accustomed to having a real roof over his head, too.

He stepped up onto the porch and stopped himself before entering and knocked on the door.

Molly was startled by the knocking, not having heard his footsteps on the porch, she closed the door to the oven, walked to the door and opened it for Mr. Jones.

"How's Tom?" Mac asked as he entered, setting down the travel bag, fishing gear and fireworks.

"He's still sleeping. Thank you for saving him, Mr. Jones. I should have thanked you earlier and I apologize."

Mac closed the door behind him, and said, "There's no need to apologize, ma'am. You were very distraught."

"I hope you don't mind, but I'm preparing dinner."

"Not at all, Mrs. Phillips. I would have been surprised if you hadn't," Mac replied.

Molly then said, "I'm not Mrs. Phillips, and have never been Mrs. Phillips as it turns out. Please call me Molly."

Mac smiled and said, "Then please call me Mac, Molly."

"Alright," she replied, then quickly asked, "Mac, what happened to your woman?"

Mac was startled by the odd question and answered, "Woman? I didn't know I ever had one. You're the first female that's even set foot in the cabin."

Molly wasn't sure if he was telling the truth, so she asked, "Then what about the women's clothing and the scented soaps and shampoo?"

Mac shook his head, laughed and said, "Oh. Now, I understand why you asked that question. When I was in LaPorte, Mr. Armstrong, the owner of the dry goods store, told me about a man selling his house and contents separately, and I bought everything but the house. Jake Abernathy, the owner, had crated many items that I didn't see. I found the soaps and shampoos, along with a lot of other women's things in the crates. I didn't even open the dresser drawers for a week and had a good laugh when I found them full of women's clothes. I left the soap and shampoos because they were still soaps that I could use for other things. I was going to use the clothes as rags, but you're welcome to all of it if you'd like. They seemed in good condition."

Molly bit her lower lip and said, "I could use some more clothes."

"Most of them are in the dresser in the bedroom where Tom is sleeping. The rest are in the bottom two drawers in the dresser in my bedroom, which is now your bedroom. I'll take my clothes out of the room and stay in my tent while you're here."

Molly was surprised by his statement as it flew in the face of what she had been expecting, but said, "I'm not comfortable with this, Mac. We didn't come here to push you out of your house."

Mac looked at her and asked, "Then why did you come here, Molly?"

She looked down at the floor and replied softly, "We had no place to go. I didn't know what was going to happen to us tomorrow."

"Well, now you know. You can both stay here as long as you like, Molly. It's a wonderful place and you and Tom wouldn't cost anything extra to feed. I wouldn't mind the company, either."

She lifted her eyes and looked at Mac, then said, "I'm not that kind of a woman, Mr. Jones."

Mac was startled at her assumption, but replied, "I didn't say you were, Molly. I said I wouldn't mind your company, nothing more. Now, you and Tom can stay in the house as long as you like. If you want to leave tomorrow, I'll give you a couple of hundred dollars, you can take all the women's clothes and I'll take you and Tom back to Fort Collins and buy you stagecoach tickets to wherever you'd like to go."

"Why would you do that? You don't know us at all."

"Maybe it's because I believe you've been dealt a bad hand and I believe that you and Tom deserve a good draw. The money and clothes don't matter to me, but if I can make your lives better, that does."

"But what do you want in return?" she asked almost begging for an answer that made sense to her.

Mac couldn't understand why she was being so resentful, but answered, "Life isn't always like a ledger book with debits and credits, Molly. I'm not some saint who runs around trying to do good things, but I'm not about to deny assistance to someone who needs it, either. Now, I'll tell you once more. If you are concerned about staying here, then I'll take you to Fort Collins tomorrow."

Molly realized that she had gone too far, and said, "I'm sorry. We'll stay. It's just that I'm not accustomed to someone giving me something without wanting something in return. Your offer to help is like the fishing pole you bought for Tom, isn't it?"

"Somewhat, but in the store, there was that added recollection of when I was a boy, too. I could tell that you didn't have enough money to buy him what he wanted, but wished you had. I watched his face break into that big grin and your face light up when you saw how

79

happy he was. How do you think that made me feel, Molly? The money didn't matter. It was only thirteen dollars and change. But to see Tom realize his small dream was priceless, and to watch how pleased you were because he was happy was a very satisfying sensation for me. It was really a selfish thing to do. I drew at least as much happiness as Tom did out of the exchange. As his mother, I'm sure you understand that."

Molly nodded slowly, and replied simply, "Yes."

"I'll go and take my things out of my room. Then I'll leave you and Tom alone, so you can rest after your long walk."

Before Molly could say anything, Mac walked down the hallway, entered the second bedroom, she heard the drawers open and close, then he walked back out with his clothes in his arms.

Molly wanted to tell him that she had cooked for three, but didn't as he walked past, opened the door, walked out, then closed it behind him.

Molly felt like a first-class ingrate.

———

Mac thought it was an unusual conversation, but the whole situation was unusual, if not downright bizarre, but even if she thought she had behaved poorly, he hadn't. He expected that she was just shaken by her being tossed out by the man who she thought was her husband, having no place to go and walking fifteen miles to his cabin, then having her son almost drown. He imagined that discovering his odd construction was the final piece of a very trying day for Molly and Tom.

Even her quick 'I'm not that kind of woman' was understandable. A woman in her situation would naturally expect a man to demand favors for assistance. It was a sad commentary on society.

He ducked into his tent and began reorganizing his things, so he'd have enough room to be able to lie down and not bang his head. He took out two of his small tarps and stretched them out on the ground and began moving tools out of the tent. After they were all on the tarps as they had been before the cabin was finished, he folded the tarps over and started a fire in his dormant fire pit. He had to replace the grate before tossing in some bigger sticks and branches.

He walked down to the creek, filled the coffeepot and then realized he didn't have any food except the bag of coffee in his saddlebags along with some jerky. It'd have to do until he moved some food out into the tent.

But on the positive side, it was a warm night, so he'd be comfortable. Besides, he had helped Molly and Tom when they needed it the most. The only question now was how long they would stay. It wasn't just some social nicety when he said he'd enjoy having the company. This may be a refuge, but he never had any intention of being a hermit. In fact, he was already thinking about trying to find a woman to share his cabin before their arrival.

———

Molly had watched through the kitchen window and seen Mac moving things out of the tent and starting a fire, making coffee and chewing on jerky. If she had felt like an ingrate before, she felt worse now. *Why didn't she just walk out and tell him to come inside and have dinner?*

But more than that, she wondered why she told him that she wasn't that kind of woman. When she had set eyes on him less than an hour ago, she was that kind of woman, and when he had held her on the back of his horse, she was even more that kind of a woman. *What possessed her to suddenly get all high and mighty and proclaim her moral superiority?*

Maybe it was the presence, albeit a sleeping presence, of her son, but knew better. It was just a recurring desire to think that she was a good person and not the flawed, shameless woman that she was. She had married Chester Saunders, her first husband, well, her only husband now, when she was seventeen. He had been a boyfriend in school in Boulder and had dropped out when he was sixteen to work in his father's freight company with his three older brothers. As soon as Chester had turned eighteen, they had married, and Molly admitted to herself even then that she was anxiously awaiting becoming a woman. She had expected so much and had been sorely disappointed, and not just in that aspect of her marriage. Chester the boyfriend was much different than Chester the husband, especially after she had told him of her pregnancy after just two months.

When she had begun to swell with Tom, he had become indifferent at best, and after Tom was born, he became abusive. It was all words for the first year or so, then it progressed to slaps and swats on her behind with a switch. By the time Tom was seven, he would beat her if she so much as asked for a dime to buy some milk.

When he had died of influenza almost two years ago, she thought she would be provided for by his father, the owner of the freight company, but he had acted as if she were a stranger. Her own father had died when she was fourteen, and she'd lived with her grandmother for three years before she passed away, so she was destitute and in real trouble. All she had was the three hundred dollars that her grandmother had left her. It had lasted over a year of a very miserly existence.

She had gone to the freight yard to make one more unsuccessful appeal to her father-in-law and had met Bob Phillips. She thought he'd be different and better than Chester and had accepted his offer of marriage after a single week's courtship, if one could even dignify it with that title. Essentially, it had amounted to a week of rutting like rabbits, at least on his part. She had succumbed the first time with just the promise of marriage and had to keep him satisfied until they wed. She was so ashamed of herself back then that she thought it couldn't get any worse.

At least Bob/Ed hadn't beaten her. He had behaved strangely and lied to her often, and even walked out on her a few times, always returning when he needed satisfaction, but he hadn't struck her. He had ignored Tom, though, and that had hurt as much as one of Chester's earlier beatings. He seemed to regard her as his personal painted woman, and that was how she had begun to view herself. She hadn't gotten pregnant with him, which had surprised her. Chester, once she became pregnant, treated her like a pariah, and was sure that he passed demeaning stories about her to his father and brothers which was why they shunned her after his death. She couldn't understand why she hadn't gotten pregnant with Bob Phillips because he never seemed to leave her alone.

So, her history of quickly offering herself to men in the hope of marriage and security had led to this. She had quickly announced to perhaps the nicest man she had ever met that she was a good woman; a moral woman, and not the harlot she knew she was, which had culminated in her giving herself to the landlord.

All that aside, Molly knew she couldn't leave tomorrow, or not for a long time, if ever. Or at least not until Tom was old enough to provide for her. *But why would she burden Tom with having to provide for her?* He deserved his own life. He needed to find a genuinely good woman to marry, not like the defective woman he called mama.

Molly's dinner was ready, so she stuck her head in the first bedroom and saw that Tom had awakened and was looking at her.

"Mama, can I have my travel bag, so I can get dressed?" he asked when he saw her peer into the room.

She smiled at him, picked up his still soggy clothes, and replied, "I'll be right back."

Molly took Tom's travel bag into his room and left it with him, closing the door as she walked into the kitchen.

———

As Molly and Tom sat at the table having dinner, Tom asked, "Where's Mr. Jones?"

"He moved back to his tent, so we could live here."

"Why? It's his house."

"He was just being polite, Tom. Now eat your dinner."

"Why isn't Mr. Jones eating with us, Mama?"

Molly sighed and replied, "He already had his dinner, Tom."

Tom took a big bite of a baked potato, swallowed and said, "Okay."

Molly was glad the Mister Jones questions had ended as she ate. She didn't need the reminders of her callous treatment of the man.

———

Molly had rummaged through the two drawers of women's clothes and found two nightdresses. Her last nightdress had been lost to her two months ago when Bob had ripped it from her and rendered it useless, then told her not to bother buying another. She fingered the soft flannel and was looking forward to sleeping under those deep quilts and blankets wearing a flannel second skin.

Ten minutes later, Molly was snuggled deep under the blankets and quilts in her flannel nightdress and looked around her in the dim light. This one bedroom was half again as large as the bedroom she had been sharing with Bob, and the kitchen/living/bathing area was larger than their whole apartment in Boulder. Then, there was the bath itself and that bizarre, yet very useful indoor privy. Everything about the new situation for her and Tom was infinitely better, especially Mac Jones. Her only question was why he had so readily given up so much just to help her and Tom? He was outside sleeping in his tent while she and Tom were enjoying the amazing comfort of soft beds and thick covers. He sounded sincere when he had told her why he had done it, but there was still a lingering bit of doubt in her mind. But she knew one thing for sure as she felt warm and comfortable; she didn't deserve it.

CHAPTER 5

Mac was up early, as he had become accustomed to doing, and had cleaned and shaved as dawn arrived. He had just reheated last night's coffee, eaten some more jerky, and prepared to start his day. He had planned on setting off his fireworks in the evening but wasn't sure he'd be able to do it now. He did know that Tom still had his fireworks, so maybe he and Tom would set some off later.

———

When Molly's eyes popped open on that Saturday morning, the Fourth of July, she was momentarily disoriented and then took in a deep breath and sighed as she enjoyed a few more minutes of the cozy comfort under the blankets.

Then she heard what must have awakened her, and it wasn't the sun blazing through the window. It was the sound of rhythmic pounding in the distance. *What was that noise?*

She didn't take too long to think about it as she quickly slid from under the blankets and trotted out of her bedroom to make use of that wonderful indoor privy.

———

Molly had dressed, made the bed and had put on a pot of coffee when Tom walked out, yawning.

"How are you feeling, Tom?" she asked.

"I feel good, Mama. Is Mr. Jones here?"

"No, sweetheart, he's outside working already. Did you want some oatmeal for breakfast?"

85

"Can I have eggs and bacon, Mama?" Tom asked, not wanting any of that little kid breakfast food.

"Of course, you may. I'll get them going now."

"Is Mr. Jones the one who's making those banging noises?" he asked as he took a seat at the kitchen table.

Molly laid the bacon strips onto the biggest frypan and replied, "I'm sure he is. I just don't know what he's doing."

"I'm gonna go and see after breakfast. How come he's not havin' any?"

Molly answered, "I'll ask after we've eaten. I should have asked earlier and I'm ashamed of myself for not doing so."

"It's all right, Mama. I don't think Mr. Jones will be mad or anything. I think he likes us."

Molly said, "I hope so, Tom."

———

One of the first concessions that Mac had to make that morning because of the presence of Molly was to wear his shirt as he worked. Even in the chilly morning air, he was already soaking the shirt in perspiration as he pounded the wedges deeper into the log, finally being rewarded with the loud crack as the foot-thick trunk cracked open along the wedge line. After driving the wedges into the log until their heads were flush with the log, he cracked it open the rest of the way with his axe and then chopped it into two halves. Now, he had to split those halves into two more rails which would give him eighty altogether. Just four more trunks before he had to cut some posts. He was also getting a lot of firewood from those branches and treetops, too, stacking them nearby to let them dry. He hadn't done anything much with that huge Ponderosa lying on its side near the house, other than taking those five short logs to add as middle supports for the cabin's support raft. He had used his entire team of draft horses to drag the great tree trunk a couple of hundred feet away from the cabin, though.

He was almost finished splitting his third log of the morning when he caught movement out of the corner of his eye and quickly stopped what he was doing, looked up, and saw Molly and Tom heading his way.

He leaned on his maul and said, "Good morning, Molly and Tom. Happy birthday to you both."

Tom was confused until his mother laughed and replied, "Good morning, Mac, and happy Fourth of July to you as well. You seem to be awfully busy already this morning."

Mac was pleasantly surprised by Molly's better mood as he said, "I'm used to putting in twelve-hour days and needed to split a few more rails for a corral for the horses."

"Would you like some breakfast?" she asked.

"I'm fine, Molly."

"You must go through a lot of shirts, Mac. That one's already soaked and covered in wood chips."

Mac blushed and replied, "I normally don't wear a shirt when I'm working, but I didn't want to embarrass you."

Molly noticed the reddened ears and cheeks and was surprised that he'd feel embarrassed for saying that he normally worked shirtless.

"It's perfectly all right, Mac. I'm not some innocent teenaged girl, and I apologize for being so rude yesterday, but I'll be better now."

"You weren't rude, Molly. You had a lot of things happen to you recently, but things will be much better for you and Tom from now on."

"I need to be useful, Mac. Let me at least do the cleaning and cooking. I'm a good cook, you know."

Mac understood her need, and replied, "That's fine. Just to let you know, if you go down the back-porch steps, right at the edge of the creek is a blocked section with a milk can, butter and some fresh meat. I harvested a white-tailed deer a couple of days ago and what I didn't smoke is in one of the pails covered with a cast iron pot to keep away the critters."

"I'll cook some for lunch then, but you'll have to start joining us. I'm cooking for three, you know."

Mac almost made a joke in poor taste, but said, "Okay, Molly. Just send Tom out to find me."

Then he turned to Tom and said, "Just follow the noise, Tom."

"Can I watch for a while, Mr. Jones?" he asked.

"Sure. I'm just splitting the last of the rails for the corral before I cut some posts."

Molly smiled and said, "Then I'll head back into the cabin and I'll see you in a couple of hours."

"Yes, ma'am," Mac replied and returned her smile.

Molly left the worksite and Mac pulled off his shirt to begin work, feeling the cool breeze against his skin and took a deep breath as he picked up his maul, set his first wedge in place and began to split the log into rails.

———

After entering the house, Molly had walked to her bedroom and looked out the window, watching Mac work as Tom sat on the stump watching. She felt like a sinful voyeur as she kept staring as he smoothly worked his muscles, slamming the heavy maul into the wedges. She found him mesmerizing even as she chastised herself for her loose morals.

After watching for almost twenty minutes, she turned, left the bedroom, and walked out of the back door to retrieve the deer steaks for lunch.

————

Bob was pleasantly surprised when he found that the boss had given the men the afternoon off because it was Independence Day, so Bob thought he'd do a little detective work to make sure Molly had gone. He was already regretting telling her his real name. He should have made something up, but then figured she didn't know anyone anyway, so it shouldn't matter.

His first stop, naturally, was the Overland Stage depot. There wasn't a railroad to Fort Collins yet, but it would be there before the year was out, probably in three months.

He entered the offices and was greeted by the manager.

"Howdy," Ed said, "me and the missus had a real tussle the night before last, and I think she's run off with the kid. I've been lookin' all over for her to tell her I'm sorry, but can't find her anywhere, and I'm gettin' worried. I hope she didn't go back to her parents' place. Did a good-lookin' woman and a boy about ten get on the stage to Boulder yesterday?"

The manager replied, "Yup. They sure got on a stage, but they didn't go to Boulder. They took the short run to LaPorte."

"LaPorte?" asked a surprised Ed Richardson. *Why would she go to LaPorte?*

"Yes, sir. They should've been there before noon."

"Well, I guess I'll just have to take a ride to LaPorte now and get on my knees and beg her to come back again."

89

The manager laughed and said, "That's the way of it, ain't it?"

Ed shook his head and said, "Way too often. I appreciate the help," then turned and left the office, still wondering why she had gone to LaPorte. At least it was out of Fort Collins and she wouldn't interfere with his growing relationship with Mildred.

———

With all of the rails split and set in their respective positions, Mac headed off to the creek to wash up, stopping to pick up a clean shirt on the way while Tom trotted into the house to see if lunch was ready.

After his cleanup and with his shirt back on, Mac walked up the front steps and knocked on the door again.

Molly was expecting him this time, but Tom bolted past her to open the door before she could take two steps from the stove.

"Come on in, Mr. Jones. Mama says the food is almost ready. I was just gonna come and get you."

"Well, here I am," Mac said as he entered.

Having spent that much time watching Mac work, Molly was embarrassed herself on the off chance that he had seen her at the window. But after two minutes, he hadn't said anything to indicate that he had, so Molly relaxed as Mac began setting the table.

"Mr. Jones, can I explore around here?" Tom asked.

"Explore wherever you want, but I'd recommend that you don't go anywhere without a pistol or a rifle, and that means I'll have to be close by," Mac replied.

"Why? Is it the bears?" Molly asked.

"Partly, but it's also about men. When I had the wood delivered a couple of months ago, one of the…"

Then he stopped in mid-sentence as his brain made the connection – Bob Phillips.

Molly saw something click in his mind and asked, "Mac?"

Mac began again, saying, "One of the men who delivered the lumber two months ago was probing to see if I had any money. He tried to be coy, but I could see it in his eyes. I had him pegged as a potential problem. The man was your husband, or the one who claimed to be your husband, Bob Phillips."

Molly wasn't shocked by the revelation, and said, "That wasn't his real name, he told me that his real name was Ed Richards."

Mac blinked as his brain made another connection and asked, "Are you sure he said, 'Ed Richards' and not 'Ed Richardson'?"

"Oh, that's right," she replied, "it was Ed Richardson."

Molly took the steaks from the frypan and then began moving the hash browns to a large bowl as she asked, "How did you know his name?"

Mac looked at her and answered, "Ed Richardson is a wanted man. The last time I knew, and that was more than two years ago, the price on his head was five hundred dollars. He was wanted for murder, robbery and rape."

She may not have been surprised by Mac's first revelation, but this one hit her hard. *She had been living with a murderer!*

Then she asked quietly, "Are you sure it's him?"

Mac nodded and replied, "I'm sure. When I began talking to him, I thought there was something familiar about him. I couldn't quite figure it out until you said he was really Ed Richardson. Ed Richardson had a scar on the left side of his forehead that he had picked up a ricochet. He was wearing a beard when I saw him a couple of months ago, and I didn't make the connection. He had been running in a gang headed by a man named Wild Willie Patterson."

"How would you know such things?" Molly asked quietly as Tom listened intently.

"I worked as a deputy sheriff and a bounty hunter, too. Wanted posters are a bounty hunter's way of life and you have to study them carefully but leave a lot of wiggle room for bad descriptions. Some of the men who chased after those rewards weren't very particular and wound up shooting innocent men. I only concentrated on those with distinguishing characteristics, like that scar."

Molly quickly asked, "Did the gang break up or something? Why did Bob, I mean Ed, marry me and stop doing those things?"

Molly slid the venison steaks onto the plates as Mac answered, "It wasn't by choice, Molly. The story was that after a stage holdup, they stopped in a small town and somehow, four of the five got caught by the sheriff. Ed was the only one not apprehended. He lit out after taking all the gang's loot from the robbery. The way I heard it, the sheriff somehow got jumped by the gang in his office, and they killed him. My guess is they weren't happy about Ed not helping them with the sheriff and then taking their money. As to why he married you, you'd know better than I would."

Molly knew why Ed Richardson had wanted a wife, and it wasn't just a single reason, either. He may have needed to blend in for one, and the other was, well, the more obvious reason. Ed Richardson rarely gave her a night off.

But Tom was more intrigued with the other part of Mac's explanation and asked, "You were a sheriff and a bounty hunter? Really?"

"I had my reasons for doing both jobs, Tom. How are you feeling today?"

"I'm as good as ever, Mr. Jones. I shoulda thanked you for savin' me, but I forgot. So, thank you for gettin' me out of that river. It was really cold, too."

"I had to save you, Tom, because I'm the one who put you into that situation when I gave you those waders. I should have warned you not to go out too far in swift currents because you're not heavy enough to withstand the push from the flowing water. So, I apologize for that omission."

Molly took a seat while Mac poured coffee for him and Molly. Tom already had a tall glass of milk with drops of water condensing on the outside of the glass.

As she ate, Molly somehow felt even more flawed than she had earlier. She had married, or thought she had married, a murderer, a thief and a rapist. As much as that bothered her, it was the proximity of that monster to Tom all that time that really frightened her. *But why had he stayed with her for so long?*

After asking herself that question, she asked Mac, "Mac, why didn't he just run away after a month or so? Why would he stay for so long?"

Mac was chewing a piece of venison when she asked, so he put up a finger, swallowed and replied, "You would know that answer better than I would, Molly. I can understand why a normal man would want to marry you, and that may have been the only reason, but he probably needed to blend in better, too. A man walking down the street with a woman doesn't even earn a second glance from the law. After he grew that beard and married you, he'd be practically invisible to a lawman. Maybe he stayed married because you had changed the way he saw things. Maybe he decided to quit the outlaw trail and go straight, but after the way he talked to me, I would have been surprised."

Molly took a bite of hash browns and thought about it, but still had a hard time believing that he had changed all that much. He was always furtive and distrusting, as if he expected a man with a badge to put his hand on his shoulder at any minute. Then there were his relentless bedtime pursuits that were so frequent but so short. Bob didn't care about her as a person. She finally concluded that Bob had stayed because he had no place else to go. It was that simple. *But why had he suddenly run?*

"Mac," she asked, "why did Bob suddenly run away to Fort Collins? Did the sheriff recognize him?"

Mac shook his head and replied, "Not likely. Not after a year and with that beard. I wonder if he ran into Wild Willie and his boys. Ed would have been much happier having a sheriff find him than his old partners. I don't know why he stayed, and I really don't understand why he suddenly told you who he was and then basically told you to leave."

Molly said, "He left us in Boulder and told me that he had to do a job in Fort Collins and would be coming back. When I found out from the freight company that he had really quit the job, I thought he'd abandoned us. I thought I was still married to him, so I really had no other choice but to go to Fort Collins. We were barely off the stage when he saw us and that's when he told me we were never married and even gave me twenty dollars to leave town."

Mac mulled this one over in his head. It didn't make a lot of sense at all. He glanced at Molly and could easily understand why Ed would want to marry her, even if he didn't want cover. And, if he did decide to give up his lawless ways, that would explain his staying. He could even understand the sudden flight if he had seen Wild Willie. He finally decided not to think about it anymore and just deal with the issues created by her and Tom's arrival. One of which might be the sudden appearance of Ed Richardson on his land if he changed his mind again and wanted Molly back.

That added a new potential problem, but one he could handle.

After lunch, Mac returned to his work and began cutting his posts for the corral, finding it much easier than splitting rails, not requiring anything more than a quick measure and a minute of sawing. In just four hours, he had enough posts for the corral out in the clearing.

Tom had been watching from a nearby stump and was in awe of Mac's strength as he easily tossed the cut posts into a pile.

"Mr. Jones, how can I get bigger and stronger?" he asked.

Mac tossed the last one onto the stack and replied, "Just keep eating and working hard, Tom. You won't notice it at first, but after you've stopped growing tall, you'll fill out."

Mac was brushing off the sawdust when Tom asked, "Mr. Jones, are we gonna set off them firecrackers later?"

Mac grinned at him and replied, "Now, Tom, don't you think it would be wasteful to buy those firecrackers and not use them?"

Tom broke into a grin and asked, "When are we gonna light 'em off?"

"Oh, I think just after dinner. We can light off the small, loud ones early, and I have some that are better after it gets dark. Okay?"

Tom nodded vigorously and answered, "Okay. Where are we gonna do it?"

"I think it's best down near the river junction, so we don't start any fires."

"Okay," Tom replied, but he really didn't care where they did it. He was going to get to set off some firecrackers!

Then, Mac made his day even better when he said, "Tom, seeing as how we're going to be setting off explosives together, I think you should start calling me Mac. Okay?"

Tom had an explosion of pride in his chest as he replied, "Okay, Mac!"

———

While they were gone, Molly had done some cleaning and more in-depth examination of the cabin. In her entire life, she'd never lived in a place with so much room and with so many comforts, and she hadn't even tried out that extraordinary bathtub.

It was when she was staring at the bathtub that she suddenly realized that she was now a single woman again and had been one since Chester had died. She was a single woman and Mac Jones was a single man. It was a revelation that titillated her and unsettled her at the same time. She found him so exciting and at the same time, so very considerate and kind. She was certain it was because he was so considerate and compassionate, that he had treated her so well. *How could such an extraordinary man ever think of her as anything more than a pathetic woman worthy of pity for her bad judgment and loose morals?* And he didn't know about how she had to give herself to Bob to ensure he married her or even worse, how she had sold herself to the landlord.

Molly was finding it harder to maintain her pleasant countenance and wondered how long she could keep it up.

She sighed and began to prepare dinner.

———

Molly hadn't heard any noise from outside and thought Mac and Tom were coming in for dinner, but when she looked back outside, she couldn't see them anywhere.

She left the house, and walked out into the front yard, where she stopped and listened for any sounds of Mac's industry but hearing nothing.

Then, after almost a full minute of silence, she heard Tom laughing loudly behind her, turned and still couldn't see anyone, so she walked around the house and finally spotted Tom as he was watching Mac stick his head into the creek and then yanking his head out quickly, throwing his hair back and running his fingers through his long black locks to bring them into some semblance of order.

She felt a flush of heat rush through her and wished she wasn't so easily turned into a weak-kneed teenaged girl at the sight of a bare-chested man. Well, at least this bare-chested man was worthy of attention, she told herself.

Tom then spotted his mother and said, "Hello, Mama. Mac is just getting rid of all the sawdust. I can't believe that he stuck his head in that cold water."

Mac turned to face, Molly, water still racing across his face, chest and back, and said, "It'll curl your toes, I'll grant you that, but it's the quickest way to get rid of wood chips and sawdust."

"Would you like some dinner?" she asked.

"I'd love some, but I've got to dry out first and put on a clean shirt. I'll be in shortly, but Tom's hungry. I could hear his stomach from thirty feet away. Then, in a little while, we're going to go and set off some fireworks."

Tom laughed again and trotted over to his mother while Mac walked slowly away from the creek.

"Are you finished working for the day then, Mac?" she asked as they began to walk around the side of the house.

"Yes, ma'am. I have all the rails and posts done, so all I need to do is build the gate, set the posts and hang the rails. I should get most of that done tomorrow."

"Don't you go to church?" she asked.

"I haven't been to church since I left to go to war."

Molly replied with a simple, "Oh."

Mac then pointed at the house and traced a long, slow arc across the landscape with his finger, saying, "Why would I go to a building and listen to a preacher tell me what to believe when I have this incredible cathedral right here, built personally by the hand of God?"

He reached down and picked up a blade of grass and held it between his fingers, then said, "And look at how perfect this is. Did you ever stop and think of how everything we see or touch, is all part of one great creation and even this blade of grass has its part to play in the perfect machine that we live in? I can look at this apparently simple, tiny sliver of greenery and be in awe of the Creator who designed it. So, I don't feel the need to go to church and be told that if I cuss or look at a woman that I'll roast in fiery torment forever. But those are my personal views. If you would like to attend church, I can drive you to LaPorte in the morning."

Molly was in awe herself, but not of the blade of grass, when she replied softly, "No, I haven't been to church since I was a girl. I just didn't want to keep you from going."

Mac looked at Molly, smiled, and said, "That's very considerate, Molly. I'm sorry I was so preachy myself. I'll be back shortly."

He then handed her the blade of grass, turned and walked away, heading for his tent.

Molly stared at Mac's sliver of greenery laying on her palm and, as he had just described, began to look at it with new eyes, understanding what he had meant and what he believed.

"Mama, Mac is a smart man," Tom said as he watched his new friend go into the tent.

Molly replied quietly, "I think he's an extraordinary man," then closed her hand around the blade of grass, took Tom's hand in her free hand and walked back to the house.

———

Molly had dinner on the table by the time Mac arrived in his clean shirt.

"I did some baking this morning while you were splitting your rails," she said as Mac and Tom took seats at the table.

"I can smell that, Molly. It really adds a wonderful aroma to the house. What did you bake?"

"Nothing fancy, just some bread and some biscuits. You have a lot of food in your pantry, Mac."

"I think we'll still make a run on Monday to LaPorte with the wagon and get some more. I'll get some fresh milk, butter, eggs and anything else you might like, too. How about you, Tom? Is there anything you'd like?"

"Could I get some penny candy?" he asked.

Before Molly could step in with a motherly admonishment, Mac replied, "I already have some out in the tent with me. I bought a big bag when I first arrived here and sometimes like to suck on a peppermint or a lemon drop while I'm working, but there's still a lot left. It's so dry up here that it hasn't even stuck together in a giant multicolored candy rock. Maybe that's what rainbow trout eat to make them look that way."

Tom laughed, remembering the bear-eating trout story, but said, "Could I have some later, Mac?"

"That, my fine friend, is a decision left entirely with that nice lady who is about to let us taste her bread and biscuits."

Molly smiled and said, "You can have one after lunch, Tom. Just one," as she placed the plate of biscuits on the table.

Mac snatched one of the biscuits and took a bite before Molly placed plates of ham sandwiches on the table, watching Mac's reaction to her efforts.

Mac rolled his eyes as he chewed and said, "Molly, this is exquisite. You put a little honey in the dough, didn't you?"

Molly was more than just a little pleased and said, "I did. I'm glad that you noticed. Would you like some butter?"

"No, ma'am. I wouldn't want to spoil perfection," he replied as he polished off the biscuit.

Tom snatched a biscuit off the plate, took a big bite, and couldn't understand the big fuss that Mac was making. It was good, but Mac had candy in his tent.

When they were eating, Molly asked, "Where are you from, Mac?"

"I grew up on a farm outside of Burlington, Iowa. Are you from Boulder?"

"I was born in Denver, but my family moved to Boulder when I was little. I got married when I was seventeen to a boy, not a man, named Chester Saunders. He died two years ago from influenza."

"And then you sort of married Bob Phillips," Mac added as he took a drink of coffee to wash down his first bite of sandwich.

"Yes, that's the short version of my life. Did you ever come close to getting married?" she asked.

Mac shook his head once before replying, "I wouldn't say it was close, but I had a girlfriend in high school, and I believe she assumed we'd get married right after I graduated, but I went into the army instead and I never heard from her again. I know she married another Burlington man named Lenny Crawford and had three children, but I never saw her again."

"Did she break your heart?"

"No, she didn't. One of the reasons I went into the army was because I was too much of a coward to tell her that I didn't want to get married yet. I just wasn't sure about it. I tried to tell her twice, but she didn't want to hear it. Once I was in the army, she probably discovered on her own that it wasn't going to work. I hope she's happy, though."

Molly wanted to ask more, but noticed that Tom was paying close attention, and was concerned that the questions and answers might drift into adult areas, so she stopped that line of discussion.

"As complete that this house is, I'm surprised you don't have rocking chairs on the porch," Molly said with a smile.

Mac took another big bite of sandwich and had to finish chewing and swallow before saying, "They're under the house. I can drag them out if you'd like."

"You wouldn't mind? I couldn't think of a better way to spend a beautiful Sunday afternoon than sitting in a rocking chair and listening to the birds and that creek running under your cabin."

"Then Tom and I will bring you your rocking chairs in a few minutes. Won't we, Tom?"

Tom had a mouthful of ham sandwich and just vigorously nodded his agreement.

So, while Molly washed the dishes, Mac and Tom went to the tall end of the raft supports and Mac had to wind his way around some other stored furniture before he and Tom slid out the two maple rockers.

Mac had to carry them up the stairs because they were both too heavy and too awkward for Tom, but it was Tom who had the honor of being the first to try one out.

"Aren't you gonna try it, Mac?" Tom said as he rocked back and forth.

"No, sir. The second one is for your mother. I have to agree, though, that on a beautiful day with the sounds of the birds and the creek as it splashes its way past the rocks on its way to LaPorte is worthy of some time on the porch."

Molly exited the open door with a big grin on her face, saying, "I'm glad you agree with me, Mr. Jones, and thank you for reserving the rocker for me. They're very nice pieces of furniture."

Mac replied, "Now that you have your rockers for tomorrow, how about if we go and make some loud noises?"

———

Twenty minutes later, Mac and Tom were carrying their bundles of fireworks south from the cabin to a spot close to where Tom had almost met his end two days before. Molly was carrying a blanket as they reached the newly designated center of explosive delights.

There were several seat-sized boulders in the area, and Mac spent a few minutes rolling them to a central location, so they could all sit and still be close enough to talk without shouting.

For the first hour each of them took turns lighting the fuses of small firecrackers. Molly had been reticent at first, but soon was as excited as a schoolgirl as she'd set a fuse hissing and then run for safety. Mac had to spend some time before lighting the first fuse to show them how to do it. He had been surprised to find that Tom had never set one off before.

Then, Mac thought he'd have some fun and said, "I want to show you something that might find interesting, Tom."

Tom and Molly both walked over as Mac took out a penny from his pocket and then the tin cover from a can of beans from the other.

"Now, I'm going to place the penny on top of the piece of tin. Then, I'll put a firecracker on top and set it off. What will happen, Tom?"

"They'll both be blown up!" he said cheerfully.

"Okay. Molly, what do you think will happen?"

Molly replied, "I think the penny will be smashed into the tin and make a circle."

Tom looked at his mother and wished he had a chance to change his guess. His mama sure was smart, just like his friend, Mac.

Mac walked ten feet away, set the tin on the ground, the penny on top, and then the firecracker. He lit the fuse and quickly trotted back to the others as it sizzled until it reached the firecracker and it exploded with a loud crack and the penny, the tin and a bunch of small rocks nearby all flew away.

Tom felt vindicated and cheered as Mac walked to retrieve the tin and the penny.

He showed the penny and tin to Molly, who admitted that it wasn't deformed much at all.

"Okay, I'm going to do the same thing, with one difference," Mac said as he replaced the tin, the penny and the firecracker, but then placed a large flat rock on top of the firecracker, and after setting the fuse alight, again trotted back to Molly and Mac.

After a muffled explosion, Mac returned to the flat rock, where smoke was seeping around its edges. He flipped it over and picked up the penny and the tin and walked it over to Tom and Molly. He was grinning as he showed them the tin with the backwards face of the Indian and lettering firmly imprinted onto the tin.

"Wow! Mac, why did it do that this time?" Tom asked as he gazed at the deformed tin.

"The force of the explosion has nowhere else to go. When I set it off the first time, almost all of force from the explosion went into the air. This time, a lot more had to go into the penny, mashing it into the tin. It'd be better if I had been able to block the sides, too. But there's a reason for my showing you this little experiment."

"And what's that?" asked an impressed Molly.

"The reason the river is named the Cache La Poudre is that some French trappers, who were caught here in a snowstorm early in this century, buried their large supply of gunpowder so they could make it out of this pass. They never returned to find it and now, somewhere nearby, is buried about eighty pounds of gunpowder in four casks, and because it's buried the power of an explosion would be pretty impressive."

103

Molly, with wide eyes, then asked, "You mean it could blow up at any time?"

Mac shook his head, "No, ma'am. Gunpowder is pretty safe stuff, really. You could shoot a cask of gunpowder and most of the time, it wouldn't go off. It needs a spark. If you did shoot a gun into the buried casks, though, it's possible that if the bullet ricocheted off a rock, or if it hit one of the iron bands around the casks it would set it off."

"Do you know where it is, Mac?" Tom asked.

"No, sir. No one does. I'm not sure it's even good anymore after all this time and as many floods that have come through here. The last big one was so bad, it flooded Camp Collins and they moved it to where Fort Collins is now. But that was twenty years ago. With the cabin in the air like that, I don't think we have anything to worry about floods."

"Well, that makes me feel better," said Molly, "we may not get blown up, and we don't have to worry about floods either."

Mac laughed and said, "Everyplace has something to worry about; earthquakes and mudslides out west, hurricanes back east, and where I grew up, we were blessed with tornadoes every summer, in addition to the floods from the Mississippi River that were so common, we'd just get used to them. I'll settle for a good flood every couple of decades anytime."

———

As Mac laughed, just below his feet, what looked like a brown flat rock was really the top edge of the rusting iron band of the first of four casks of perfectly dry gunpowder.

———

In Boulder, Wild Willie Patterson, Jimmy Page, Cookie Priester, and Vern Porter were spending their holiday in Willie's hotel room reviewing the details of the stagecoach job on Tuesday.

"No witnesses this time," Willie said firmly, "that almost got us hung last time. If we didn't get that sheriff, we'd be pushin' up daisies by now."

Cookie quickly added, "Maybe you would, Willie, but I think Jimmy would be pushin' up skunk weed."

Vern joined Cookie in a series of guffaws before Willie glared them both into silence.

"Nothin' about this job is gonna be funny, Cookie. You remember that. We kill everybody on that stage, grab the money and head for Fort Collins fast. We need to get there at least a few minutes before the stage is due to arrive. They won't get worried for at least an hour, and we'll just walk our horses through town real peaceable, maybe stop at the saloon and have ourselves a beer. We won't use any of that Fort Collins Bank money, though. Then, we'll just take our time and ride cross country back to Boulder. We're gonna have to rough up those new bank notes, too."

"Why are we goin' to Fort Collins, boss? Shouldn't we just turn around and head back to Boulder right away?" asked Vern.

"I figure that the law from Fort Collins will find the coach and wire Boulder and all other law offices around the area that the coach was robbed, and he'd have an idea of how many men were involved by the hoofprints. If we head back to Boulder, we may walk right into the arms of the law. They got a lot more badge carriers in Boulder than they do down in Fort Collins. If we split into two pairs, it'll throw them off, too."

Vern wasn't satisfied by Willie's answer and asked, "But we could do that goin' back to Boulder, too, boss. Hell, we could hit it just ten miles outta Boulder and let them discover it. Why do we go to Fort Collins?"

Willie finally said, "Because, Vern, that's where I think our old pal Ed Richardson is hanging out. If he had a wife and kid with him, he'd need a town. He wouldn't go to any big town like Denver and it had to be close. So, I'm bettin' that he's in Fort Collins. Ed took our money and left us out to dry. Nobody does that to me! Nobody!"

Cookie glanced over at Vern and glared at him for upsetting the boss while Vern just nodded at Willie's gruff response.

"Now," Willie continued after he had calmed down somewhat, "we got the rest of the day and Sunday to get ready. We ride out of here on Monday and find our spot for the ambush. Everybody clear with all that?"

There were three heads bobbing in agreement as Wild Willie scanned his gang members.

"Okay, then. Let's play some poker," Willie said as he took out the deck from his jacket pocket.

———

After the sun set, Mac gave Molly and Tom each a Roman candle, and everyone watched as the colored balls of fire popped out of the tube and arced across the darkening sky.

But Mac had saved the exploding rockets for last, and as Molly sat on her boulder and Tom on his as Mac lit rocket after rocket, launching a new one after the last one had blinked out. He had one left, and as he set lit the fuse to the largest rocket, he trotted back to stand between Molly and Tom.

The fuse spluttered into the base of the rocket, the gunpowder ignited, and the rocket lifted off of the rocky ground soaring higher than the others, reaching almost three hundred feet before it detonated, spreading red, white and blue streaks of light across the sky, blotting out the stars behind them.

The patriotic firework ended the night's festivity and they began to head back to the cabin. Mac was carrying the blanket and was walking between Molly and Tom.

Molly said, "Mac, this turned out to be the best day of my life, and I want to thank you. You've made us feel so welcome since we've been here and we're so very grateful."

"I enjoyed myself immensely, Molly, and it wouldn't have been nearly as much fun without you and Tom here to share it with me."

"Did you want to come in for some coffee, Mac?" she asked.

"Coffee is always appreciated, Molly."

Tom had gone to bed and Mac and Molly were sharing coffee. Molly found that when she was with Mac, she didn't spend any time dwelling on her past or her failings. She simply had her focus elsewhere and found that she was actually happy, and not some false front.

The current topic was the cabin.

Mac had explained how he had built the cabin and why it was where it was, then Molly asked about the two biggest oddities in the structure.

"The indoor privy was the easy idea and construct. I just cut the hole and didn't put any flooring over the hole. I had to build the seat, and the oak seat itself took a day. I'm going to surround the open part under the cabin with logs to keep out the wind. I can imagine how shocking it would be to sit on that seat with a cold wind shooting under the cabin."

Molly laughed and replied, "Trust me, I already have a good idea of what to expect."

Mac grinned and said, "Now, I've got to show you how to use the bath. In fact, I'll have to set it up because it takes all four pots of water, including the Dutch oven to get a reasonably warm bath. It's just too big. I've got to come up with a way of getting more hot water into that tub."

Molly had her elbow on the table and her chin on her palm as she asked, "Would it be too much to ask if you could get it set up for me tonight? I know it's late and you get up early to work, but I've been looking at that bathtub and can't wait to try it out."

"I'll get the stove fired up and those pots filled. It'll take a while, but I think you'll find that it's worth it."

Molly was genuinely excited as she replied, "I'm sure it will be."

Mac had a fire roaring in the cookstove's firebox in minutes, then closed the firebox door and as Molly watched, he filled the pots and Dutch oven with water and set them on the stove and even in the oven.

Then, Molly filled their coffee cups as Mac sat back down.

"You know what, Molly. While I was filling those pots, I think I have an answer to how to get a lot more hot water into the tub."

"Another invention, Mr. Jones?" Molly asked with a smile.

Mac smiled back and said, "Yes, ma'am. When I was in Ledbetter's hardware store buying tools, I remember that he had a few of those big washtubs. Now, if I were to buy one and insert a valve near the bottom. I could run a hose from the valve through a hole in the wall to the bathtub while the washtub was on the stove. Once the water was almost boiling, I'd open the valve and let the hot, hot water flow into the tub. I'd bet I could get a good two feet of warm water out of it."

"That sounds like a marvelous idea, Mac," Molly said enthusiastically.

"We'll see," Mac replied before taking a sip of coffee.

"What's next after the corral, Mac?"

"After the corral, I'll probably build the smokehouse next. With as much wood as I have, I can make it bigger than I had originally planned, too. That seems to be a pattern with me since I've been here. I expected to build a small cabin and built this beast. The corral is going to be enormous, and the barn will probably be twice the size I had envisioned, too. I have all that lumber to use. I may build a chicken coop, too."

"And after the chicken coop, what will you do?" she asked.

"Tend the gardens and live in peace," he answered softly.

Molly paused before she asked, "I see you've got a lot of things growing. What do you have planted?"

Mac replied, "Potatoes, onions, carrots, tomatoes, and strawberries."

"You're growing strawberries?" she asked in surprise.

"It's sandy soil, and the strawberries don't take a lot of room. I've got two whole gardens of just potatoes, another of carrots and onions, the last one has tomatoes and the strawberries."

"Tom and I can help with the gardens," Molly said.

"Any assistance would be appreciated. I still have to figure out a way to keep the furry critters out of the carrots and tomatoes."

Molly laughed as Mac stood and checked on the water.

"Okay, Molly, I'm going to start moving the water into the tub. You can go and get your soaps and things."

"Alright," she said as she stood and walked down the hallway to her bedroom.

Mac began lugging the heavy, steaming pots to the bathing room. He had a pedestal near the tub for support as he set the first pot on top and tipped its contents into the tub.

After he had poured the last pot into the tub, Molly arrived with a folded nightdress, a bar of scented soap, and shampoo in her arms.

"It's all yours now, Molly. Pump in enough cold water to get the temperature you want. Enjoy your bath and good night."

"Good night, Mac, and thank you very much."

"You're welcome."

As Molly went inside and closed the door, Mac put the pots away and left the cabin to return to his tent.

Molly quickly undressed and then began pumping cold water into the still steaming tub. She tested the water twice and with it only a foot deep, she slipped into the tub and discovered to her delight that the smooth river rocks on the bottom not only provided a much more comfortable sitting surface, but they still retained the heat from the boiling water giving her legs a warm, massaging sensation.

She then took advantage of the luxury of a warm bath and when she finally left the cooling water, pulled the plug, and began drying herself, she said out loud, "Mac Jones, you are a genius!"

———

Twenty minutes later, a clean and thoroughly contented Molly was buried in the heavy quilts and blankets and luxuriating in the sensation. She was happier than she had any right to be, she suddenly thought. *What have I done to deserve this?*

She was warm, clean, comfortable and safe. She'd thoroughly enjoyed the time she had spent with Mac and wondered if it was possible for him to ever think of her as a woman worthy of marrying. She knew that she already wished he was her husband, but a man like Mac Jones needed to respect the woman he would marry, and she knew he would never respect her.

With that thought, Molly's mood again shifted back to the morose as she began to revisit her many flaws and the poor decisions she had made in her life, the worst being the one that turned her into a whore.

———

If only Molly had known that two hundred feet away, as Mac lay in his tent, he was thinking of exactly the same thing, only his obstacles were different. He genuinely liked Molly, and although he did feel sympathy for what had happened to her, he didn't pity her at all. He wanted to make her life better and he wanted it to be here, in his sanctuary.

His problem was that after listening to Molly, and the problems she had with her husband and then Ed Richardson, he believed that she needed time to lick her wounds.

Then, there was his biggest failure, the one that drove him to seek his refuge and do his penance. He had almost finished the work and still hadn't felt he had earned his own forgiveness. *Could he share an already encumbered Molly with his own soul's burden?*

Mac decided all he could do was to live each day as it came in the hope that a solution would present itself.

———

Ed Richardson had spent the rest of his day off at the saloon, figuring he'd ride over to LaPorte tomorrow to see where Molly had gone. He couldn't afford to have her return to Fort Collins and ruin his plan for the well-endowed, well-off widow.

CHAPTER 6

The next morning, Mac had aligned the rails along the ground, following the pines to the clearing, then going fifty feet out into the clearing before circling around back into the trees. Then, when he reached the starting point, he began moving the fence posts to their new locations out in the clearing.

Molly and Tom were still sleeping as Mac began to dig his holes with the pickaxe, spade and post-hole digger. He had only managed two holes when Tom appeared from the trees.

"Good morning, Tom," Mac said as he punched the beginning of the third hole with his pickaxe.

"Mornin', Mac. Mama wants to know if you're gonna come and have breakfast."

Mac slammed the tip of the pickaxe back into the ground and said, "Tell her I'll be there in a few minutes. I need to get cleaned up a bit and get a shirt on."

"Okay, Mac!" Tom shouted as he disappeared back into the trees.

Mac took off his work gloves and hung them over the pickaxe handle before heading for his tent.

Five minutes later, he was knocking on the cabin door, which was immediately opened by Tom.

Mac smiled at Tom, scuffed up his hair and entered the cabin and took a seat at the table.

"Good morning, Mac. I see you've been working early again," she said as she poured him a cup of coffee and set it on the table in front of him.

"It's my nature, I guess."

"Well, that nature has created some wonderful things. The bathtub, by the way was amazing. I thought the stones would be hard, but they were so incredibly soothing."

"I found it that way, too. After I get that washtub contraption made, it should be a lot better."

"What are you doing today?" she asked as she set a plate with eggs and ham in front of him.

"I should get those posts all done today and then, after I get the spikes in, the rails hung, and the gate built. The corral will be done, and I move onto the next project, which will probably be the smokehouse because it'll be so quick."

Tom then asked, "Can I help today, Mac?"

"Sure. You know what you can do, Tom? I really need a lookout when I'm working so no critters or Indians sneak up behind me. But a lookout isn't any good unless he's armed. Now, that Winchester is too much gun for you, so I think that if your mother thinks it's okay, I'll find you a nice .22 rifle the next time we go to town and I'll teach you how to shoot it."

Tom's mouth dropped, and it stayed agape as he turned to face his mother, and closed long enough to ask, "Is it okay, Mama?"

Molly replied, "Yes, it's a good idea."

Then she turned to Mac and asked, "Mac, you said you thought that Ed might come here because he wanted to rob you. Do you still think that's possible?"

"I think so, although I thought it was more likely the first two days after he helped drop off the lumber. Now, with you here, he might decide to visit after all."

She then asked, "I think it might be a good idea for me to learn to shoot a gun, too. Don't you?"

Mac replied, "It's not a bad idea, Molly. Tom will need a smaller rifle, but you shouldn't have any problem with the Winchester or the shotgun."

"Okay, Mac. When do we start?"

"Well, I'll give you both the quick version of using guns in general, but then, I've got to get back to work."

Molly nodded and said, "Okay."

Mac then spent ten minutes explaining the do's and don'ts of using firearms while Tom and Molly paid close attention as they all ate breakfast.

———

Mac finished his post holes before three o'clock, working right through lunch, and used the rest of the time before dinner dragging the rest of the rails into position, so each spot had two rails. He had four spare rails left over when he was finished.

Tom had helped with the post holes, handing Mac different tools, but couldn't do much with the rails, so he had returned to the cabin for lunch.

Molly had asked Tom why Mac hadn't returned for lunch and Tom had just shrugged, so Molly made the not-unexpected leap to think that Mac was angry with her for something and spent some time reviewing what had been said during breakfast and not finding anything.

It was getting into something of a routine now, so after he had cleaned up and donned his shirt, he walked to the cabin door, knocked and in seconds, Tom yanked the door open.

MAC'S CABIN

Molly looked over and said, "Honestly, Mac, I don't know why you knock. It's your cabin."

"Just habit, I guess," he said as he closed the door, then walked over to the shelves and began taking down plates to set the table while Molly was spooning mashed potatoes into a large bowl.

After they were all seated, Molly asked, "Mac, why didn't you come back for lunch?"

Mac replied, "I'm sorry, Molly, it's just that sometimes I get into a rhythm and in this case, it was digging the post holes. What happens is I play this game in my head. I have sixteen post holes to dig, so after I've done two, I'll think two down, fourteen to go. Then I start doing percentages, like, I'm twenty-five percent done. Once I get past fifty percent, I feel as if I need to finish. It's just a personal quirk."

Molly relaxed and smiled, saying, "Oh, that's all right, Mac. I thought you might be angry or something."

Mac smiled back and said, "When I get angry, you'll know, although I can tell you that you and Tom will never be the cause."

Molly then asked, "Are we going to LaPorte tomorrow?"

"Yes, ma'am. We need to buy some more supplies, some clothes for Tom, and a rifle he can use, too."

Tom grinned at the idea of the rifle. Clothes were clothes, but a rifle! Now that was something else!

———

Ed Richardson walked into Armstrong's Dry Goods in LaPorte and approached the counter.

"Can I help you, sir?" asked Z.T.

"I hope so. My missus run off a couple of days ago with my boy, and I'm gettin' kinda worried about her. She don't know anybody

115

around here, and the stage manager said she took the stage here. It's kinda my fault. I had a bad day at work and wasn't very nice to her. You haven't seen her around, have you? She's about thirty years old, slim, but pretty and the boy's ten."

Z.T. replied, "I saw 'em walking west while I was out sweepin' the boardwalk. I was wonderin' where they were headed, 'cause there ain't much up that way."

Ed was even more confused than he had been after hearing they had taken the stage to LaPorte.

"What's west of here? I helped deliver a load of lumber up to some feller named Jones a while back, but I didn't know anyone else livin' up that way."

"There isn't. The only person living up there is Mac Jones. He's a right nice feller, too."

Ed then asked, "He must be pretty well off to be livin' up there buildin' that house by himself. Don't you think?"

Z.T. took affront at the question, and plumb just didn't like the man, so he replied, "Now, mister, I don't know you, and I've answered your question about your wife. I'm not gonna talk about Mr. Jones. I like him and he's a good man."

Ed held out his palm and said, "No need to get all riled, mister. I was just tryin' to figure out why my wife went that way."

"Well, if you don't know, I sure as hell can't tell ya," Z.T. snapped back.

Ed didn't say another word, he just turned and headed out the door. As he climbed on his horse, he glanced at the river flowing down from the north and then wheeled his horse to his left and headed back to Fort Collins.

———

MAC'S CABIN

After he'd gone, Jolene stepped out of her office, placed her hand on Z.T.'s shoulder and said, "A man who doesn't know where his wife is isn't much of a man, Z.T."

Z.T.'s eyes were still fixed on the open door as he replied, "You got the right of that, Babe. I don't trust that feller one bit, neither. Him askin' about Mac like that makes me think he's up to no good."

"Maybe you should ride up there and warn him. Besides, I think that man's wife and boy are up there."

"I kinda figured that out. With that for a husband, I don't blame her for runnin'. If Mac hasn't stopped by before Wednesday, I'll ride up that way. I'm kinda curious about that cabin of his anyway."

Jolene smiled before turning back to the office and said, "A lot of folks wonder what he's building up in those woods."

As Ed rode back to Fort Collins, he wondered why Molly would take the kid to that cabin. She didn't even know the man. He was still uneasy with having her so close while he was making such good progress with Matilda Richards.

He had only used the 'I love you' line, not the 'let's get married' line on her yet, but she had taken him to her bed willingly. She seemed to be a bit put off by his rush to satisfy himself, but he had explained that he had remained celibate for so long after his wife had passed and that she was such a desirable woman that he couldn't constrain himself and it had seemed to solve that problem.

The only real problem left was Molly, but even as he saw her as a potential problem, he now began to think of her decision to go to the cabin as a possible benefit. He could go up there, shoot Jones for stealing his wife and find his money. Of course, he'd have to kill Molly, which was too bad, but he'd enjoy the hell out of her first. Killing the brat wouldn't bother him in the least, and as far away as that place was, no one would ever hear a thing.

It was just a question of timing. Everything seemed to be coming together for Ed; the widow and Molly's decision to go to that cabin. Maybe he'd bring Mildred to his new cabin and live there.

———

Mac was helping to clean up after dinner and Tom was outside when Molly said, "Mac, I'm still feeling guilty about you having to live in the tent while I sleep in your bed."

"There really is no reason for it, Molly. I'm perfectly fine out in the tent."

"What about when it gets cold?" she asked.

"I was thinking of that. I'll probably just build the barn a little bigger and build a small fireplace and close off a room on the end. I can build a bed into the wall, too. I'll be fine, Molly."

Molly then said quietly, "I should never have come here. I pushed you out of your house and now that bastard that called himself my husband is going to come here and cause trouble."

Mac sighed and said, "Molly, you're here because I want you here. Period. No more blaming yourself for anything that has happened or will happen. It's just a waste of time. Okay?"

Molly nodded and said, "Okay."

Mac didn't believe she meant it, though, and he was right in his assumption. He needed to get her off the subject and cheer her up somehow. Time for a story.

"You know, ma'am," he began, "there just ain't no sense in worryin' cause it ain't gonna help none. Now, one time, I was hot on the trail of an outlaw named Worry Walt. He had a price of eleven dollars and thirty-two cents on his head for takin' liberties with a skinny ol' schoolmarm named Nelly Nobottom. Well, I knew I was gettin' close to nabbin' old Worry Walt and had already made big plans for all that reward money. I was ridin' along on my trusty mount, Horse, when I get to hearin' this hollerin' and then a gunshot. Now, I'm kinda surprised 'cause I didn't think Worry Walt was a violent kinda feller. So, I jump down from Horse and get to runnin' to where I heard the yellin'. And what do you think I saw with these very eyes? Why it was Worry Walt hisself, with his draws down on his ankles and a smokin' pistol in his hand. I figgered Walt ain't gonna shoot me, cause he was carryin' a flintlock and he'd shot his wad, so to speak. I come runnin' up to him and see that he just shot this big ol' rattler."

Molly was holding back from laughing but had a smile on her face as Mac looked into her eyes and continued.

"Well, ma'am, I shout to Worry Walt, 'What happened?', and he says, 'That damned snake bit me in the butt without a single rattle!'. And sure 'nuff, he had two big ol' bite marks on his bee-hind where that dead rattler done bit him. Then, I looked at the snake and said, 'Well, lookee there, Walt! That rattler ain't got no tail at all!' Walt looks back at the butt end of the snake and says, 'Well, don't that beat all. Here I was worryin' about everything and I'm gonna die from somethin' that I didn't see comin'.'"

And you know what, ma'am? Worry Walt didn't die from that bite. That snake was so old, he musta been almost outta poison. So, bein' a kindly soul, and figgerin' that Walt done got punished enough, I forgot about that giant ree-ward, and just let Worry Walt go. But he learned a lesson from that run-in with the snake and told me that worryin' didn't stop somethin' he didn't see comin' from bitin' him in the ass. If you pardon my language, ma'am."

Molly still refrained from laughing, but asked, "Is that the end of this obviously true story?"

"Well, almost, ma'am. A few months later, I'm walkin' along the boardwalk of Surprise, Arizona when I spotted Walt and a tall, thin woman headin' my way. It turned out that after we parted company, ol' Worry Walt headed back and married Nelly Nobottom, and she now proudly bore the name of Mrs. Walter Broadtail."

Molly then allowed herself the laughter that had been held back until the story ended. It was a silly tale, but she could see that it had some merit even as she laughed.

Mac felt his mission was completed and set the last plate into the drying rack.

"Well, I'll leave you with that story, Molly," Mac said as he dried his hands.

Molly then asked, "Did you want to sit on the porch and talk for a while?"

"Alright," Mac replied.

He waited while Molly dried her hands and then they both went outside and took seats in the rocking chairs. It was a beautiful evening and the sun was just about ready to drop below the horizon.

Before either could say anything, Tom trotted up the stairs and said, "I'm gonna go inside and wash up. I kinda got dirty."

"Then you get ready for bed, young man," Molly said as he nodded and walked past, closing the door behind him after entering the cabin.

Once he was gone, Molly said, "Thank you for that story, Mac. I was worrying too much. Don't you ever worry?"

"I keep myself too busy to worry, Molly."

"Not even at night when you're alone getting ready for sleep?"

"I wouldn't call it worry. I think about things that I need to do."

"What about your past, Mac. You haven't told me much about what brought you to this place. Why did you come out to this isolated area to live? It sounds like you've had the opportunity to live anywhere you chose, but you chose this place. Why?"

Mac replied, "I like hunting and fishing, and this place was perfect."

Molly was disappointed in his answer. It smacked of a typical Bob Phillips non-answer. *What was Mac Jones trying to hide?*

Molly needed to know right now. She wasn't going to go through this again.

"Mac, why are you telling me that? You've called this cabin your refuge or your sanctuary. You didn't come here for the fishing or hunting. It sounded like you came to hide from someone. Please don't be like Bob Phillips. Tell me the truth. Please."

Mac replied, "I'm sorry, Molly. You're right. That was just a flippant answer because I don't like explaining the reason I'm here. It's nothing like Bob or Ed Richards. I'm not wanted or anything."

Molly asked quietly, "But you didn't say you haven't committed a crime, Mac. Is that what it is? You committed a crime and weren't caught, so you're hiding here?"

Mac sighed and stared out into the forest and replied, "It wasn't a crime as much as it was a sin, Molly."

"Aren't they the same thing?" she asked.

"No. There are a lot of crimes that aren't sins, and a lot of sins that aren't crimes. My sin was so terrible that I had to find a refuge to make penance, so I could forgive myself. I needed to be alone."

"Is that why you came here, then? To escape from people?"

"No, not at all. I like people and get along with almost everyone. It's hard to explain. I never felt at peace since I left the farm when I was eighteen and was searching for it ever since. Then I found this spot, and spent two months working twelve hours a day, seven days a week to build the cabin. It was supposed to be like a penance, but I found I enjoyed it too much for it to qualify as any form of atonement, and yet, when I finished building the cabin, it was so much more than just a building or a home. It was as if it were an offering to show that I was willing to at least try to make amends."

Molly asked quietly, "Amends for what, Mac?"

Mac hadn't wanted Molly to know the reason, but now felt he had no choice.

"I'll tell you the reasons, Molly, but it's going to be difficult."

Mac stood and walked to the edge of the porch faced the trees and folded his arms.

"I've been trying to make amends for the wrongs I committed beginning on the day in July of '61, when I happily left the family farm and joined the Seventh Iowa Volunteer Infantry Regiment. I had been born and raised on that farm; my mother died giving birth to my twin younger brothers when I was just a year old. My father and brothers were all I had. My father wasn't a bad man or a good one; he was just a farmer and a typical father."

It was difficult for him to bring up his three sons and he remarried when I was three and his second wife, Delores, died when I was fourteen, but I never knew why she died. I can barely remember her anymore. My father assumed that I and my brothers would all be farmers as he was, and that was what I expected, too. I had my girlfriend and it looked as if my future was all set down in stone. Then, the war happened. I had just turned eighteen a few days before the attack on Fort Sumpter, and I wanted to sign up, but my father begged me not to go. Like many young men at that heady time at the start of the war, I was incredibly naïve about the realities of war, and just wanted to wear a uniform and carry that big Springfield rifle. I thought it would show everyone that I was a real man. I told my father that he'd be fine with my brothers there to help and left the farm to go to war. He was raging at me when I walked out the door."

After our unit finished assembling in Burlington, we were shipped east to fight with Grant's Army of the West. We were so proud of ourselves as we marched in a long line winding its way to an unknown destination, and when we saw the mass of bluecoats, the dozens of cannons and the hundreds of mounted cavalrymen, we all knew for certain that those rebels would be finished in three months."

MAC'S CABIN

Mac paused and looked down at the porch's edge before continuing.

"Of course, that, like almost everything else I believed, was wrong. War wasn't some glorious triumphant charge with bayonets flashing and flags waving; it was a dirty, slow, horrific thing where your friends died from getting sick as often as they did from bullets or artillery fire, but mostly it was waiting. It seemed as if we were always waiting for something, whether it was for chow, letters from home, orders to go somewhere, or a train to arrive to take us there. And then, there were the battles: Belmont, Fort Henry, Donelson, Shiloh and a bunch of others all the way across Georgia before Sherman turned us north for another march through the Carolinas. The big battles were horrible with whole lines of my friends being rendered into pieces by canister shot and others being hit by Minie balls from a hundred yards away, never seeing the face of their executioner. But all of the skirmishes in between were just as likely to get you killed and wounded, too. And underlying every battle and every skirmish was the confusion. We never knew what we were doing or where we were going. We just did what we were told as if we weren't even humans, just cattle being driven to the slaughterhouse."

He paused as if remembering something, then continued.

"I didn't get any mail at all; not a single letter. So, I didn't know what was going on back at the farm. I didn't find out until we mustered out in July of '65, and when I did return, it was even worse than what I'd experienced over those four long years."

Molly felt his pain dripping from every word and couldn't imagine what could be worse.

Mack exhaled sharply and said, "When I returned to the farm, I expected to finally find peace after those four soul-destroying years. I walked to the farmhouse and saw men working the fields, and thought it was my father and brothers, and it looked like he had hired some help, too. So, I began running, still wearing my blue uniform, and waved wildly, expecting my father and brothers to see me and begin waving back, but no one waved. They were all looking in my direction, but no one waved. When I was closer, I finally saw my father and he just stared at me as if he didn't know me. I recognized some of the men working with my father as neighbors but couldn't find my brothers. When I finally drew close, I asked my father where my brothers, Jimmy and Henry were, he just said, 'you killed them', and went back to weeding as if I wasn't even there."

Mac then looked up at the tops of the trees that disappeared into the darkening sky.

"After I had gone off to war, my two brothers waited until they turned eighteen and both joined the army to follow in the footsteps of their big brother. I had never written to them of the horrors that I had seen; the sickness, or the boredom. If I had, maybe they wouldn't have enlisted. I don't know. I learned that Henry had died from dysentery and Jimmy died in a skirmish that wasn't even worthy of a name. They both died just three weeks apart in October of '63, and I never knew. I felt responsible for their deaths, just as my father had said."

After that first day back, I worked harder than I'd ever worked before to make up for the loss of my brothers, but my father never forgave me. When he got the word about my brothers' deaths two years before I returned, he took to the bottle, and by the time I got back, he was drinking a bottle every three days of rotgut corn liquor. He lasted almost a year, and as he was dying, I asked him to forgive me for what I had done, and his last words to me were, 'I wish it had been you that died'."

Mac took in a deep breath and blew it out before continuing.

"I worked the farm for a little while longer, but it was a sad place with terrible memories, so I sold it and then just bought a horse and saddle, packed up my clothes and left, riding west, looking for my refuge. Ever since I left the army, I never wore a hat again, either, except to keep my head warm when it was cold. I wasn't ashamed of being in the army, Molly. I knew it was a war that had to be won. It's just war itself and how it destroyed my father and took my brothers from me, and it was all my fault. If I hadn't been so damned determined to prove how brave I was or how much of a man I was, they'd all still be alive. I was the only one in the family to survive that war, but I should have been the only one to die."

Molly couldn't say a word as she watched Mac continue to stand on the edge of the porch and began to fear that he might do something to harm himself.

But Mac finally just said, "I'm a bit tired now, Molly. I'll see you in the morning."

"I understand, Mac," she replied softly.

Mac smiled slightly, then hopped down without using the stairs and slipped into the night.

Molly stayed sitting in the rocking chair, without rocking, as she just listened to the sounds of his footsteps fade into the night, still stunned by Mac's revelations. *How could he blame himself for something like that?* He had joined the army. He didn't force his brothers to sign up. He surely wasn't responsible for their deaths, yet he still thought it was his fault almost ten years after going back home.

Her own worries pushed aside, Molly thought she would do what she could to make Mac's life better.

CHAPTER 7

Monday morning's sunrise found Mac still in his tent for a change.

He was still unsure if he had done the right thing by telling Molly about what drove him to this place, even if she was concerned that he might be hiding a dangerous secret. He'd only known her for three days and here he was baring his soul. Maybe it was because she was a woman, but he was most concerned about the story adding to her already formidable concerns.

He finally just realized there was no point in worrying about it. He had told Molly and he couldn't take it back.

He finally left the tent and headed to the creek to get some water to wash and shave.

After he finished his morning ablutions, he looked at the cookstove pipe and saw smoke, which meant Molly was awake, so he figured he might as well head that way and see what kind of damage he had caused by telling Molly his story.

When Mac knocked on the door, it was Molly who opened the door, and he was pleased to see that Molly was wearing one of the dresses from the collection of clothing that had been donated by Jake Abernathy. It seemed to fit her better than her own dress, and coupled with her brushed hair and smile, it made for a pretty picture, but mostly, he was relieved to see her in a happy mood.

"Good morning, Molly."

"Good morning, Mr. Jones. Now take a seat and I'll feed you properly," she commanded.

"Yes, ma'am," Mac replied with a smile and a mock salute.

Molly smiled at him and was glad to see he still was in his normal good humor after last night and wondered if he had just pushed everything back inside again.

She slid a plate with four eggs and two thick slices of ham in front of him, along with a plate of biscuits and a crock of butter. Then, she poured him a cup of coffee before sitting down with her own cup of coffee. Tom was sitting with a cup of heavily milked coffee across from Mac.

"No breakfast for you, Molly? You need the food. You're still about ten pounds too light."

Molly laughed and replied, "And how would you know, Mr. Jones?"

"Don't forget who lifted you down from the horse, ma'am," he answered as he cut a big piece from the ham.

Molly said, "I'll never forget that, Mac, but Tom and I have eaten already. I had three eggs and some ham along with a biscuit. Is that enough?"

Mac nodded then forked some eggs into his mouth.

Tom said, "Mama says I should eat more oatmeal, but I'm not a little kid anymore."

Mac said, "Did you think I bought that oatmeal for you, Tom? I seem to recall that I already had the oatmeal on the shelf before you arrived. I bought it for me to eat. I love oatmeal, and I don't believe I qualify as a little kid either."

Tom asked in surprise, "You do? Really?"

Mac nodded and said, "Really. I like it with some brown sugar and butter. Maybe I'll talk your mama into making some for us both tomorrow morning."

Tom looked at his mother and asked, "Can you do that, Mama?"

"Oh," she replied, "I think I can handle oatmeal."

Then she looked at Mac who winked at her, bringing another smile to her face.

After breakfast, Mac harnessed the team and brought the wagon around to the cabin.

By nine o'clock, Mac was driving the wagon across the north fork's ford with Tom on his left eagerly watching the oncoming current that had nearly drowned him just days earlier while Molly sat on his right watching the team of draft horses easily pulling the empty wagon.

He had raided his bank that morning, checked his balance and discovered it had dwindled to less than fifty-four-hundred dollars after he had withdrawn four hundred. He was planning on buying horses and saddles for both Molly and Tom, so they could get around better, but was concerned about the rapid decline in his cash over the past two and a half months. He wondered how he could push it back up, while still acknowledging it was still a large amount of money. There was always the gold. The nine nuggets he'd found since he'd been working on his cabin were quite a lot for the area. One or two wouldn't have surprised him, but nine? And he wasn't even looking. He simply didn't want the news to leak out.

Molly was almost dozing already as the wagon rocked and pitched as it rolled down the long slope because she hadn't slept well at all as her mind was busy with so many divergent thoughts. Now, she was even worrying that she might bump into Ed Richardson in LaPorte and was concerned that he might make trouble for Mac. Her non-husband was a murderer, after all. She knew that Mac was well-armed, but she didn't know how good he was with the pistol he wore at his waist.

So, after they were about halfway to LaPorte, she asked, "Mac, how good are you with your guns?"

Mac glanced over at Molly and wondered where that question had come from, but replied, "Better than most. I practiced a lot when I was a deputy sheriff, and even more when I was a bounty hunter, but not with this pistol. I've only practiced twice with this one but found it to be very accurate. I'm better with the rifles, though. The Sharps I've only put a few rounds through, but it's a good long-range weapon with a lot of power. So, overall, I'd say I'm reasonably good. What brought on that question, Molly?"

Molly chewed on her lower lip and then answered, "I'm worried that Bob, or rather Ed, might be looking for me and might be in LaPorte."

"Why would he be looking for you, Molly? Didn't he basically throw you and Tom out into the streets?"

"Sort of, well, never mind," Molly said, sorry she ever brought up the subject.

But Mac couldn't let her non-reply go, and asked again, "Why would he be looking for you, Molly?"

Molly clenched her hands into fists and snapped, "It's his way, that's all. He wants to get rid of me and then he gets, well, lonely, and he wants me back. But this time it was different. This time, he told me he really hadn't married me, so I knew I couldn't go back, even if he tried to get me to return. Can't you understand the difference?"

Mac understood more easily than she could have anticipated and replied, "I do understand, Molly, but don't worry about Ed at all. I'll handle him if he shows up."

Molly didn't reply, but just nodded.

Mac knew he'd done all he could short of holding Molly and trying to make her feel protected but was convinced that was the last thing he should do, especially after hearing about what Ed had done to her. He couldn't imagine treating a woman like that. She had been so desperate she had walked fifteen miles with her eleven-year-old son to the unseen cabin of a virtually unknown man. For all she knew, he could have been living in a miner's shack with a common law wife.

———

Just before eleven o'clock, Mac parked the wagon in front of Armstrong's Dry Goods, and after Tom leapt from the driver's seat, Mac slid out that way, then walked around the other side and helped Molly down.

They entered the store and Mac told Molly and Tom to wander the aisles and pick out anything they needed while he dropped off his order with Z.T.

Z.T. had seen Mac walk in with that man's wife and kid and had a whole wasp's nest of questions as Mac walked up to the counter with a slip of paper.

"Morning, Z.T., I've got an order for you," Mac said as he smiled and laid the list on the counter.

Z.T. waved him closer and then leaned over the counter and said quietly, "Mac, that lady's husband came in here Sunday and was askin' for her and the kid. I told him that I seen her headin' west out of town on foot a few days before. She's at your place now?"

Mac wasn't surprised after what Molly had told him and said, "He told her that he had lied about his name when they got married and that he wasn't really her husband before he threw her and her son out into the street, Z.T. She had nowhere else to go and didn't know anybody. She only knew me because I met her and her son in Fort Collins and we had a nice talk."

Can you imagine how alone and frightened she must have been to risk that walk all the way to my place? They didn't even have a pistol to protect themselves. Her boy almost drowned in the river when he tried to cross, too. I'm providing sanctuary for them both now, Z.T. She and her son are living in my cabin and I'm living in my tent, if that soothes your concerns."

Z.T. replied, "I wasn't worried about that, Mac. I was worried 'cause that bastard began askin' about you and how much money you might have. I got the feelin' that he was aimin' to pay you a visit."

"That's the same feeling I got when he and some men from the lumber mill delivered wagonloads of lumber to my campsite a couple of months ago. The worst part is that the guy's a wanted criminal. His name is Ed Richardson and he used to run with Wild Willie Patterson's bunch."

Z.T.'s eyes shot wide and he said, "Well, that's bad news. You figure they're all around here?"

"I don't think so. If anything, he's running from them, and I don't think Ed will be too pleased if they find him. He kind of left them in the lurch when he could have saved their hides. Then he ran off with their loot to add insult to injury. If you see him again, just tell Marshal Ackerman. I might head that way and tell him myself."

"That's not gonna do any good, Mac. The marshal left to take a job in Denver last week, and Deputy Smith just up and quit 'cause he didn't want to do the job by himself. We're havin' to depend on the county sheriff right now."

Mac hadn't heard that bit of news, but said, "Well, I'd send a telegram to the county sheriff in Fort Collins, but he doesn't know me at all, so all we can do is keep an eye out. Thanks for the information, Z.T. I still need to get this order filled, though."

Z.T. returned to his storekeeper mode and took the list.

Mac began his own perusing of the aisles, but not to buy anything. He found Molly in the boys' clothing area and she turned when she heard him approach.

Mac said, "Molly, you were right about Ed Richardson looking for you. He told Z.T. some nonsense story about you running off after an argument, then he went back to Fort Collins."

Molly closed her eyes and asked, "Does he know where I am?"

"He does, but it doesn't matter, Molly. I'd rather deal with him sooner, so you don't have to think about him anymore. But don't worry, Molly. We'll be all right. He won't be able to sneak up on us."

131

"Why not?" she asked, as her eyes revealed her fear.

"Because," Mac replied with a comforting smile, "when we get back, after target practice, I am going to build a tree house for Tom, so he can see almost all the way to LaPorte."

Molly was still unsettled about the news but nodded and said, "Okay."

Mac bought a simple, single-shot Remington rifle that used a .22 rimfire cartridge that was suited to his size. He handed it to Tom, had him verify that the chamber was empty and told him that in a couple of years, he'd graduate to a Winchester. Tom didn't care one bit as he took the rifle from Mac's hand, and just looked at the weapon with awe.

Mac added four boxes of .22 cartridges, anticipating that Tom would be shooting a lot, then added a pair of field glasses to the list.

Molly brought her large stack of clothes for Tom and set them near Mac's things on the counter, feeling a bit sheepish.

"Tom's never had so many clothes and I know he'll be shooting up again soon."

"That's quite all right, Molly. Get him some better boots, too, and give him some wiggle room in the toes."

Molly smiled, turned around and three minutes later set a pair of boots on the counter.

"Those are perfect. Now, we just need to help Z.T. with the rest of the order and we'll be on our way back home in a little while."

When Mac said 'home' it had a soothing effect on Molly. She hadn't had a real home since she was a girl and recalled the comforting blanket of security she felt when she was home.

Yes, Molly thought, *we're going home.*

It took another half an hour to finish the order and get it loaded onto the wagon. Mac made one quick stop at Ledbetter's to buy that big wash tub, a valve and hose. He had Ledbetter drill a hole in the side of the tub for him and they mounted the valve on the side. The store owner was as pleased with the creation as Mac was when it was done.

When Molly saw the thing being loaded onto the wagon she had to laugh, but she knew that strange contraption would make her baths even more enjoyable.

Tom didn't notice as he was admiring his new Remington.

Mac then treated for a nice lunch at the café before they headed back just two hours after arriving.

Tom was really anxious to try his new rifle, and he held onto his newest prized possession all the way back, pretending to shoot any target of opportunity on the three-hour trip.

For the duration of the drive, Molly would glance at their backtrail every couple of minutes, afraid that Ed Richardson was coming after her, even though she knew it was an incredibly remote possibility.

Mac noticed and knew that nothing he could say would eliminate her worry about the man. The only thing that would be to eliminate the man entirely. He began to think about riding to Fort Collins and just grabbing him and taking him to the sheriff's office. It would take a wanted criminal off the streets and it would remove Molly's worries.

———

Wild Willie and his boys had ridden out of Boulder at eight o'clock, ahead of the stage to Fort Collins, so they could get a good idea of how fast it would be traveling when it reached them and how they could get it to stop. It was a last-minute change in plans by Wild Willie, as was their escape. He thought they'd skip Fort Collins, riding around the town so no one would see four strangers ride in around the same time that the stage was held up. They'd hole up in LaPorte for a

couple of days before they returned to Fort Collins to find Ed
Richardson.

They rode for three hours before finding a good location just twelve
miles or so before Fort Collins. It was a thick copse of aspens that
jutted out from a forest that normally ran a couple of hundred yards
from the roadway. The site was perfect as it only left them thirty or
forty yards to go before they reached the road.

They pulled into the trees and tied off their horses deep in the
woods, waiting for the stage to pass. It wasn't long before they
spotted the dust cloud coming down the roadway.

"Here she comes," said Cookie needlessly as they watched it
approach.

They all watched as the six-horse team had the coach moving
briskly along the dirt road, throwing up a huge cloud of dust behind it.

It swung past the trees and continued on to Fort Collins as the four
outlaws followed its progress with measuring eyes.

"It's gonna be close," said Willie, "we don't have a lot of wiggle
room on this one. As soon as it's about a quarter of a mile out, we
make our move. Now, he can't leave the roadway to the right over
there because of the berm and that two-foot drop-off, and it's not wide
enough to go around us. We just gotta make sure he doesn't try to
plow through us. We need to shoot the driver and the shotgun rider
right away. That's where the shotgun comes in. Now, let's relax and
get some chow."

———

Mac had the wagon unloaded, the team unharnessed and happily
grazing as Mac, Molly and Tom walked away from the house and
headed for the same area where they had enjoyed their fireworks on
Saturday.

Mac was carrying the shotgun and a two-foot tall, eight-inch
diameter log that was a leftover from some of his cuttings, while Molly

carried his Winchester Yellowboy. Tom, of course, lovingly carried his Remington .22.

When they reached the new designated target range, Mac set the shotgun against a boulder then walked the log about a hundred feet away.

When he returned, he said, "Okay, Tom, you get to go first because I think you're primed yourself. Now before you shoot, I want you to repeat to me the rules for using a gun."

Tom quickly went through the rules about always assume a gun is loaded, knowing what you are going to shoot, and never point any gun at someone even if you know it is unloaded.

Then, Mac handed him his loaded rifle, stood behind him as he prepared to fire.

"Don't fire yet, Tom. I'm going to correct your stance," Mac said as he leaned against Tom's back.

He moved Tom's left foot forward another six inches, and his left hand further down the small rifle's forearm to reduce the swaying Mac was already seeing, then stepped back.

"Okay, Tom. Fire when you're ready."

Tom aimed his Remington and when he squeezed the trigger smoothly as Mac had told him to do, he was rewarded when the rifle cracked, and a cloud of white smoke popped out of the muzzle. Mac had been watching downrange and had seen the puff where the bullet struck.

"Just about a foot to the left, Tom. But very good shooting for the first time. Go ahead and reload and try again."

Mac was a bit amused by the small report of the .22 short cartridge with only twenty grains of powder, but he was sure that Tom didn't care one bit. He was shooting his own rifle.

After he fired three shots, finally hitting the log on the third try, Tom wheeled about, remembering to drop the muzzle of the rifle, which pleased Mac.

"I hit it! From way back here, too!"

Molly said, "Good for you, Tom."

"Is Mama going next, Mac?" he asked.

"Yup, that's the plan," he replied as he turned to Molly and asked, "Are you ready, Molly?"

"I think so," she answered.

She was still unsettled as she watched Mac as he demonstrated how to hold the carbine, lever a new cartridge into the firing chamber, then aim and fire. Normally, when instructing a new shooter, as he had with Tom, he'd hold their arms and hands to get them into a proper shooting position, but he didn't want to make Molly more uncomfortable than she already was, so after demonstrating the technique he handed her the Yellowboy.

Once she had the Winchester and assumed a firing position, he verbally gave her the adjustments she needed to form a more stable platform.

Molly took aim at the log, then closed her eyes and yanked the trigger, sending the bullet high, so Mac had no idea where it had gone.

Mac stepped closer to her and said, "Molly, you closed your eyes and jerked the trigger, so the barrel lifted, sending your shot high. Just relax and squeeze the trigger gently. Keep your eyes open and the rifle's sights on the target. Let it be a surprise when it fires. Okay?"

Molly turned to Mac and asked, "Can you help me like you helped Tom, please?"

Mac nodded and stepped behind Molly on her left side, put his right arm around to her right hand and his left hand under her elbow and made some small adjustments, but suspected her biggest problem was her nerves.

While he was still close to her, Mac said, "Don't be afraid of the rifle, Molly. It's just a tool. It's noisier than most, but that's all it is. But this tool will give you security and freedom if you know how to use it. So, you need to just relax and let it do its job. Keep your eyes open and hold your breath to keep the muzzle steady. Then just squeeze the trigger softly. Okay?"

Molly had taken what Mac had told her to heart as she blew out her breath and looked downrange at the log. She imagined the face of Ed Richardson as she looked past the sights.

"Okay," Molly replied.

Mac quickly stepped back and said, "Okay, Molly. You're ready."

Molly sighted on the log, held her breath and slowly pulled back on the trigger, keeping her sight on the log until the Winchester bucked and smacked her shoulder as the loud report echoed across the rocky ground. She didn't see where the bullet had hit and turned to Mac.

"Where did that one go, Mac?" she asked.

Mac smiled at her and said, "You hit the log just a little right of center, Molly. You did a great job."

Tom grinned and said, "My mama is a sharpshooter!"

Molly smiled and asked if she could take some more shots.

"Go ahead, just remember to cycle that lever quickly."

Molly did as Mac said and was rewarded when the empty brass was ejected from the gun and she aimed and squeezed off another shot. After three more rounds, she was satisfied in her newfound ability, and so was Mac. Molly felt more than just pleased, she felt a sense of confidence growing inside her, and her fear beginning to slide away. Mac had been right. This long, skinny tool was her key to protecting herself.

Mac strengthened her newfound confidence by saying, "Excellent shooting, Molly. You're doing really well. Now, I want you to try one round with the shotgun. I don't think you want to risk firing both barrels at once, though. It has a bigger kick than the Winchester and both barrels would really hurt."

He took the Winchester from Molly and handed her the twelve-gauge. With Tom watching carefully, she cocked the right-hand hammer, aimed it downrange and squeezed the trigger, feeling the more powerful kick against her shoulder.

"You're right, Mack, I think both barrels would do some serious damage," she said as she handed the shotgun back to Mac.

"For someone as light as you are, it would definitely be painful. Now, let's get these guns back into the house and get them cleaned before Tom and I build his lookout treehouse."

This was the first that Tom had heard about it, but he was already excited before they took two steps back toward the house. *A rifle and a treehouse in the same day?*

As they walked back to the house, Molly asked if she could carry the Winchester, which was a good thing for Mac to hear, so he handed it to her. As her fingers wrapped around the Yellowboy, she felt, well, different. She was no longer helpless.

After cleaning the guns, a task watched studiously by both Molly and Tom, Molly said she'd start cooking dinner, while Mac and Tom took some boards and tools and headed toward south looking for a tree that had a clear view south toward LaPorte.

———

While Mac and Tom were building the observation platform, Molly alternated preparing dinner and looking at the Yellowboy sitting in the gun rack on the wall. Mac had told her that it was her gun now. At first, she had thought there must be something wrong with her for enjoying having the rifle in her hands that first time Mac gave it to her, but when he had told her what it was, she understood why she had felt that way. The rifle was independence. It was a liberating sensation that filled her as she recalled the power she held in her hands. She was in control of her life, not Ed Richardson or anyone else. There would be no more fear of bogeymen, no more self-pity and no more morose wallowing in self-doubt. No more constant self-examination and condemnation. She had made mistakes, as everyone did, but she had raised Tom to be a good young man by herself, too.

She was almost thirty now. Half of her life was past, and she suddenly knew it had been wasted in fear and worry about what the next day would bring.

She looked quickly around her and knew what she wanted and who she wanted. Then, she looked at her reflection in the kitchen window and flipped her dark brown hair behind her ears, appraising herself honestly without a filter of self-loathing or disgust. She saw a pretty, dark-haired woman that had wasted too much time feeling sorry for herself and blaming herself for things that had happened to her.

"I'm just a woman, not 'that kind of woman'," she said aloud, "I am who I am, and I can live with that."

Molly then shook her head and decided that the second half of her life wasn't going to be the same as the first half. Molly was going to live.

Molly slid the roast into the oven and after the door closed, she stood straight, turned and marched to the open door, stepped out onto the porch, stopped and put her hands on her hips.

As she glared defiantly at the forest, she shouted, "To hell with you Ed Richardson! And damn you, too, Chester, if God hasn't already. No more self-pity or worrying about what happened before or what will happen tomorrow. I am Molly Ann Bradford and I am starting my life over beginning right now!"

Then, she turned and strode purposefully back into the kitchen, no longer Molly Phillips or Molly Saunders. She was starting her new life with the same name that she had begun the first.

The Winchester may have been the spark, but the smoldering urge to fight back finally ignited into a raging inferno. The world was going to see a different Molly now.

———

Mac and Tom sat on the floor of the new treehouse and could see a good twelve miles south. Both had heard Molly's shouted declaration of personal independence, but neither knew what had prompted it.

"Tom, I'm sure you heard what I told your mother about Bob Phillips; his real name and what he did. Now, it seems that he's looking for your mother again and probably knows where you both are. I still want to get some work done, but I don't want to be surprised by a sudden visit by Ed Richardson. You won't have to stay up here all day, because that would be a waste of time, but you can stay on the ground down near the target range and even practice for a while. I bought two hundred rounds of those .22 cartridges, so you have plenty, but don't go all silly on me. You need to be responsible. Once you feel you can hit the target most of the time, save your ammunition for when you really need it. Once an hour or so, climb up here and take a quick look down toward LaPorte. If you see a dust cloud coming this way, you run and find me, so I can get ready. Do you understand all that?"

Tom nodded seriously and replied, "Yes, sir."

"Good. Now, let's climb down and get some dinner."

Mac climbed down first so he could catch Tom if he fell. He needn't have worried as Tom climbed down a lot faster than he did. The kid was like a chimpanzee the way he scrambled down the ladder.

When they arrived back in the house for dinner, Molly smiled at them and asked, "So, is Fort Jones ready to defend the realm?"

Tom grinned, then saluted, and replied, "Yes, ma'am!"

Molly returned his salute, laughed, then turned back to the cook stove to remove her roast from the oven.

Mac watched as she lifted the roast onto the cutting block and began to slice the beef. There was something different about Molly. Her shouted announcement was obviously behind it.

He glanced at Tom, who had also noticed a change in his mother. She seemed happy, and Tom was glad that she was better.

Mac noticed the cheerful mood immediately but had seen something else in those brown eyes. Molly wasn't afraid anymore. He just hoped it was permanent.

Molly served the roast beef, mashed potatoes and gravy, and biscuits and when she took a seat, she smiled at each of her men in turn.

Then she asked, "How much ammunition do you have for the Winchesters, Mac?"

Mac blinked as he began slicing his large cut of beef, looked up and replied, "I bought eight boxes when I arrived, so I have nine boxes plus what's in the pistols and rifles."

"Do you think I could do some more target practice?" she asked before taking a big forkful of potatoes and gravy and shoveling it into her mouth.

"Whenever you want, Molly. The only thing you might want to consider is that too much practice will wear out the rifling in the barrel which would harm its accuracy. I've had that Yellowboy since '67 and have put a few hundred rounds through it already. I'll tell you what I'll do. You shoot as much as you'd like, and the next time we're in LaPorte, I'll buy you a new '73 like mine, okay?"

Molly smiled and said, "I like the '66 a lot. I know it sounds silly, but with those brass sides I think it's prettier than your '73. Do they still sell the Yellowboys?"

"Um…yes. Yes, they do. If you'd like a new '66, I may have to go to Fort Collins. I know that Pete Hinton has some in stock."

"Then I can practice with this one and when you get a chance, you'll get me another one?" she asked, then put a chunk of roast in her mouth.

"Yes, ma'am."

Molly chewed and swallowed her roast beef before asking, "Now, the shotgun doesn't have rifling, so it doesn't have that problem, does it?"

"No, but I only bought eight boxes of shells, so I have a lot fewer shots. But using the shotgun doesn't need a lot of practice."

Molly laughed lightly and said, "I know. I was just curious."

Mac looked at Molly and the change was extraordinary. She looked beyond just happy. She looked confident. This was a different Molly, and he thoroughly approved of the transformation. Kudos to whatever had given her the impetus for the change.

After dinner, Tom went to his room to inspect his new rifle and the field glasses that Mac said he could use up in the tree outpost while Mac helped Molly with the cleanup.

As he washed, and she dried, Mac asked, "Molly, you seem different. Is everything okay?"

Molly kept drying a plate and replied, "Everything is wonderful, Mac. When you gave me that rifle, something happened to me. I just decided I'd wasted all of my life up until now worrying about what was going to happen, or what people thought about me, and realized that neither really mattered. You've given me an extraordinary gift without realizing it, Mac. You've given me an opportunity to start my life over.

MAC'S CABIN

I'm sure I'll still have some worries and fears, as everyone does, but I won't let them dominate my life anymore. Ever since you and Pete carried me across that river to your sanctuary, I've had nothing to fear, but didn't realize it until I returned from shooting. Then, I began to look at what worried me and made me afraid and knew they didn't matter."

Mac looked at Molly and asked, "Then, you're not afraid of me?"

Molly set the plate down, looked at him and asked, "Are you serious, Mac? Why on earth would I be afraid of you?"

Mac replied, "When you first arrived, you told me what had happened, and I knew you were scared and worried. Then, after I told you about why I came here, I thought it made me seem a bit crazy, which would scare anyone."

"Mac, I could never be afraid of you. It's just the opposite. I enjoy every second that I'm with you."

Mac just smiled and continued to wash the dishes, looking at this new Molly and was curious just how deep the change went.

―――――

Wild Willie and the boys had set up a small campsite in the trees, so they could have some semblance of a meal before the big day tomorrow.

"After we finish the job, we just ride around Fort Collins and head for LaPorte. We wait a couple of days until things quiet down and ride into town and see if we can find Ed," said Willie.

He'd said almost exactly the same thing at least eight times already, and if anyone else had said it twice, he would have been smacked in the head with something hard, but no one was about to challenge Wild Willie.

―――――

Two hours later, Molly and Mac were sitting in the rockers, but neither of the chairs was moving.

The new Molly wanted Mac to understand her better, and why the old Molly had to go.

"Mac," she began, "I told you that I wanted to start a new life, but for you to understand why I feel the need to do that, you need to know what my old life was like. So, please bear with me. Okay?"

"Okay," Mac replied.

Molly began by saying, "I had a pretty normal childhood for the first few years, except I didn't have any brothers or sisters. My mother died in childbirth when I was eight, and I was raised by my father, who drowned when I was fourteen. After that I lived with my grandmother until she died when I was seventeen.

Like most girls, I grew up with romantic notions of what it would be like to be married and have children of my own. We always imagined our husbands to be strong, handsome young men with kind hearts, yet still brave and very masculine. As I began to change physically, I was still a girl inside with those same girlish notions."

I met Chester Saunders in school, and while he may not have been my ideal, he liked me, and he became my boyfriend. I was excited about the thought of being a woman, getting married and having children. I wanted so badly to fulfill my fairytale expectation of love and marriage that I gave myself to Chester after he said he wanted to get married when I was seventeen just before my grandmother died. I didn't think there was anything wrong because we were going to get married. But Chester balked, and then I got worried that I might be pregnant, so I said he could come to my bed again but only if he married me. It was a terrible way to start a marriage."

So, I married Chester and for two months, everything was fine. It was disappointing to me with my lofty expectations, but it wasn't bad. Then, I was overjoyed to discover I was pregnant and told Chester, which seemed to surprise him, like he didn't know how it could have happened. He was very unhappy with the situation, and never told me why, but after I was pregnant with Tom, everything changed. First, he became insulting and cruel. Then, a few months after Tom was born, he slapped me for the first time. Then, he began to use a switch on my backside and eventually began to beat me for anything he thought was wrong, especially if I asked for money."

Once I was with child, he pretty much ignored me as a woman, and took his pleasures elsewhere, and I lived a strange life with a husband who wasn't a husband at all. He resented having to feed me and Tom and I was never sure if my getting pregnant wasn't just an excuse for him to return to his bachelor days before I had trapped him into marrying me. It was that way for ten long years. When he died, I'll admit, I wasn't displeased, and thought that his father would at least provide a living for me and his grandson."

But Chester had been telling stories about me to his father and brothers, probably to excuse his philandering. He even told them that Tom wasn't his son at all. So, I was shunned by the Saunders. For over a year, I lived with Tom on the money that my grandmother had left me. I was alone and desperate when I met Ed Richards, who was working at the freight yard owned by my father-in-law and married him a week after we first met."

I was so ashamed, Mac. I had granted him husbandly privileges that first night on just the hope of marriage, just like I had done with Chester. Then I discovered that he was rapacious in his needs, and I had to continue to let him take me until we were married, and after that he never gave me a night's peace. But it was a terrible thing because I felt as though I wasn't a wife, I was nothing more than a whore to him. We both knew what I was, and I was disgusted with myself. I hated what I had become, because I knew it was all my fault."

Over the year we were together, there were many times he would either walk out or threaten to kick me out, but he'd always come back, and it wasn't because he missed me or came close to loving me. It was because he needed gratification, and I gave it to him, so I wasn't much better than he was, either. I didn't care for him at all, but I needed him to provide for me and Tom. So, maybe I was a whore after all, only I sold myself cheaper."

C.J. Petit

Mac started to object, but Molly held up her hand to silence him as she continued.

"When he left us to go to Fort Collins, and I found out he had lied about having a job there, I was relieved and terribly frightened at the same time. I was right where I had been two years earlier, only Tom was older. My biggest problem was that I thought I was married, so I couldn't even find another husband. Then, with the rent looming and my money dwindling, I did the most shameful thing I had ever done in my life, which was already hideously disgraceful. The landlord offered me five dollars a week to provide him with services, and I sold myself."

I was so disgusted with what I had done, I packed our bags, and spent almost all of our money to come to Fort Collins, believing I was still married to Bob Phillips. I was so afraid and weak; you have no idea how I saw myself then. I knew what I was and what was likely to happen when we got to Fort Collins, but when Bob or Ed told me that I had been his personal whore for a year, and then even paid me to leave, I had reached the valley of disgust with myself."

Mac finally interrupted saying softly, "You hid it well, Molly."

Molly laughed lightly and said, "Yes, I hid it well. I had learned over those ten years with Chester and the one with Bob or Ed how to hide the fear, emptiness and revulsion I had for myself. I never let Tom know how cheap I felt, but the feelings were always there."

She paused and then asked, "Remember what I said when you first offered to let me stay?"

Mac nodded and replied, "You told me that you weren't that kind of woman."

"Yes, that's exactly what I said, and it was the biggest lie I've ever told. I was exactly that kind of woman but knowing it and saying it are two different things."

"Why did you lie, Molly?" Mac asked.

Molly looked over at Mac and replied, "Because I didn't want you to think less of me."

Mac sighed and said, "You could have said nothing at all, Molly. I was just offering you and Tom a refuge."

"I know, and I felt bad for saying it right after it popped out of my mouth. By saying that, I was implying that you had malicious intent toward me and that was totally unwarranted. I may as well have slapped you in the face, and I am sorry for that lie, Mac."

"Molly, I'll forgive you for your falsehood because you didn't know me at all and with your history with men, I can completely understand why you might say something like that. So, why don't we do this. You said that you were starting a new life today and wanted it to be different. Two months ago, I came to this place, looking for a place of penance and I believe that we can help each other, so let's start right now."

Even the new Molly was surprised that Mac hadn't been revolted when she had told him that she had sold herself to the landlord but was incredibly happy that he hadn't been.

Mac then stood, made a slight U-turn on the porch and stood in front of Molly, who looked up at him from her rocker.

He extended his right hand and said, "Ma'am, my name is Mac Jones. How do you do?"

A small smile formed on Molly's lips as she took his hand and replied, "It's a pleasure meeting you, Mr. Jones. My name is Molly Bradford. Please call me Molly."

Mac bowed his head slightly and said, "Thank you, Molly. Please call me Mac. It's short for MacKenzie, which is my mother's maiden name."

"It's a beautiful name, Mac. I'm honored to know you."

"And I am honored to know you as well, Molly."

Mac then returned to his rocking chair, looked over at a smiling, wet-eyed Molly and said, "Now, Molly, how about if I try out the new bathtub water heater?"

Molly grinned, popped up from her chair, stuck out her hand and said, "Let's!"

Mac took her hand and they walked into the house.

———

Wild Willie and the boys were sitting near their small campfire playing poker. In a deviation from the norm, Cookie and not Willie was winning. Usually, none of the others would call when they knew Willie was bluffing. But Cookie had called two of Willie's bluffs already, one when Willie was only holding a ten high, and Wild Willie was getting sore.

Cookie glanced at his hand. He was holding three jacks and knew that Willie, the only other player in the hand, was bluffing again. Willie always pulled at his beard when he bluffed, and they all knew it. But something had gotten into Cookie that night and he had decided to tweak Willie's nose a bit.

Willie tossed a dollar onto the pot and said, "I'm raisin' you fifty cents, Cookie. You'd better have a good hand this time."

Cookie flipped a silver dollar onto the cash in the middle and said, "It'll cost you another fifty cents to find out, Willie."

Willie tugged at his beard, looked back at his hand, then reached onto his dwindling stack, picked up two more silver dollars and dropped one, then the other onto the pot.

"Another buck and a half to you, Cookie."

Cookie knew he had Wild Willie, so he tossed six quarters into the pile and said, "I'll call," before triumphantly laying down his three jacks.

MAC'S CABIN

Willie grinned and began snapping his hand down one card at a time; the six of diamonds, seven of spades, eight of spades, nine of clubs and then, held the last card high above his head and slammed the ten of hearts onto the others before scooping up his winnings.

Cookie was stunned. Either Willie had finally figured out that he'd been giving away his bluffs, or he had cheated. Cookie glanced over at Vern and then Jimmy for support, but neither even looked at him.

Cookie finally accepted defeat, but not gracefully. He knew that Willie had just cheated him out of over seven dollars that should have been his, and there was nothing he could do about it. At least not today.

———

It was after ten o'clock, and all of the guests had gone to their rooms, and Ed Richardson and Mildred Richards were alone in the parlor.

"Well, Bob, it's getting kind of late and I do need to go to bed."

Bob smiled and replied, "I'll escort you to your room, Mildred."

Mildred smiled and took his offered arm as they left the parlor and climbed the stairs to the second floor. Once they reached her room, Mildred opened the door, leaving it open for Bob to follow, who closed the door behind him.

Mildred was ready for the slower, gentler Bob Richardson and spent the next ten minutes trying to slow him down, but to no avail. Twelve minutes after entering the room, she found herself even more frustrated as she lay next to a satisfied Bob Richardson.

She made up her mind then that she wouldn't put up with this much longer, and closed her eyes recalling the soft touches and caresses of her late husband.

———

149

"Are we ready for the big release?" Mac said as he stood next to the valve.

Molly was in the bathing room and watched the other end of the hose and exclaimed, "Go ahead!"

Mac turned the valve and he watched the almost-boiling water start to drop in the big tub.

Molly heard the gurgle first and then a sudden burst as the steaming water flowed from the hose into the tub. It finally reached ten inches of depth, and she began to pump cold water into the bathtub until she had almost two feet of warm water.

Mac set the heating tub on the floor as Molly stepped out of the bathing room and said, "Mac, it's perfect! I'm going to enjoy it now."

Mac smiled and said, "Good night, Molly."

Molly smiled back and replied, "Good night, Mac."

As Mac left the house, closing the door behind him, and Molly entered the bathing room, closing the door behind her, each knowing an important page had been turned in each of their lives and a new chapter had begun in their lives together.

That night as the new Molly pulled the quilts over her, she knew that she had made the best decision of her life, new or old. Telling Mac had been the second big step down the new trail she would be blazing for herself. The next step would be up to Mac.

———

Mac had already come to the same conclusion. He had been very aware of Molly's femininity when he had held her on Pete's back as they crossed the river. She was pretty, smart and compassionate, but she had been so troubled that he had a hard time really getting to know her. Things were totally different now. He was smitten with the new Molly and hoped things worked out. His only concern was that he might go too fast and rekindle memories of the Bob Phillips situation.

CHAPTER 8

Mac had slept well after his talk with Molly. Now that he understood her better, and knew that she wasn't afraid of him, he could relax when he was around her and not be so concerned about what he said or did. He had taken a bath in the canvas tub after leaving the one in the house to Molly, and hadn't heated that much water, but it was still a lot better than an ice water bath. He had taken extra care that morning when he had shaved and put on a clean shirt and even brushed his hair. He needed a haircut, but that would have to wait.

A little past seven o'clock, Mac did everything but pick flowers for Molly when he nervously walked up the steps to the porch, then knocked on the door.

Molly quickly swung the door open and smiled at Mac, who noticed that she had a ribbon in her hair and seemed just as nervous as he was.

"Good morning, Mac," she said as she showed her white teeth behind a big smile.

"Good morning, Molly," he replied as they both stood there like teenagers on a first date.

"Mama! Is Mac coming in?" shouted Tom, breaking the spell.

"Oh. I'm sorry. Come in, Mac. I have breakfast ready."

Mac walked behind Molly as a delicate scent of lavender floated behind her.

"That bath was amazing, Mac. You have to try it sometime," she said as she approached the stove.

151

Mac walked over behind her, took a few seconds taking in her flowery scent, took the coffeepot, stepped back to the table and poured two cups of coffee.

"I'll be right back, Molly. I'll get some milk for Tom and you can put some in your coffee if you'd like."

Molly turned and smiled at Mac and said, "Thank you, Mac. I'd love some."

Mac smiled and almost tripped as he turned to leave the kitchen to go to the stream and get some milk, then sheepishly returned to get a jug for the milk.

After he'd gone, Tom asked, "What's wrong with Mac, Mama? He seems all mixed up."

Molly smiled at Tom and replied, "There's nothing wrong with Mac, Tom. Nothing at all."

———

After breakfast was almost over, Molly asked, "What are you going to do today, Mac?"

"I'm going to start putting up the rails for the corral along the trees, then when that's done, I'll have to put spikes in the posts and set them in the holes. Tom is going to keep an eye on the road while I work."

Tom said, "I made a strap for my rifle from the cord Mac gave me, so I could take it with me up into the observation post. Then, if I see anyone coming, I can fire a shot and Mac can hear it from anywhere."

"That sounds like an important job, Tom. You're not going to stay up there all day, are you?" she asked.

"No, Mama. I'm going to walk around mostly, but every once in a while, I'll climb up to the tree house and take a look."

"Mac, can I help with the rails?" Molly asked.

MAC'S CABIN

"You can hand me the spikes if you'd like. I went to Ledbetter's a few weeks ago to buy some sixty penny nails, and after he asked me what I needed them for, he sold me a two-hundred-pound keg of railroad spikes. He said he'd ordered nails and one of the kegs contained spikes, so he made me a deal. They'll actually work better for my needs anyway. Because I'm only driving them a couple of inches into pine, I can use a hand sledge rather than a big one."

Molly laughed and said, "You just can't do anything like anyone else does, can you?"

Mac grinned and replied, "This from a woman who walks fifteen miles uphill to find a man she barely knew with a cabin."

Molly dropped her smile, and looked into his eyes and said softly, "And who will be forever grateful to that man with a cabin for taking her and her son in."

Mac kept his eyes locked on Molly's for a few seconds and finally said, "Let's clean up the dishes and get to work."

Tom watched Mac and his mother and knew that something was going on and was happy that it was as he then stood and ran to his room to get his rifle and some spare ammunition.

At nine o'clock, the Boulder to Fort Collins stage pulled out of the depot. The driver and shotgun rider were up top, with three men inside the coach. One was a steam engine company representative who was going to Fort Collins to try to convince the flour mill to convert from water power to steam, the second was a rancher returning to Fort Collins after arranging for the purchase of a prize bull, and the third was a bank guard, who appeared to be just a normal passenger with a common travel bag. But inside the travel bag was eight thousand dollars of freshly printed Fort Collins National Bank notes. It wasn't even locked. The guard was armed, however, with a Cooper Pocket pistol in his jacket pocket.

153

Twenty miles south, Wild Willie's gang were ready in their trees, alternating lookouts down both directions of the road. They wanted no witnesses, and that included any unfortunate passers-by.

———

Mac and Molly had developed a smooth routine for the spiking operation. Before they began, Molly suggested that he might not want to get his shirt all sweaty, so Mac had willingly complied as Molly smiled.

Mac only needed three strikes with the eight-pound sledgehammer to drive the spike into the pine, keeping it at a slight up angle as he did. He was only using two rails for the corral, so the work progressed quickly.

As they moved through the trees, Mac and Molly conversed about many topics; some serious, many not. But it was very much like two inexperienced young people getting to know each other better with the advantages of being more mature and having already learned the most intimate aspects of each other's lives.

———

Tom was taking his duties seriously and didn't let his eleven-year-old mind wander, but still found things to keep his attention as he paraded across the stony ground, looking toward LaPorte often. He'd been up into his tree house twice, leaving the field glasses on the observation post.

———

All of the trees were spiked and ready for the rails when Molly returned to the cabin to make lunch. After lunch, he'd move to the posts and then he'd just have to hang all of the split rails and the corral would be done.

After he'd cleaned up in the creek, he put his shirt on and then walked out to the observation post to get Tom.

———

Cookie Preston picked up the dust cloud from the approaching stage first, while Jimmy Page announced that the road was clear on the other side.

They had another twenty minutes or so for the stage to reach their location, but Willie had them all on their horses ready to go after Cookie announced the imminent arrival of oncoming stage.

They didn't bother with masks as they sat on their horses listening for the approaching stage as there would be no witnesses. No witnesses to identify pintos or anything else.

After fifteen minutes, the hoofbeats of the six-horse team and the cries of the driver urging them on were heard from about a half a mile away.

"Okay, boys, let's get ready," Willie said as he slid a shotgun from the bedroll and pulled back both hammers while Cookie, Vern and Jimmy pulled their rifles.

Just as the stage reached the edge of the trees, the three men trotted their horses quickly onto the road just ahead of the oncoming stage and pointed their guns at the two men on the driver's seat eighty yards away.

The driver and shotgun rider were taken by surprise at the sudden appearance of the gang. No one had held up the stage in three years, and that lack of readiness cost them.

The driver yanked hard on his right-hand reins, beginning a hard swerve to the right of the highwaymen, bouncing off the berm and slamming the coach onto the rough ground off the roadway. As the coach flew off the road, the shotgun rider pulled his shotgun to bear and began to cock the two hammers, but neither action was any use as three rifles fired at the distance of less than forty yards and Willie let loose with both barrels of the shotgun.

C.J. Petit

Which of the two men on the coach took which bullet or how many pellets didn't matter as both were peppered with lead from one smoking barrel or the other.

The driver tried to maintain control of the stage for five more seconds before passing out and falling off to the side, leaving the seat of the coach, plummeting the eight feet to the dirt and rolling another six feet.

The shotgun rider was knocked back slightly by the force of the bullet and pellet strikes and fired his own weapon into the air before slumping back down over the front of the coach and almost diving onto the rump of the last horse in the team and then bouncing under the left front wheel causing the stagecoach to bounce into the air, careen on its two right wheels for several seconds before the yoke cracked and the stage crashed onto its right side and began to tumble, rolling over twice before coming to rest on its left side in a huge cloud of dust as the team raced away in panic.

Willie shouted, "Let's get in there!" and raced his horse to the stricken stagecoach.

Inside the coach, the two passengers and the bank guard were in bad shape. The steam engine man had broken both of his arms and was screaming in pain, while the rancher lay paralyzed but alive after his neck had snapped when his head had hit the top of the coach as it rolled.

The bank guard, knowing he was going to die, did something beyond rational thought as he struggled with a broken femur, three broken ribs and a punctured lung, to open the travel bag trusted to his keeping and as soon as he managed to pull it open, began hurriedly ripping two bundles of cash out and scattering them on the what used to be the left side of the coach, but was now the floor. He finally dumped the remaining bundles on the loose bills and pulled out a match from his jacket's vest pocket, ran it across the side of the coach, and when it flared to life, tossed it onto the banknotes.

As the guard was preventing the thieves from getting their loot, Jimmy Page was the first to climb to the top of the coach, look inside

156

and immediately saw what the bank guard was doing. As the guard looked up at him and smiled, Jimmy let loose with his pistol, emptying five shots into the guard and the other two men.

"Son of a bitch!" Jimmy shouted as he yanked open the door and threw it wide as he scrambled into the coach and tried to save some of the bundles of money from the growing fire.

He plunged his hand into the fire, grabbed two bundles, tossed them through the open door over his head and then grabbed one more before the fire grew too hot. He climbed back out, the smoldering tightly wrapped bundle of cash still in his hand as the flames began to lick at his feet.

He tumbled out onto the ground where Wild Willie was picking up the other two bundles that Jimmy had rescued.

"What happened, Jimmy?" he shouted.

"That damned bank guard dumped the cash out and set it on fire. That's all I could get," he replied as he handed the last bundle to Willie and began brushing debris from his pants.

"Let's get out of here before that coach really goes up," Willie said as he glanced at the smoking coach.

Cookie, meanwhile, had opened the stagecoach's boot and had been pulling travel bags and a mail pouch from inside and tossing them away from the coach as flames began to show through the back of the doomed vehicle.

He trotted over to the travel bags and began to open one when the others noticed what he was doing and walked over to him and each took a bag and began tossing aside its contents.

After they had emptied the bags and found nothing of note, Willie opened the mail pouch and found the expected pile of posted letters, handing a bunch to each of his partners and began to rip them open, hoping to find cash inside, but again coming up empty.

"Damn it! If that damned guard hadn't been so fast with that match, this would have set us up for a long time," groused Wild Willie as he examined the three bundles and finding one bundle of single dollar notes, and two of five-dollar bills totaling five hundred and fifty dollars.

It wasn't a bad haul but burning in that stagecoach was probably another five or six thousand dollars.

"Well, toss that mail into the fire," Willie said, "we don't want any U.S Marshal or Secret Service folks chasin' after us because of some open love letters."

Vern Porter laughed as he, Jimmy and Cookie picked up the letters and the empty pouch and tossed them into the now raging fire along with the travel bags.

"Do we go and chase down that team, Willie? That was some mighty good horseflesh," asked Cookie.

"Nah. It'd be like writing a confession. At least these bills won't draw too much attention, especially if they think they're all burned to cinders. Let's get to LaPorte before they figure out what happened.

———

In the boarding house, they were sitting down to lunch, and Mildred was having second thoughts about Bob Phillips. He had cornered her in the hallway and tried to talk her into returning to his room for mutual pleasure, and when she had refused his suggestion, he had taken more liberties out in the hallway, for God's sake! Now, as they sat down, he had placed his hand on her thigh and began to pull up her skirt even as the other guests were eating. *The man had no shame!*

As soon as Mildred finished, she hurriedly left the table, returned to her room and closed the door. She walked to the bed and sat down, her heart still pounding as she thought of the horrible situation that Bob had put her into. If anyone had seen what he was doing, she would have been ruined.

MAC'S CABIN

She closed her eyes and began to cry softly and didn't even notice when the door opened silently but did hear it when the door latch snapped closed and looked up, not surprised to see a smiling Bob Phillips.

"Get out of my room, Mr. Phillips! How dare you do what you did at lunchtime? Have you no sense of decency?"

Bob walked slowly toward Mildred and stood over her smiling.

"Why, Mildred, I'm surprised. I thought you enjoyed it. Don't you love me as I love you?"

Mildred seethed and snapped back, "You must be joking! You are a dirty, abrupt man not worthy of my contempt. Now, leave my room at once!"

Bob wasn't about to leave. He slapped Mildred hard across the face and then threw her back on the bed, thinking that she would just cry and let him take her again.

But Mildred wasn't about to let that happen. She suddenly slapped him even harder than he had slapped her, and then she screamed.

Bob was busy wrestling with her knickers when she hit him and let loose her banshee scream right in his left ear.

He knew that he had to get out of there fast, and get out of Fort Collins, too.

He slapped her harder once more, then raced out of the room, crossing into his room across the hall quickly as he heard footsteps on the stairs. He threw his things into his travel bag, opened the window and looked down to the alley fifteen feet down. He dropped his travel bag outside, then climbed out through the window, hung for a moment by his hands and then dropped the remaining seven feet to the ground, slightly spraining his right ankle.

He snatched his travel bag and hobbled out onto the street and headed for the livery to get his horse.

C.J. Petit

———

Wild Willie Patterson, Cookie Priester, Jimmy Page and Vern Porter were riding along at a fast trot two miles out of Fort Collins as Ed Richardson reached the livery and hurriedly paid his stabling fees and began saddling his horse, needing to do it in record time.

———

Mildred was telling her story of the attack by Bob Phillips to a sympathetic Mary Templeton, the wife of the owner of the boarding house, not mentioning what she and Bob had been doing. Mary, of course, knew full well what they were doing, but was still incensed when she saw Mildred's red face where Bob had slapped her.

"Did you want me to go and get the sheriff, Mildred?" Mary asked.

"No, Mary. I don't want anyone else to know of this. It's just too horrible. I just don't want to ever see that man again."

Mary had fire in her eyes as she replied, "You won't, Mildred. I'll see to that."

She then stormed out of Mildred's room, knocked loudly on Bob Phillips' room, and when he hadn't opened it after a minute, swung the door wide and noticed that it had been stripped and the window was open.

She returned to tell Mildred that Bob Phillips was gone and wouldn't dare to show his face again.

———

The four P-gang members split up as they reached Fort Collins. Two went east around town and two went around the west side, merging again on the other side on their way to LaPorte.

After they'd ridden two miles, Vern Porter checked their back trail and saw a rider coming fast.

160

"We got company, Willie," he said loudly as the rider galloped closer.

The other three men all turned in their saddles and spotted the man, expecting to see a badge but not seeing one.

———

If Ed Richardson had seen a pinto among the four horses being ridden by the men on the road before him, he would have turned right around and headed back to Fort Collins, but Cookie had traded the pinto for a plain brown gelding and had vowed never to have a conspicuous horse again.

Ed was more worried that the Larimer County Sheriff would be looking for him than the four men just walking their horses to LaPorte. He even thought that he might join up with them on the ride and let his horse rest.

It was Jimmy Page who first guessed the identity of the approaching rider and said in a normal voice to Wild Willie, "I think that's Ed Richardson comin' up behind us."

Willie didn't turn, but just released his pistol's hammer loop and waited for Ed to get closer.

Ed was just a hundred and fifty yards behind the four riders when he began to recognize certain characteristics of the men, like the way they sat in the saddle, or the way they wore their holsters, he was beginning to reconsider his decision to ride with them, when he saw the two outer riders suddenly wheel their horses around and charge toward him, pulling their rifles from their scabbards.

"Damn it!" he shouted as he thought about making a break, but knew it was too late.

Ed was trapped and needed to come up with a way to talk his way out of certain death, so he stopped his horse, put his hands off to the side, and waited for Wild Willie.

Wild Willie and Cookie Priester trotted straight toward Ed Richardson while Jimmy and Vern kept their Winchesters trained on him.

Willie was grinning as he drew close and said loudly, "Well, if it ain't our yellow pal, Eddie. Now, I bet you've come up with some big lie for lettin' that sheriff sneak up behind us and then runnin' off with our money."

Ed replied, "Nope. I ain't gonna lie to you, Willie. When I walked out of the store with that ammunition, I spotted that lawman walking you into the jail. I was gonna try and bust you guys outta there, but a passel of folks had all started heading that way and there wasn't nothin' I could do. I figured if I took the money, they couldn't convict you. Then, when they did, what could I do after that? I still have most of the money right here in my saddlebags."

Willie knew he was lying, because when they all walked out of the jail, there was no one there.

He snarled, "You're lyin', Ed. Are you gonna pay us back for the money you took?"

Ed leaned back in his saddle and replied, "Maybe I can do a lot better than that. I saw you leavin' town and figured I'd cut you in for a deal I'm workin'. It could be worth five or six thousand and some fringe benefits, too."

After the short haul from the stagecoach robbery, Willie was interested, and asked, "How did you see us? We didn't go through Fort Collins."

"I know, I kinda had a problem with some widow I was busy with, so I had to get out of there fast and cut out through an alley."

Cookie laughed and said, "You were with some widow? What happened to your wife and kid we heard about?"

Ed replied, "I tossed her out 'cause she was whinin' too much, but that's part of the deal, see? When she run off, she headed for this

162

guy's cabin. I been up there, and this character is livin' alone and has a bunch of cash. I seen it when he gave us all a tip for bringin' all this lumber up there. I tell ya, he's got thousands."

Willie knew he'd lied earlier, but he partially believed the rest of the tale.

"Okay, Ed, you bought yourself some time. Now, you said that this guy is livin' alone up there?"

"Not anymore. He's got my wife and her kid up there, but that's all. Nobody ever goes up there, either and it's far enough away from town that they won't hear any gunfire."

"How far away is this place?" asked Willie.

"About fifteen miles outside of LaPorte. We can be there in four hours and it won't take that long. I know where his cabin is, too."

Willie looked at his boys and asked, "What do you all think about Ed's plan to rob this poor feller?"

"I like it, boss," said Vern, "unless Ed is lyin'."

Cookie said, "Same here, boss."

Jimmy Page nodded his assent and Willie said, "Okay, Ed, let's head that way. What about your wife and kid after we kill this guy?"

"I don't care about the kid, but I'll take that woman back and make her sorry for sassin' me."

Cookie laughed and said, "Hell, Ed, you made her sorry for marryin' ya."

Everyone, including Ed, laughed as they turned their horses toward LaPorte.

———

Mac was hammering spikes into posts while he talked with Molly, who had her Winchester Yellowboy with her and two full canteens of water. He was swinging the sledge when he heard the distinctive light crack of Tom's .22.

He let the sledge fall then said, "Let's move, Molly. Someone's coming."

The old Molly might have crumbled in fear, but this was the new Molly, so she just handed him a canteen, picked up her Winchester and they began to walk quickly back to the cabin.

They got there two minutes later, quickly entered, and Mac took down the shotgun, cracked it open and made sure two loads of buckshot were there, then, still shirtless, he grabbed his medium jacket, put it on, and handed a box of .44s to Molly while he took a box of twelve-gauge shotgun shells and put them in his left jacket pocket. Molly had taken a dozen .44 cartridges and put them in her dress's pocket, then handed the rest of the cartridges to Mac, who dumped them in his right jacket pocket. With his Winchester, Smith & Wesson and the cartridge loops on his gunbelt, Mac now had almost fifty shots available, plus the two barrels full of buckshot.

They stepped out of the house and began fast walking toward the observation post.

———

Tom had just climbed into the treehouse when he spotted the large dust cloud coming from the south and fired his warning shot. Mac had told him not to expect an instant response as he had to get his weapons and ammunition, but to stay put in the treehouse and keep them under observation. He was doing exactly as he was instructed and began counting the riders. There were five of them, and then he began to get worried. *How could Mac handle five bad men?* He looked over at the box of .22s and decided to help.

———

MAC'S CABIN

The five riders had been following the wagon tracks and Willie began to wonder if he really needed Ed any longer, but then figured it really didn't matter. They were going to kill him anyway, so they may as well send him in first just in case this loner spotted them coming and was ready for them.

Ed suspected that he was on borrowed time and thought he might be able to make a break as soon as he reached that forest where that Jones character was building his cabin. Once he got into those thick woods, he could pick off anyone who came after him.

Cookie had decided to hold off on any revenge for Willie's cheating until after they found out how much money this guy really had.

————

Mac and Molly neared the treehouse and Mac looked up at Tom and asked in a normal voice, "How many?"

Tom held out five splayed fingers and Mac was surprised.

Molly looked over at Mac and asked, "Five of them? Where did he get four more men?"

"If I'd have to guess, it'll be Wild Willie's bunch. I have no idea why they'd be riding together, but among thieves, you never know. Now, Molly, I want you to go into those trees and get your rifle ready to fire. Do not show yourself. I'm going to force them to leave and then if they come back, I'll use the Sharps to pick them off at range."

"Why don't you just shoot them now?" she asked.

"Well, the Sharps is back in the cabin for one, but the other reason is that I think I can get them to turn on Ed, if they aren't planning on killing him anyway. If I can convince them that it's not worth it to try and come back here, then nobody has to die. I want Ed, though. He needs to be punished for what he did to you and Tom, and he's still got a price on his head. So, go to the woods right now and tell Tom to stay up there and hide. I'll talk loudly enough so you both can hear me."

Molly replied, "Okay, Mac," then began to trot toward the treehouse as Mac watched her.

He was amazed at the transformation she had made. Here Ed Richardson, whose name had made her quake with fear two days ago, was riding in with four notorious outlaws and she was as cool as that creek flowing under the cabin.

He stepped away from the trees another fifty yards until he reached a spot where he had a good line of sight around the edge of the tree line and was close enough for Tom and Molly to hear him. He stood facing the direction they'd have to come, his shotgun in his hands with both hammers cocked and his Winchester laying on the ground with the muzzle pointed the way he was facing.

If they were following his wagon tracks, they'd come around the tree line only forty yards in front of him. If they had rifles drawn, he'd let them have both barrels and drop to a prone position with his Winchester. If not, he'd have a little chat with the boys.

––––––––

The five riders reached the ford and stopped.

"It's pretty quiet around here," said Willie as he glared at Ed.

"He's probably in that cabin of his havin' a good ol' time with that wife of mine. She sure did enjoy my attentions," Ed replied before laughing.

"Yeah, I'm sure she did," Willie replied sarcastically as he led his horse into the swirling, cold water.

The others followed and when they were about a third of the way across, they began lifting their feet to avoid the water. When they reached the deepest part of the northern fork, their heels were almost touching the saddle seats even though the water was barely past their horses' bellies.

When they reached the other side, they dropped their boots back into the stirrups and walked their horses toward the trees.

"His cabin is about a thousand yards around that tree line," said Ed as he pointed.

Cookie pulled out his Winchester and Willie said, "Hold off, Cookie. Let's see how close we can get. He don't know us from Adam."

Cookie slid the rifle back in the scabbard and asked, "What about Ed? Won't his wife recognize him?"

"By the time she could, we'll be too close for it to matter. If you wanna feel better, take off your pistol loop, but other than that, just act like we're real friendly fellers."

―――――

Tom had lost sight of the men when they had ridden to the ford, and he began to worry that they'd come around from the back. Then he heard voices and calmed down.

Mac had heard the voices and prepared for their arrival by waving and smiling at Molly and then Tom, but not waiting for a wave in reply. The riders were close.

Then he saw movement ahead as the head of one of their horses came into view fifty yards away. He just calmly watched as one became five and then the riders began appearing.

"Hello, boys!" Mac shouted, not moving the shotgun into position, "What can I do for you? This is private property, but I'm sure you have a good reason for being here."

Willie was startled by Mac's shout, as were the others, but quickly assessed the threat. The man was standing with a cocked twelve-gauge that could do some serious damage at this range. Willie had to play the hand that was dealt.

"We just come up here and was followin' those tracks, curious who was up here. You know how it is," Willie shouted as they all continued to walk their horses closer.

Mac watched as they drew within forty yards before shouting, "Now, Willie, you never impressed me as the curious type. I know why you're here. That idiot you used to ride with, Ed Richardson, has been feeding you a bunch of horse manure about me having gold or something. My guess is that he told you that right after you were getting ready to pay him back for running off and leaving you under that sheriff's shotgun."

Willie asked, "Who the hell are you? How come you know so much?"

Mac shouted back, "I used to be a deputy sheriff and then a bounty hunter. I made money off of your like. But I don't have a grudge with you or your boys. The same can't be said for Ed over there. I have a big grudge against him. You four can turn and ride away while I deal with Ed. I don't want to have to kill every last one of you today."

Willie laughed and yelled, "You've got sand, I'll give you that, but not a lot of brains. Now, you've got that scattergun in your hands and a Winchester on the ground. If you touch off that twelve-gauge, you may hurt one or two of us, but you ain't gonna kill any of us and we'll be mighty displeased with you and have to fill you full of lead."

"That might be true, Willie, if I didn't have another Winchester aimed right at your head right now. If you want a demonstration, I can have Molly fire and you'd be impressed with her accuracy, unless she's aiming at Ed. Then, she'll probably just shoot his head off. Did Ed tell you that he's not even married to her? He lied on the marriage license, making it worthless. She's mighty pissed off about that moron lying to her for so long, and a truly angry woman, Willie, is something to behold."

Willie licked his upper lip and said, "No woman can shoot a Winchester worth a pile of donkey crap."

MAC'S CABIN

"Oh? Would you be willing to bet your life on it, Willie? So, I'll tell you what. I would be within my rights as the owner of this land to shoot you where you sit right now, but I'll give you one more chance for the four of you to ride off while I just deal with Ed."

Cookie was slowly moving his hand to his pistol; confident he could get a shot off before the shotgun-wielding cabin-builder could turn and fire his shotgun. He had his hand just two inches from his Colt's grip when Mac noticed the proximity of the hand to the gun and quickly brought the shotgun's two barrels around to the riders.

The sudden move created a chaos of movement as each man reached for his sidearm and Mac responded by squeezing the trigger of the shotgun.

The two muzzles blew out a huge cloud of smoke, an explosive report and two full loads of #4 buckshot.

Mac was already dropping the shotgun and himself to the ground as they opened fire amid a spray of lead pellets. The spread wasn't as wide as Mac had hoped, but it was too narrow to suit Cookie Priester, the one who had been the spark for the gunfight.

He took almost all of the brunt of both barrels as there was sufficient space between him and the other four men to let the other pellets pass by without hitting any of the others.

Cookie flipped back onto his horse's rump but was held in place by his stirrups. His horse, like all of their horses, was spooked by the shotgun blast and soon bucked him free, letting him crash to the stony ground on his head before he flipped over onto his stomach. He lay dead on the smooth stones having never gotten revenge for the seven dollars he had lost in last night's poker game.

The other four men began firing their pistols at Mac, but they couldn't get clean shots because of their uncontrolled horses.

Mac ripped his Winchester into his hands as he lay on his stomach, cocked the hammer and picked out a target, who happened to be Jimmy Page. He fired, and Jimmy spun from his horse as the

.44 caliber round caught him high on the left side of his chest, breaking one rib, ripping through his lung and then leaving his chest and smashing into his left upper arm, shattering his humerus. He fell off his horse and bounced off the rocky soil, blood pouring from his wound. He'd die in another twenty seconds.

Willie, Vern and Ed all raced their horses to get them around the tree line, so they could get their Winchesters ready to return fire.

When Mac saw them run for cover, he grabbed the shotgun and his Winchester and sprinted for the trees where he could see Molly waving him in. He glanced up at Tom who was staring down and waved him down from the tree house.

When he reached Molly, he was huffing from the sprint and said, "I want you to get Tom and we're heading for the cabin. Those three won't come back this way again, so I'm going to get the Sharps. I want you and Tom to stay in the bathtub. It's safe there."

"No, Mac. I want Tom in the bathtub. You'll need me to cover your back. Let's get Tom and get to the cabin."

Mac smiled at her and said, "Yes, ma'am."

She smiled back and when Tom touched his foot to the ground, they all began walking quickly back to the cabin.

———

"What are we gonna do, Willie?" asked Vern after they had the safety of the blocking pines behind them.

Willie growled, "We ain't gonna go back that way, that's for damned sure. I don't know if that bastard has any money, but he's gonna pay for killin' Cookie and Jimmy. Now, what we're gonna do is ride along that river another eight hundred yards, dismount and take our Winchesters into those trees and find that cabin of his. He probably figured we run off and won't be expecting us to come back. Once we pick him off, we have the place to ourselves. Let's not make any noise gettin' there either. Walk the horses in line in the water. Ed, seein' as how this was your idea, you take the lead."

The orders given; Willie waited for Ed to precede him walking his horse into the north fork of the river just six feet from the water's edge.

———

As they walked back, Mac said, "Molly, I'm gambling that if they're coming back and not returning to Fort Collins, they'll follow the river until they think they're close, and then come on foot to cut down the noise. So, I'm going to take the Sharps and my Winchester and go into the trees on the river side of the creek and circle around."

Now, here's where it's going to be dangerous. I have to be close enough not to miss them, but I don't want to bump into them, either, so I'll be moving slowly. You get in a prone position on the back porch with your Winchester. If you see them coming, fire and I'll hear your shot and get behind them. Don't stop and see if you got a hit. Cycle in a new cartridge as soon as you've pulled that trigger. Do you have all that?"

"I've got it," Molly said as they approached the cabin.

"What about me?" asked Tom.

"Tom, your mother and I need to know you're safe. Your .22 won't kill them and will only tell them where you are. I want you to stay in the bathtub until this is over. You can keep your rifle with you in case one of them makes it into the house. No arguments, Tom."

Tom was disappointed, but understood and replied, "Yes, sir."

They all bounded up the stairs and into the house. Mac reloaded the shotgun and set it against the wall near the back door in case Molly needed it. He emptied his pocket of the shotgun shells and put in six of the .52-70 cartridges for the Sharps. Then he and Molly trotted out to the back porch, Mollie stayed put on the porch while Mac used the steps down rather than his usual leap to avoid the potential of a sprained ankle which would slow him down.

He didn't look back as he entered the trees on the river side of the creek. Molly stretched out on her stomach and cocked the hammer of her Yellowboy. She had about thirty yards of relatively clear ground before the trees began to thicken and visibility became sporadic, but she knew she'd pick up motion if anyone moved between those trees.

As she lay on the wooden deck, Molly ran her hand across the wood and knew that Mac had put it there. This piece of wood and the boards and logs surrounding it had been assembled by Mac to create his own refuge and now it had become her sanctuary as well. It was now her home and she'd defend it against those who tried to take it from them.

————

Ed was really nervous having Willie behind him with a rifle in his hands. He was sure that the only reason he was still alive was because they had already lost Cookie and Jimmy. He couldn't turn and shoot Willie without getting a chest full of .44 first, so he'd have to hope he'd get a chance soon. After watching that Jones take out Jimmy, he knew there was trouble ahead, too. Guns in front of him and guns behind him, and all of them were pointed at him.

Willie had been watching Ed and even with the loss of Jimmy and Cookie, was debating about putting a bullet in Ed's back. What held him back was the tell-tale noise the rifle would make, letting Jones know where they were. Ed would get to live a few more minutes at least.

Willie guessed they were close and said, "Here!"

They turned their horses out of the river and stepped down as soon as the hooves were dry on the shore. They led the horses to the nearest tree and tied them off.

Willie turned to Ed and asked, "Where do you figure his cabin is?"

"He was buildin' it over a creek, and I figure that was the creek we crossed a couple of hundred yards back."

Willie was livid as he snarled, "You mean we coulda followed that damned creek right to his place and you didn't think to tell me?"

"I didn't think about it. Besides, he'd see us comin' a lot further off."

"Alright, let's go," Willie groused as they stepped away from the river.

———

Mac had heard the muffled conversation, even above the sound of the river's background noise. They had to be closer than he thought, so he set the Sharps against a tree, levered a fresh cartridge into his Winchester's firing chamber, hoping they didn't pick up the noise and began walking through the trees in the direction of the voices, assuming they'd be moving toward the cabin.

After he'd walked ten yards, he stopped and waited, watching for movement between the pines. He had his Winchester in firing position as he just stood against a thick trunk expecting a flash of color any second.

———

About a hundred feet away, Ed, Willie and Vern were walking slowly through the trees, their Winchesters cocked and ready, expecting to see a cabin pop into view with the next step. They were just five yards apart, and Vern was the unfortunate outlaw to be the closest to Mac's position.

They were trying to be as quiet as possible, but they were all watching for the cabin, and there were enough twigs on the ground to make their approach noticeable.

———

Mac picked up the crunching and cracking of their boots and aimed at a line between the obscuring pine trunks. The noises were getting louder, and he braced his Winchester against the tree trunk as Vern

Porter suddenly appeared from behind a thick pine and Mac squeezed off the shot.

The relative silence of the forest was shattered by the loud crack of his Winchester as it spat the .44 caliber missile through the air crossing the ninety-six feet separating the repeater's muzzle from Vern's left side in a tiny fraction of a second. It ripped into his gut, just below the ribs, tearing through his stomach, and drilling into his liver, severing the hepatic artery. He screamed as he hit the pine-covered ground and began to gush blood from the wound.

Willie and Ed both turned, spotted Mac and fired quickly before racing behind a nearby tree for cover as Vern continued to scream.

Mac then trotted a few feet back toward the cabin and set up behind another tree. He knew he didn't have to move, but they did. They had to either leave or continue on to the cabin. If they chose to leave, he'd chase them down, but he didn't believe they would. They had already invested too much. They'd have to go to the cabin, but they'd have to kill him first, and Mac had no intention of letting that happen.

———

When Molly heard the shooting and the screaming of a wounded man, she felt a chill run up her spine. She found that she was frightened again, but this was a different kind of fear. She wasn't afraid of what would happen to her. She was afraid of what could just have happened to Mac.

She felt an overwhelming urge to run and help Mac but knew that she would cause more trouble for going out there and decided to stay.

Fifteen feet behind her, Tom had heard the shots and screaming as well, and looked at the small rifle clutched in his hands as he lay in the bathtub and knew that it wouldn't do any good to protect anyone, so he laid the rifle on the floor, clambered out of the bathtub and left the bathing room. He took two steps outside the room and saw the shotgun leaning against the wall near the doorway. He picked it up and returned to the bathing room. But instead of lying back in the tub, he just sat on the edge of the tub with his feet inside and his back pressed against the back wall, so he could look out the door. He had the shotgun in his hands with the muzzles resting on the floor. Now, he felt useful.

————

In the forest, it was a stalemate. Each man generally knew where the other was, but no one could move without giving away his position. Something had to change. The first change was when Vern stopped screaming, returning an eerie silence to the forest with only the sound of rushing water in the background.

Mac had one huge advantage in that he knew the ground. His cabin was just another eighty yards to his left as he faced north to where Willie and Ed were. Ed had seen the cabin location and the creek, but he hadn't seen the forest between the creek and the river where they were now, so he still had no idea how close they were.

While he waited, he began inserting cartridges into the loading gate of his Winchester while watching for any signs of movement from the last two outlaws.

The first sign of movement wasn't what Mac expected, nor did Wild Willie, who should have.

When Ed and Willie had made their break for cover, Willie's tree was just to the left of Ed's and what was worse for Willie was that he was now in front of Ed, his back now a broad target for Ed just fifteen feet away. Since he'd been behind the pine, Ed had been debating about shooting Willie and then making a break for the cabin or waiting for Jones to move.

The longer he waited, the more he thought about it. After almost three minutes of nerve-wracking tension, Bob smiled. He could do both.

As Wild Willie strained to spot Mac, Bob turned his Winchester's sights to take aim at Willie, but he didn't want a killing shot. He wanted Willie to be in pain and screaming like Vern did, and he wanted Willie to be able to shoot too, when Mac Jones came to see how badly he had been wounded.

He aimed his rifle low, right at Willies right buttock. He squeezed the trigger and the sudden report surprised Mac but shocked Willie when Ed's bullet ripped through his behind and shattered his right hip. As Ed knew he would, he screamed and went down.

Ed bolted immediately, heading directly away from Mac's rifle and disappearing into the woods.

Mac quickly recovered from the surprise and took a quick shot at the fleeing Ed Richardson before leaving his covering tree and racing toward Willie, who was writhing on the ground, his Winchester four feet away.

Forgetting about Ed for the moment, Mac reached Wild Willie, knelt beside him and found there was nothing he could do for him.

Willie saw Mac and grabbed his jacket, snarling, "Shoot me! I ain't gonna make it and this is killin' me! Just go and kill that back-shooting bastard!"

Mack knew he was dying, and it was going to be a long, painful death, so he angled his Winchester downward and pulled the trigger, ending Willie's life, then took off after Ed.

Ed had raced north and then angled west toward the cabin. He knew that Molly was alone in the cabin now and he finally saw another use for the woman. Jones was the sort that would give himself up rather than watch her die.

He finally spotted the cabin and slowed down to a walk.

———

Molly had heard the renewed gunfire and screaming followed by another single shot and was getting more worried about Mac's chances as she strained to look in the direction of the shots.

———

But Ed had gone further north, and when he exited the trees, he was too far on the other side of the cabin for Molly to see him.

Ed crossed the creek, silently cursing the cold water as he reached the front porch. He stepped quietly up the stairs, his Winchester cocked as he crossed the porch finding the front door conveniently open.

———

After complying with Willie's request, Mac had quickly picked up Ed's trail and then had to slow to avoid walking into an ambush, but as he followed, he realized that Ed had passed Molly's line of sight and could enter the cabin behind her.

He took a serious gamble and shouted, "Molly! Ed's coming up behind you!", then began to run.

———

But by the time Mac shouted, Ed was already in the house and saw Molly lying on her stomach on the porch directly in front of him. He had her in his sights as she jerked up at Mac's shout and tried to bring her rifle to bear, then saw Ed already there with his Winchester pointed at her. She dropped her gun and glared at him, hoping Mac would arrive soon. It was her only chance now.

"Well, Molly, it looks like you've learned some tricks since you've been away," he said as he walked closer, keeping his repeater's sights on her.

Then he shouted, "Now, you shout real loud to Jones and tell him not to come any closer or you're a dead woman. Do it now!"

Molly stared back at Ed and said defiantly, "You don't order me around anymore, Ed. You are nothing but a stupid, dirty man. Go ahead and shoot. It doesn't matter. Mac will kill you and leave your carcass for the coyotes and the worms."

Ed had expected a look of absolute terror in her eyes and was startled by her boldness but recovered quickly.

He continued to step toward Molly and just as he reached the open doorway to the bathing room, said, "If that's what you want, Molly, then I guess I'm just gonna have…"

The cabin suddenly exploded with the sound of both barrels of a twelve-gauge shotgun as clouds of smoke rushed out of the bathing room following two full loads of buckshot.

Ed Richardson never knew what happened to him as the spread of the massive loads never exceeded eight inches in diameter, turning his entire left side into a mass of pulverized red meat. His lifeless body slammed against the opposing wall six feet away and slid to the floor as Molly watched in utter shock.

Mac came racing through the front door with his rifle ready only to find Ed Richardson staring lifelessly into the underside of the cabin's roof. He lowered his Winchester and walked toward the bathing room where clouds of gunsmoke still billowed from the open door.

He looked inside as a shaken Molly walked up beside him.

They saw a white-faced, wide-eyed Tom sitting with his back against the wall, his feet dangling into the bathtub, the shotgun laying before him, smoke drifting from the two barrels as his small hands still gripped the gun.

Tom looked up slowly and said softly, "He…he was gonna shoot Mama, Mac. I had to do it."

Mac crouched down and took the shotgun from his hands, wondering how he had avoided breaking his thin shoulder, and said, "Are you all right, Tom? You saved your mother's life, and you should be proud of what you did. I know I'm proud of you."

Tom looked into Mac's eyes and asked, "Then you're not mad because I disobeyed you?"

MAC'S CABIN

Mac smiled at Tom and replied, "No, I'm not in the least mad, Tom. You did exactly what had to be done to protect your mother. I think you should get a regular Winchester now."

Tom shook his head and said, "Not yet, Mac. I'm still too small."

Molly had stayed in the doorway listening to her son and was still stunned by what had just happened. She had just closed her eyes, preparing herself for Ed's fatal bullet, and then, he was gone, just like that.

Mac helped Tom to his feet and then when he stood, Mac saw why Tom hadn't hurt his shoulder when he fired.

"Tom, you had the butt of the shotgun against the wall, didn't you?"

Tom nodded and said, "It was too heavy for me to hold, so when I heard Mr. Phillips coming, I put it under my arm and against the wall, so I could hold it straight. How did you know?"

Mac replied, "Remember when I showed you the firecracker and the penny trick? Look around you and you'll see how I knew."

Tom turned around and saw the impression of the shotgun's butt pressed into the wood behind him.

"It'll be a reminder of your cool-headedness and bravery, Tom."

As Tom smiled, Mac turned to Molly and said, "Molly, why don't you and Tom have a seat around the bathtub while I move Ed's body out of the cabin. Okay?"

Molly nodded and stepped past Mac, who closed the door behind her, so mother and son could spend some private time to deal with the aftermath of what had just happened and not witness the removal of Ed Richardson's body.

Mac dragged Ed out the back door, past Molly's Yellowboy and unceremoniously dumped him off the edge of the porch onto the ground. He then returned to the cabin and spent a few minutes cleaning the floor of the blood. He examined the far wall and saw where some of the pellets had punched into the wood leaving holes. He'd worry about that later. Maybe.

Once the house was cleaned, he opened the bathing room door and said, "Molly, it's clean in the house now. Why don't you make some coffee and wait while I harness the team and start loading up those bodies? It'll take me about an hour to track them all down. I'll have to unsaddle their horses and get them into the clearing, too."

"I can help, Mac. I'm all right now," Molly said.

"I know you are, Molly, but this is a question of muscle. I'll be back as soon as I can."

Molly nodded, and Mac walked out the front door to harness the team. He had planned on making the run to Fort Collins tonight, but thought it wouldn't make any difference if he just left the bodies in the bed of the wagon overnight. New Molly or old, she had undergone a horrific experience and she shouldn't be left alone.

It took over two hours to get all five bodies into the back of the wagon. Mac brought all of their horses to the clearing and unsaddled them, leaving their tack near the tent, but going through their saddlebags. He found the bundles of bank notes and set them aside but the rest of the saddlebags' contents, including Ed Richardson's $237 dollars, and the other $142 from the others, he jammed into his pocket. The bundles of notes were all Fort Collins National Bank notes, while the loose cash was mostly Federal bank notes. He had a feeling that the bundled notes were recently stolen by the gang.

He also left the five Winchesters and assorted handguns in the tent for later sorting and cleaning along with the Sharps which he had almost forgotten as it leaned against a young lodgepole pine.

He joined Molly and Tom for dinner and coffee when he was finished.

"Mac, can Tom and I come along with you?" Molly asked.

"You'll need to write a statement, Molly, but even if you hadn't, I wasn't about to go anywhere without you and Tom, but I hadn't planned on going tonight. It would be late before we got to Fort Collins, and it would be hard to track down the sheriff and the mortician."

"Why do we have to go to Fort Collins?" she asked.

"I found these in Wild Willie's saddlebags," he replied as he tossed the three stacks of bank notes onto the table, "notice anything odd about them?"

"Some are singed along the edges," Molly replied.

"I think the boys robbed the Fort Collins National Bank before they got here. We need to bring these to the sheriff. I'm sure he's looking for those boys."

"So, we can have a normal night and leave in the morning?" she asked.

"That's the idea, ma'am," Mac replied and followed it with a big smile.

With the day's terrible, fearful events behind them, they attempted to return to a normal routine, trying to forget the wagon outside with five bodies lying under the tarp in its bed.

———

Three hours later, in what was becoming almost ritualistic, Mac and Molly sat on their rocking chairs talking after Tom had gone to bed.

"He almost shot me, Mac," Molly said quietly.

"But he didn't, Molly. We're sitting here on the porch, drinking coffee and enjoying each other's company. Don't dwell on what could have been. I thought I was talking to Molly Bradford, not Molly Phillips."

181

Molly looked over at Mac, smiled and said, "You are talking to Molly Bradford, but even she can be scared. I told you that, if you recall."

Mac took a sip of coffee then said, "I'll grant you that. Let me ask you something, though. When you saw Bob pointing his Winchester at you, I didn't hear any screams or begging for mercy. I seem to recall hearing a defiant woman shouting at Ed Richardson. At the time, you weren't afraid, were you?"

"No, I guess I wasn't. I was mad. I wanted to shoot him."

"*That*, Miss Bradford, is what you should remember about that moment. Not that you almost were shot, but that you stood up to him even then. I can't tell you how proud I am of you, Molly. You and Tom both showed remarkable courage today."

"Thank you, Mac. I'll do that. But I can also tell you how proud I was watching you stand up to those five killers. I think you really had them scared because you never flinched. When I watched you swing that shotgun, my heart stopped. Everything happened so fast, I couldn't get a shot off."

"Well, it's over and we can just get back to working on improving our home."

"*Our* home, Mr. Jones?" Molly asked softly.

"Yes, Molly, *our* home. Remember my original offer, that you could leave if you wanted to? It still stands, but I never want you to go anywhere. If you did leave, I'd follow you to the ends of the earth to convince you to return with me."

Molly sighed and said quietly, "You won't have to go to the ends of the earth, Mac. I'm not going anywhere without you."

Mac smiled at Molly and took her hand, then said, "I love you, Miss Bradford. Would it be premature to ask if I could call on you?"

Molly found breathing difficult as she held his hand tightly and whispered, "Not premature, Mr. Jones, just unnecessary. I've loved you since that ride across the river on the back of your horse and your arm around my waist. I'm not some innocent, virginal young girl, Mac. I'm almost thirty and I want so badly to spend the rest of my life with you."

Mac then stood, turned in front of Molly, pulled her to her feet and said, "Miss Bradford, would you grant me the honor of becoming my wife?"

Molly put her hands on the sides of his face and replied softly, "Yes, Mr. Jones. With all my heart, yes."

Mac then kissed her softly and pulled her into his arms and held her close.

"Tomorrow, Molly. We can get married tomorrow in Fort Collins."

Molly rested her head on Mac's chest and simply replied, "Tomorrow."

He kissed her once more and said, "I'll be heading back to my tent now."

Molly looked at him, raising her eyebrows as she tilted her head and asked, "You're leaving?"

Mac answered, "I was going to go back to my tent."

"I thought you'd stay with me tonight. We are getting married tomorrow, after all, and I don't want to waste another night."

Mac grinned and said, "I didn't say I was going alone to the tent, Miss Bradford. I thought that we'd have a bit more privacy away from the cabin."

Molly grinned back at him before he took her hand and led her down the steps. She wanted to skip like a schoolgirl, because that was how she felt. She was free of fear, free to be herself, and free to love.

CHAPTER 9

Mac and Molly walked hand-in-hand back to the cabin in the early morning, their night's passions still in evidence as they looked at each other.

Mac had boiled some water and let Molly take a quick bath in the canvas tub while Mac watched. Mac had then used the same water and finished by shaving while in the tub as Molly watched, no longer the voyeur.

Mac let Molly go to their bedroom to get changed while he prepared breakfast.

Tom walked out of his room as the smell of frying bacon wafted through the cabin.

"Good morning, Tom," Mac said.

"Good morning, Mac. Are we goin' to Fort Collins today?"

"Yes, sir. In about an hour and it's going to be a momentous day, too," Mac said as he looked up and saw Molly walking towards him with a smile after hearing what he had just told Tom.

Molly then said, "Tom, why don't you have a seat, we have something we need to tell you."

Tom glanced at his mother and then back at Mac and he knew something was in the air. He'd noticed the change in the way that Mac and his mother talked to each other and looked at each other. And as happy as his mother had been before, this morning she looked like she was ready to start dancing, which was a good thing.

Mac said, "Tom, last night, your mother and I did a lot of talking. We love each other very much and while we are in Fort Collins today,

185

we're going to get married. We just wanted to let you know, because I'll be moving back into the cabin."

Tom grinned and said, "That's great, Mac! I'll bet my mama is the happiest lady in the world!"

Molly said, "She is the happiest lady in the world, Tom."

Mac added, "And I'm the happiest man in the world, too."

Tom thought he'd add that he was happy, too, but that would have sounded silly.

———

Three hours later, they drove through LaPorte, not stopping because of their cargo in back. It had been a cool morning, so the stench coming from the wagon wasn't bad, but Mac knew it would get worse as it grew warmer, especially with the sun beating down on the dark green tarp.

But even the presence of five corpses didn't detract from the new relationship between Mac and Molly. Tom was very happy with it, but still felt a little odd when his mother and Mac would kiss and hug on the ride. He'd never seen his mother so affectionate with a man before.

They reached Fort Collins just after noon, pulling in front of the sheriff's office, where six horses were hitched out front. Mac assumed it was because of the bank robbery.

After Tom hopped down, Mac raced around the front of the wagon to help Molly, who smiled at his eagerness when she took his hand and stepped down from the wagon.

They entered the office and found Larimer County Sheriff Mike Gunderson standing with three of his deputies looking at a map and tracing something with his finger. There were two other men looking over his shoulders. They all looked up as Mac, Molly and Tom entered the office.

"Can I help you?" asked the sheriff.

"Sheriff, my name is Mac Jones. I have a place northwest of LaPorte where the Cache La Poudre forks. Late yesterday, five men attacked my cabin. I have their bodies out in the back of my wagon. We brought them here because I found this in one of their saddlebags."

He dropped the three singed bundles of bank notes on the desk and all of the lawman stared at the partially burned bundles of bank notes for about five seconds before looking back at Mac.

"Do you know who those men were?" he asked.

"They're Wild Willie Patterson's gang. Four of the five must have just arrived. The fifth one, Ed Patterson, was running under the alias of Bob Phillips, and was living here and working at the wagon builder. He must have joined up with the gang again and told them of my cabin and they thought I was alone, and they could use it as a hideout."

The sheriff stood up straight, grinned and said, "Damn! That's great news! We were just tryin' to figure out how to track them down. Knowin' they were Wild Willie's bunch makes me glad that I didn't find 'em. Let's go and look at those bodies."

All of the other men, who must have been preparing to depart on a posse all had similar expressions of relief and they all followed the sheriff outside.

They all walked to the back of the wagon, the sheriff flipped open the tarp and whistled.

"That's Wild Willie for sure."

"The odd thing about Willie was that if you notice, he was shot in the butt. That was courtesy of Ed Richardson who wanted a chance to get to my cabin. Willie asked me to end his suffering, so I did."

"Is that Richardson?" he asked as he pointed at Ed's body.

"That's him. He had reached the cabin and was about to shoot Tom's mother when Tom let him have both barrels of a twelve-gauge from eight feet away. I'm really proud of my boy."

Tom heard him say 'my boy' and exploded like one of those big fireworks inside, and Molly wasn't far behind.

"Well, that gang knocked off the Boulder stage before noon and killed five men in the process. The bank guard carrying the currency for the bank set them on fire before the gang could get it. We thought it was all gone and it would be the devil to find out who did it, too. You saved me and my deputies a lot of headaches, Mr. Jones. How'd you manage to get all five of them? They were nasty folks."

Mac then had to go through the story from Molly marrying Bob Phillips all the way through the shootout, which still only took five minutes.

"Well, Mr. Jones, if you don't mind, I'll have Deputy Spruell drive those bodies to the mortician while you and the lady write out your statements."

"Not a problem," then he turned to the deputy and said, "Deputy Spruell, tell the mortician he can keep the tarps."

The deputy smiled and replied, "I can understand that," then climbed into the seat and drove the wagon away.

While Molly wrote her statement more quickly because she only had witnessed some of what had happened. Mac, with his lawman background, wrote a more detailed report that took him three pages to finish. Molly sat watching Mac as he wrote, knowing that another step had been taken to their future. The threat of Ed Richardson reappearing in their lives was over, and a much more important step would happen soon.

When Mac finished, he looked over at Molly and said, "Let's drop these off and get something to eat. We have a growing boy, and you still need to put on some weight, Mrs. Jones."

Molly smiled and nodded, still tickled at Mac's reference to Tom as their boy with the added thrill of being called Mrs. Jones.

Mac handed the statements to the sheriff and said, "We need to get something to eat. We'll be back in a little while, is that alright?"

As the sheriff took the sheets he asked, "That's fine, Mr. Jones. You know, you've got quite a hefty reward comin'. Every one of those men had a price on his head."

"I know. I used to be a deputy sheriff and a bounty hunter before I came here," Mac said as he took Molly's arm as they left the sheriff's office and walked slowly across the street to Elmer's Eatery for lunch.

Forty minutes later, they returned the sheriff's office, which was still crowded. The sheriff was there as were his three deputies, as well as two other gentlemen wearing suits.

Sheriff Gunderson saw them enter and smiled, saying, "Here they are, gentlemen. This is Mac Jones, Molly Bradford and her son Tom."

The two men turned and grinned at them and immediately offered their hands to Mac.

"I'm Wilbur Jeffries, the president of the Fort Collins National Bank and this is Mr. Lawrence Elliott from the Overland Stage Company. The sheriff told us of your exploits in the elimination of the perpetrators of the heinous crime yesterday, and we are pleased to make your acquaintance."

Mac shook both their hands and just said, "Pleased to meet you both."

"Mr. Jones, the bank and the Overland Stage Line each had placed a five-hundred-dollar reward on those responsible for the robbery and murders committed by the gang. If you'd come to the bank when you're finished, I'll be more than happy to give you the reward money."

Mac nodded and said, "Thank you, sir. We'll stop by shortly."

189

After the two men left, the sheriff said, "Then, there's the rewards others had posted for the gang, Mr. Jones. I'll notify those who posted the rewards and have them send a Western Union voucher for the cash. It totaled another twenty-six hundred dollars."

"Could you have it sent to me at LaPorte? It's a closer ride."

"I'll do that, Mr. Jones. Say, they need a city marshal in LaPorte. You wouldn't be interested, would you?"

Mac smiled, shook his head and said, "No, I'm sorry. I've got a lot of work to do up in our place."

Mac shook the sheriff and the deputies' hands before leaving.

They left the sheriff's office, walked to the livery and picked up the wagon. The deputy had dropped it off there so the horses could be fed and watered while they took care of the paperwork.

Once they had the wagon moving, they stopped at the bank and picked up the reward money before driving the wagon to the new county courthouse.

Tom hopped down, and Mac slid across and then followed him before trotting around the empty wagon to assist his almost-wife from the driver's seat.

"Miss Bradford, I believe we have business here, but first we need to make a short detour to that small shop across the street."

Molly turned, saw a window sign proclaiming Henderson's Jewelry, and smiled back at Mac.

"I've never worn a wedding ring before, Mac," she said.

"Well, you will now, Mrs. Jones. I don't want any other hairy male thinking you were unattached," he replied as he took her hand.

Twenty-five minutes later, a joyous Mr. and Mrs. Jones exited the courthouse with a beaming Tom alongside.

"Now, my wife, it's time for me to buy your wedding present," Mac said as they reached the boardwalk.

"Mac, I don't need anything more than you've already given me, which is everything," said a completely happy Molly.

"Just one thing, Molly," Mac said as they turned on the boardwalk.

They walked a block and a half before Mac guided her and Tom into Hinton's gun shop.

"Good afternoon, Mac? What else can I sell you? I thought you were pretty much all set now." Pete Hinton said when he spied Mac.

"Trust me, Pete, I've got more firepower now than I'll ever need, but my wife is enamored of my Yellowboy and I know that you still have some in stock, so if you could provide her with one, I'd appreciate it."

"I've only got one left, Mac. You're in luck."

Pete then turned, walked to a rack of Winchesters and pulled the '66 carbine from the rack and handed it to Mac.

He then handed it to Molly and said, "It's a carbine, so it's only got a twenty-inch barrel, but it's the right size for you."

Molly looked at her new Winchester and smiled at the weapon, having bonded with the Yellowboy as the instigator of her new life – a life that was everything her old life had not been.

"Thank you, Mac. It's perfect."

Mac paid for the gun after adding another box of .44 cartridges, so Molly could load her carbine on the drive home.

They left the shop and climbed on board the wagon. Once in the seat, as Mac snapped the reins to get the wagon moving, Molly began sliding cartridges into her Winchester's loading gate while Tom watched, wondering if he hadn't been too hasty in telling Mac he was too small to have a Winchester.

Once they left town, Mac said, "Molly, five hundred dollars of that reward money goes to Tom."

Tom's ears perked up and he looked quickly at his mother.

"What do you think we should do with it? We can't just hand him that much money." Molly asked.

"I think you should set it aside for Tom, so he'll be able to go to college," Mac said.

Tom turned to Mac and said, "College? I don't need to go to college, Mac. I'm happy here. I don't need no more schoolin'."

Mac replied, "You're eleven, Tom. You have plenty of schooling ahead of you. If nothing else, you need to speak properly. You're a brave, smart young man, Tom. Don't let your lack of knowledge hold you back. It may be too far for you to ride all the way to school in LaPorte, but your mother and I will teach you. We'll buy a lot of books and everything else you need. Don't rob yourself of your chance to be anything you want to be because you're ignorant. One day, you'll meet a girl that you'll want to marry, and you'll want to give her the best of everything. It'll come sooner than you think, Tom. For you to do that, you'll need a good education. Now, if you still don't want to go to college when you turn eighteen, then the money will be there for you to start your adult life. Okay?"

Molly squeezed Mac's arm to thank him for his answer and advice to Tom.

Tom nodded and said, "Okay. That's fair. I only talked like that because all the other boys did, and I didn't want to get beat up."

Mac grinned at Tom and said, "Well, Tom, I'm not going to beat you up, but I can show you how to take care of yourself, too."

Tom was immensely pleased with that idea.

MAC'S CABIN

Then Mac said, "Molly, when we return to the cabin, I need to show you something that I simply forgot about until we picked up that money from the bank."

"What's that?" she asked.

"I have about five thousand dollars hidden in a rock cleft near the cabin. It's from the sale of the farm in Iowa and the money I made over the past seven years. You need to know where it is, just in case."

"But Ed and those men are all gone, Mac. What else could happen?"

"There are always men like that who want what isn't theirs, and there's something else that you need to know about, too."

Molly waited for the latest revelation.

"While I was working on the cabin, I found a few gold nuggets in the creek. Now, placer nuggets like these can be found in most fast-running water in this part of Colorado, so I wasn't surprised when I found one. But in the past eight weeks, I've found nine without even looking for them. If the word gets out that there's gold up here, our square mile of paradise will turn into a hellish battlefield."

"Where is the gold now, Mac?" she asked.

"I have it buried in a Mason jar near my tent. I still have no idea what to do about it. Gold is a funny thing. The only reason it's valuable is because there isn't a lot of it. It's really not very useful. Iron is much more valuable as far as practical use goes, but men kill for gold just because some men decided that it's worth twenty dollars an ounce."

"Well, we'll just keep it our little secret," then she leaned across in front of Mac, looked at Tom and asked, "Won't we, Tom?"

Tom looked at his mother and said loudly, "Yes, ma'am!"

Molly looked up at Mac and said, "See? The problem is solved."

"Then, there's Black Eagle and his merry little band of renegade Arapahoe. I haven't heard anything about them lately, but they're supposed to be operating south of here right now."

"Who are they?" she asked.

"Black Eagle used to be called Running Beaver, but when he and his followers left the reservation, they all took more ferocious, dark names, that showed that they weren't white and were brave warriors."

"How many does he have with him?"

"It varies, but usually it's not more than eight. I know the army's been trying to corral them for a while."

"Well, we'll deal with Mr. Running Beaver if we have to, Mr. Voice of Doom."

Mac looked over at a grinning Molly, and smiled, saying, "You are quite a woman, Mrs. Jones."

Molly replied, "Oh. You noticed, did you, Mr. Jones?"

"Trust me, ma'am. I noticed."

———

They pulled into LaPorte around four and stopped at Armstrong's.

"I need to talk to Z.T. for a minute, Molly. Do you need anything?"

"Oh, I think I'll find some way to spend your money."

Mac smiled at Molly and said, "Our money now, Mrs. Jones."

They then followed what had become their standard dismounting process as Tom jumped down and let Mac run around the wagon to help Molly onto the street, a totally unnecessary act of chivalry.

As they entered the store, Z.T. spotted Mac enter and waved him over frantically.

Mac approached and asked, "What's up, Z.T.?"

"That feller, Ed Richardson. I saw him and four others like him ride by here yesterday afternoon. I think they were headin' up to your place I woulda warned ya, but by the time I coulda got Babe saddled and ready to go, they woulda been halfway to your cabin."

Mac smiled and said, "Don't worry, Z.T. They're all in Fort Collins now and maybe already in the ground. They rode in trying to get into the cabin and didn't make it."

Z.T. relaxed and said, "Glad you got 'em all. You gonna tell me the story?"

Mac glanced over at Molly as she and Tom were wandering the aisles, picking up different items.

"I think I have the time," he replied before telling Z.T. a somewhat abbreviated version.

When he finished, Z.T. said, "Mac, you oughta be the marshal. They're havin' a hard time findin' one."

"Not me, Z.T., I've still got a lot of work to do."

Then Mac leaned forward, looked over at the doorway to the office where Jolene did the books and asked in a low voice, "Say, Z.T., did you say that you had to saddle Babe? I assumed you meant your horse, but I've heard you call Jolene that a few times. Are you just itching for trouble?"

Z.T. snickered, then he did as Mac did and glanced back at the office before replying, "Well, that's a funny story, Mac. See, I had a mare named Mama for years, and never figured she'd have a young'un. But about ten years ago, lo' and behold, she drops a foal. Well, me and Jolene was just about as happy as we could be lookin' at that little foal. She was such a pretty little thing and we named her

Babe 'cause she foaled outta Mama, see. Well, a couple of weeks later, I made the mistake of lookin' at that cute little filly when the missus was standin' nearby, and I said, 'You are the prettiest gal I ever did see, Babe', and Jolene turns around, smiles at me and give me a big kiss. So, ever since then, I call her 'babe' so she don't get to thinkin' that I thought a horse is prettier than she is."

Mac laughed and gave a light tap on Z.T.'s shoulder as he watched Molly and Tom approach the counter with armloads of assorted goods. It was worth the stop just for that story.

———

Three hours later, they were back in the cabin and Tom begged off to go and take some practice shots with his .22 while the adults shared some coffee.

After Tom was gone, Mac looked at Molly and said, "Did you want to deposit this cash in the bank now?"

"Okay."

They left the house, and after a short walk, reached Mac's bank. He showed Molly how to remove the stone and pulled out his canvas covered money belt, then flipped open the cover and pulled out the thick stack of bills.

Molly asked, "What's the paper for?"

"That's my mustering out paper," he replied.

"Could I see it, Mac?"

Mac handed it to her as he began to put the bills in sequence and get a new total.

Molly began reading the history of Mac's military service during the War Between the States showing the major battles, promotions and wounds received. It was a full sheet and Molly tried to match the cold handwritten words with Mac's heartbreaking story. He had never mentioned any wounds, yet there were three listed. She glanced over at him as he thumbed through the bills and wondered how bad they were. The sheet just listed: bullet wound left thigh, stab wound right chest, and bullet wound left lower abdomen. For four long years, Mac had lived with this, eventually leaving the army as a sergeant. It showed him reenlisting in August of 1864 and wondered why he had agreed to serve another year. She didn't believe it was for the bonus of three hundred dollars.

Mac finished counting and said, "Six thousand, seven hundred and sixty-two dollars is the new balance, Molly, and that's before the reward money."

"Can I hold onto this, Mac?" she asked holding the mustering out paper.

"Sure. I only kept it in case I used it for homesteading, and it's already served its purpose."

"Thank you, Mac," she said as she held it to her breast.

Mac put the money away and said, "I've got to get those guns all cleaned and inspected. We now have five new horses, too, Molly. Did you and Tom want to go and pick out which ones you'd like so I can adjust some saddles for you?"

Molly said, "Oh, I'd forgotten about the horses. Are any of them any good?"

"Not surprisingly, they're all good. I think you'd really like the black gelding. He's a bit smaller than the others, but he's a handsome boy. Tom will be growing fast, so he'll need one of the taller horses anyway."

He took his wife's hand and they walked back to the cabin.

When they reached the cabin, Molly turned and said, "I'll start cooking dinner. I still need to put on a couple of pounds to please my husband."

C.J. Petit

Mac laughed, kissed her and replied, "You please your husband more than you could ever know, my wife. I'm going to go and check on Tom."

She smiled, and as she turned to go up the stairs, Mac gave her a soft pat on her behind which elicited a giggle, a new experience for her.

———

Tom had already put six rounds into the post and was loading his .22 with another cartridge when he fumbled the small cartridge and it fell to the ground then bounced off of a rock making a metallic ding as it hit.

He crouched down to pick up the cartridge and noticed the odd rock that it had struck and began to brush away the dirt, so he could pick it up, but it wouldn't budge. He began to dig around the rock and soon discovered it wasn't a rock at all.

———

Tom heard Mac approaching and jumped to his feet and shouted, "Mac! Look what I found!"

Mac expected it to be another gold nugget, but when he reached the spot where Tom was pointing, he knew what it was immediately.

"Do you know what that is, Tom?" he asked.

"It's a pirate treasure chest. Isn't it?"

"No, Tom. I'm pretty sure that you found the four casks of gunpowder buried by those French trappers. You are looking at a bomb."

Tom began stepping backwards as he stared at his discovery. He had been trying to uncover something that could blow him all the way to the moon! *And he had dropped a cartridge onto it!*

"What are we going to do with it, Mac?" he asked as he continued to backpedal.

"I'm not sure. Let's get back to the cabin and we'll talk to your mother about this."

"Okay," he replied as Mac turned and they walked back to the cabin, although not as quickly as Tom would have liked.

As they walked Mac was wondering what he would do with the gunpowder.

———

"*The gunpowder was buried right where we were shooting off firecrackers?*" Molly asked, stunned by what Mac and Tom had told her.

"That is kind of scary, but the question is what to do about it?"

They were eating dinner and the discovery of the gunpowder pushed aside any normal conversation.

"Can you dig it up?" asked Molly.

"I could, but then I'd have to dispose of anyway. I have no need for that much gunpowder. I'm not going to blow anything up and all of the guns uses cartridges now. I think the safest thing to do is set it off in place."

Molly asked, "How could you do that?"

"The easiest way is for me to put a few rounds through that top keg with the Sharps. I could take the shots from the treehouse for the proper angle and it's a good two hundred and fifty yards from the kegs, so it won't be dangerous. I'll just have a big hole to fill in when it's done."

Molly wasn't so sure it was that safe, but she really didn't want that gunpowder sitting out there, either.

"Okay, Mac. When do you want to do it?"

"Right after we finish eating. I think I've still got enough light to do it. I'll need to go and mark it first, so I can see it better from distance. It may not go off with the first shot or two, but it will sooner or later."

"Can I watch?" asked Tom.

"Sure, you both can, but I'll want you both about four hundred yards away."

"Okay," agreed Tom.

Molly looked at Mac with a touch of apprehension hoping that a quarter of a mile would be far enough away.

————

Mac had marked the casks with two small logs and made an arrow on the ground pointing to the exposed iron band on the top cask. He also put another small log ten feet away, so he could sight his Sharps in more accurately.

He waved to a distant Molly and Tom as he hooked the Sharps' temporary cord harness around his shoulder and climbed the tree to the observation post.

Once in position, he lay prone on the planks and took aim at the target log.

He held his breath and squeezed the trigger. The Sharps punched into his shoulder as the .52 caliber bullet spun down the rifled barrel and exploded out of the muzzle.

A fraction of a second later, the target log jumped as the big piece of lead smashed into it.

"Okay," he said out loud to himself, "now let's see if we can get those kegs to go off."

After reloading, he shifted his aim to the point indicated by the arrow logs and again, held his breath and squeezed the big rifle's trigger.

He saw the dirt in front of the two logs explode, which meant he was too high.

He loaded a fresh cartridge and tried again. This time the bullet didn't ignite the powder, but he didn't see where it went, either. He guessed he had hit the top cask, but not the iron band.

After reloading a third time, he didn't change his aim from the last shot, knowing it was highly unlikely to hit the same spot exactly.

He squeezed the trigger for the fourth time and the large round blasted from the muzzle, traveled two hundred and sixty-eight yards and three inches as it caught the bottom edge of the iron band, causing a large spark, setting the first few grains of gunpowder alight. After that, the reaction was almost instantaneous as the twenty pounds of the top cask's exploding powder touched off the second and then the third and fourth. The explosion that followed was a sight to behold as rocks, dirt and the wood from the casks all rocketed outward from the force of the reaction. The ground shook as the three pairs of human eyes watched in awe.

The cloud was enormous as debris began to rain down across the area, but none of the large ones were further than two hundred yards from the blast. Still, small rocks and dirt began falling just fifty yards from where Molly and Tom stood, both with their fingers in their ears.

Mac hung the Sharps over his shoulder and quickly climbed down from the treehouse, waiting for Tom and Molly to join him before inspecting the damage and seeing how much work lay in front of him.

"That was great!" Tom shouted when they were close.

Mac just smiled at Molly, who took his hand as they all walked to the enormous, still smoking crater.

"Mac, that's almost twenty feet across!" Molly said as they drew near.

When they walked up beside the gaping hole in the ground, the smell of gunpowder almost overpowering, they all looked down.

"It's over eight feet deep, too," Mac said.

Molly then said, "That's going to take a lot of dirt, Mac."

"I know, but at least it's safe now."

Molly looked at the devastation and shuddered, knowing that they had all been lighting fireworks in the very spot a few days earlier, but not knowing how much more dangerous it had been when Tom had dropped the rimfire .22 cartridge onto the iron band.

Mac felt her shake and put his arm around her shoulder. Molly looked up at him, smiled and put her arm around his waist.

Tom then said, "Look, Mac. It's filling with water!"

It wasn't much of a surprise, really. Not with the two branches of the Cache La Poudre River joining just a hundred yards away. But still, the rapidity of the flow surprised Mac.

"I wonder if it's going to flow into the river after it's filled," he said as he and Molly stared into the watery pit.

With that, they all turned and walked back to the cabin, neither Mac nor Molly relinquishing their holds on the other.

———

They walked back to the cabin and Tom was surprised when they shifted away from the cabin and walked straight to the clearing.

"Where are we going, Mac?" he asked.

"Tom, you need to pick out your horse. The small black gelding is your mother's, but you'll need a tall one anyway."

Tom was stunned, because like his mother, he had totally forgotten about the horses, and was bouncing as they reached the clearing. A week ago, he had met a stranger in a store who had bought him a fishing pole, and now the same man, who was no longer a stranger, but his best friend, had given him a rifle, a horse, a home, and a future.

When they reached the clearing, it only took a few seconds for Tom to select a copper gelding as his.

Molly walked up to her new black gelding and patted him on his neck, turned to Mac and smiled.

The horse selections completed, Mac took Molly's hand and they returned to the cabin while Tom stayed with his new horse to get acquainted.

They stopped at the tent on the way, so Mac could get his clothes to return to their bedroom. Molly had already taken over the dresser, and with Tom's new clothes, she didn't know how they'd all fit.

Mac told her not to worry, as there was another dresser under the cabin that he could move into the bedroom tomorrow.

With the clothing storage issue behind them, Mac just set his clothes on top of the dresser until he moved the second one into the room.

Tom returned a little while later and promptly went to his room and climbed into bed.

Mac and Molly then went to the porch for their evening chat, neither wishing to end the new tradition.

"What will you do tomorrow, Mac?" she asked after sitting down in her rocker.

"Just finish up the corral. Then, Mrs. Jones, I believe I'll saddle the horses and you'll get to ride your new horse and Tom will ride his and I'll show you the rest of our piece of paradise."

Molly smiled and said, "I haven't seen much of it, have I?"

"No, ma'am. It's pretty special."

Molly took his hand and said, "Mac, tomorrow will be just one single week since Tom and I made that walk from LaPorte. In those seven incredible days, I've gone from a despondent, fretting, and hopeless woman to a contented, happy and hopeful one, and it's all because of you. I can't imagine how fortunate I was when you walked into that store and found Tom staring at the fishing pole."

"And I only went into the store looking for oatmeal. Isn't it extraordinary how such simple things can have such an enormous impact on our lives? You decided to take the trip to Fort Collins, knowing there was probably nothing there for you. That was the day I completed my homestead agreement, and just on a whim, decided to get some oatmeal. I shudder to think what would have happened if even one slight change had altered the sequence. What if I'd been early or late, or I didn't want the oatmeal? It can make you crazy when you look back like that. I know it's only because the events happened that you can play this mental game. We like to believe that it was fate or the hand of God, but it's really just coincidence. I don't believe God sits there and manipulates our lives. If he did, why make bad people? I'm just going to be eternally grateful for my desire for oatmeal that day."

Molly then smiled and asked, "Have you no other desires right now, Mr. Jones? It is, after all, our wedding night."

Mac stood and replied, "Trust me, my love, I haven't forgotten."

———

An hour and ten minutes later, a slippery Molly was sliding her fingers across her equally damp husband and asked, "Mac, can you show me your wounds?"

"Which ones?" he asked.

"Do you have more than the three from the war?"

"I have two other gunshot wounds from my days as a lawman and as a bounty hunter. One from each job."

He showed her the bayonet slice to his chest, the bullet scar to his abdomen and the larger bullet scar to his thigh.

"Those are the one I got in the war, this one on my calf is from a .32 caliber bullet fired by a man named Cap Lipton. He tried to drygulch me with a pistol for some reason when I was tracking him. He thought I'd see his Henry's barrel too easily. The one you can't see is under my hair in the back of my head. Of all of them, it was the closest to killing me because the outlaw that shot me, a desperado with the unlikely name of Percy Madewell, had waited until I had ordered him to drop his weapon. He did, and after I stepped forward to retrieve it, he shot me with a hidden derringer. It hit me in the back of the head, and I went down. I knew I was a dead man, but my boss, Sheriff Jed Jackson, had trailed me and shot him with his Winchester from over a hundred yards out. It was that wound that made me go into being a bounty hunter where you didn't have to announce yourself and disarm them. I still tried to capture them alive, but most wound up in shootouts. These were desperate men."

Molly kissed his bayonet scar and said softly, "No more wounds from now on, Mac."

Mac kissed the top of her head and replied, "I'm not making any promises, Molly. I didn't ask for any of the ones I have, but I won't hesitate to add a new one to protect you and Tom."

Molly sighed, rested her head on Mac's chest and said, "I know."

CHAPTER 10

The corral was completed the next morning and shortly after lunch, Mac, Molly and Tom were on their horses riding away from the cabin. Molly hadn't found any riding skirts in the drawers, so she was wearing a pair of Tom's new britches, which she had bought a bit oversized to allow him to grow.

Mac had deeply appreciated the look, and told her so, which made the ride even more pleasant.

Molly had her new '66 in the scabbard while Mac had his '73. Tom, despite his earlier denial, had been given a Winchester '73 carbine from the five that had been donated by the Wild Willie Patterson gang. He had demonstrated to Mac that he could cycle the lever and hold it properly. He had even fired a round to good effect, which pleased him immensely. He'd keep his first rifle that was still practically brand new, but he treasured the Winchester.

As they took their tour of the property, Mac intentionally swung wide, going another mile outside his property lines, looking for signs of intruders. He was still worried about that gold. He didn't find any prospectors, but he did find an old campfire that had been carefully returned to its prior natural state. He only spotted it when Tom's horse, who he had christened Copper, kicked over a rock exposing the charred ground underneath.

When he stopped and dismounted, Molly asked, "What is it, Mac?"

He was flipping rocks over to determine the size of the fire as he replied, "This is an old campfire. I'm not sure how old it is, but it's definitely a campfire."

He stepped back onto Pete and they continued their ride.

"Do we have visitors?" Molly asked.

"Yes, but not recent visitors. I know when I first moved here, I found some moccasin prints just past the northern border of the property, but they were at least a few days old, and that was more than two months ago. I haven't seen anyone since, though."

"We'll just have to keep our eyes open," she said.

"Yes, ma'am, we do."

They returned to the corral, stepped down and Mac showed them how to strip the horses and brush them down. He was still the only one who could carry a saddle, but Tom and Molly could carry the rest of the tack, which was all placed in the tent.

Tom had stored all the other saddles in the tent but had moved all of the guns and ammunition into the cabin. He was still thinking about that campfire. He guessed it was about the same age as the moccasin prints that he'd found earlier, which told him that the location was being used as a refuge by Indians, and the only ones in the area who weren't on the large reservation south of Fort Collins were Black Eagle and his crowd. He knew the army was out trying to catch the renegade but didn't know where they were. But as Molly had said, all they could do was to keep their eyes open.

———

Over the next two weeks, Mac built his smokehouse and Molly harvested and canned some of the crops that Mac had planted. She even made some strawberry preserves, which were a big hit with Tom and Mac.

He began construction of the barn when he started felling more lodgepole pines for the walls. Tom was always with Mac as he worked, his Winchester in his hands, even while Mac explained his construction techniques, which included a lot of help from the draft horses and block and tackle to lift the logs into place. But because it was just a matter of cutting, trimming branches and making the cutouts on the ends for the next row of logs to put into place, it progressed much faster than the construction of the raft for the support of the cabin.

To Mac and Tom's delight, they found that the pit had filled with water, and after a week, had become reasonably warm, or at least not so cold. They began using it as a swimming hole, but Molly preferred the warm baths in the miraculous stone tub that her husband had built, and she told him that she knew he had built it just for her even before he knew she existed.

On the 28th of July, they took the wagon into LaPorte for a resupply. Molly was finally able to buy some riding skirts, but she bought some more britches for herself because Mac seemed to like to see her wearing them. They bought a lot of books for Tom, including some text books and Mac had Z.T. order a lot more.

Mac and Molly opened a bank account with the reward money, and Mac added another three thousand from the rock bank, leaving almost four thousand in the crevice in case the bank went under or was robbed.

After they had returned and put everything away, they all walked back toward the pit and engaged in one of their favorite pastimes – target practice. Today was different, though. Molly had asked on the return trip from LaPorte if she could try to shoot a pistol. She was stronger now, and her hands were big enough, so Mac gave her one of the .44 caliber chambered Colts that they had acquired and put the gunbelt over her hips, taking an inordinate amount of time making sure it was snug around her waist.

Tom was getting so used to it now, that he didn't even notice anymore.

Molly didn't do too badly for her first time with a revolver, but said she'd practice with it more often and from that day on, Molly rarely went outside without her Colt.

The books arrived at Armstrong's and Mac and Molly spent hours each day with Tom in his studies. He found that he enjoyed it much more than he expected because it was Mac who helped him with math and science, which he had never liked before. His mother helped with his grammar and spelling, and he found that he had a talent for writing that earned their praise.

MAC'S CABIN

Molly and Mac, in their new roles as teachers, found that they were learning more themselves as they read the text books. There were also a lot of books to read for pleasure now, and when they weren't busy with other things, Mac and Molly would read in bed.

————

The barn was completed on the 12th of August, complete with troughs, feed bins, stalls and a loft. It was bigger than he had first anticipated because he now had ten horses to care for. The huge doors required a trip to Ledbetter's for the giant hinges, and Mac also bought another pump, so he could fill the troughs more easily than lugging pails of water from the creek.

Mac and Tom still managed to make trips to the river to fish for trout and whitefish but didn't overdo it. Fish was a nice change, but it wasn't about to become a staple.

They hunted for most of the meat, but still bought beef and chicken from Armstrong's. With an abundance of wild turkeys on the property, Mac's plans for a chicken coop evaporated.

They were out on one of their fishing expeditions while Molly was in the cabin, doing the laundry using the same tub that they used for filling the bathtub. As she wrung out the clothes, she wasn't really even paying attention to the clothes or anything else but staring straight ahead and not seeing anything.

Since she'd given birth to Tom, once her monthlies began again, she'd never missed one. but she just had missed her July monthly. She knew she couldn't be pregnant because she had become pregnant so fast after marrying Chester, she thought she'd have at least a half dozen children. But then Chester treated her like she didn't exist, so she hadn't been surprised when she went another seven years and hadn't conceived. But with Bob Phillips, or Ed Richardson, just the opposite occurred. He almost never gave her a night off. Granted, he had been rushed, rarely lasting ten minutes from his initial grope, but still, she hadn't missed a monthly. And what really scared her was that one time she had sold herself to the landlord.

Molly decided not to tell Mac until she was sure and that would be in another two weeks.

————

With the barn, corral and smokehouse done, Mac had two other projects to complete before the summer ended and the cold weather arrived, and both involved the cabin.

The first was the construction of a cold room. He began by digging under the cabin first and lining the large hole with rocks. Then he built shelves along the walls and steps leading out of the large hole to the ground near the porch steps. He then built what looked like a mud room, which it was, but also served as an enclosed entrance to the new cold room. When it was finished, it was no longer necessary to go outside to get under the cabin, and the added depth of the cold room meant no ducking or bumped heads to get there.

Once the cold room and the mud room were added, all that remained was to cut some more lodgepole pines and close off the space between the raft and the ground to block out the wind.

The entire project was done by early September and just in time, too as the temperatures were already getting noticeably cooler.

There were stacks of firewood for as a result of all of the construction, so their home was ready for the oncoming winter.

A few nights later, Molly was laying half across Mac under the covers, and knew she not only had to tell him, but admit to her real concern over what should be joyous news.

"Mac, I don't understand this, but I think I'm pregnant."

Mac looked down at Mollie, kissed her on the forehead, smiled and said, "That's wonderful, Molly! Why don't you understand it, though? I mean, let's face it, we've been pretty busy for the past couple of months."

"I know that, but I thought I was barren. I mean, after Tom. I thought something had happened to me when he was born because I never got pregnant again. I know it wasn't likely with Chester, but with as much as Bob Phillips used me, I was surprised I never got pregnant. I just thought I'd never have another baby."

Mac then looked at her face and said, "Then, why are you so sad, Molly. I thought you'd be happy."

"I am. Well, mostly I am. But I am worried about one thing, Mac. What if it's not your baby? Bob was already gone when my June monthly arrived, so I know he couldn't be the father, but I missed my July and now my August monthlies. What if the landlord…"

Then Molly just began to shake and cry as she buried her face in Mac's neck.

Mac held her closely and said, "Molly. Sweetheart. Listen to me. We are going to have our beautiful baby and I never want to hear you think about this again. I have made love to you dozens of times since we've been married. I think it's closing in on a hundred already. And since you've filled out so nicely, I'm thinking of reaching a hundred in the next few hours."

Molly felt his caressing touch and pulled her head from his neck and looked at his smiling face.

"I'm being silly again, aren't I?" she asked with a sniff.

"No, Molly, you're being pregnant, not silly. I can understand why you would be concerned. Now, I'm going to pass on something that I happen to know from a long time ago. Okay?"

"Okay."

"Now, your landlord problem happened right after your June monthly, is that right?"

"Yes."

"Did you know that it's very rare for a woman to get pregnant the week after her monthly?"

Molly looked at him and said, "You're making that up to make me feel better."

"No, I'm not. Remember I told you that I had that girlfriend in school that thought we were going to get married? Well, she told me that little fact, so we could, you know, do what we just did. But before I believed her, I went to the Burlington library and looked it up in a medical book and found she was telling me the truth. So, Mrs. Jones, what you have growing in your tummy is our baby. Period."

Molly smiled rested her head on Mac's chest and said, "Then, I'm very happy, Mac. I wanted this to be your baby as well as mine. I wanted to love her as much as I love you and Tom."

"Her?" Mac asked.

"Her," Molly replied before saying, "and now, Mr. Jones, you can tell me about your girlfriend that you must have visited after your library reading."

Mac slid his hand across her smooth back and down further before saying, "After."

Molly slipped close to him, kissed him softly and replied, "After."

———

Her concern over the fatherhood of her baby gone, a happier Molly prepared breakfast the next morning for her husband and son before they took the wagon into LaPorte to load it up with hay for the winter.

———

Sixteen miles due south of the cabin, Lieutenant Michael Grafton was riding at the head of his column of cavalry. They had trailed Black Eagle's band of renegades for over two weeks now and had finally trapped them in a box canyon. He had an understrength company under his command, but it was more than enough to do the job.

He turned to his sergeant and said, "Have the men draw their carbines. We'll ride in three columns of four abreast at a medium trot. Expect them to open fire when we're in range. We'll continue to advance and prepare to fire at their smoke when I give the order."

"Yes, sir!" Sergeant Tucker said as he wheeled his mount about to pass along the orders.

The men were tired of the chase and were heartened to finally be able to do what they were trained to do. Each man pulled his Spencer carbine from its scabbard and began to form into four four-abreast columns.

———

A mile and a half ahead of the cavalry, Black Eagle and his eight men knew they were in trouble. They had thought they'd lost the cavalry twice already and had ducked into the canyon and covered the tracks of their horses, or so they believed. But three of their number were riding shod horses and hadn't had time to remove the iron shoes that left deeper marks behind.

In this case, the iron shoe of Dark Cloud's horse had struck a rock, breaking a large chip off the face of the rock that none of them had noticed. For experienced trackers like the Crow scout being used by Lieutenant Grafton, it was a dead giveaway. Black Eagle had gone into a box canyon.

Now, Black Eagle had to decide. Did they abandon their horses and climb the canyon walls, or did they fight? He knew that none of them would survive the battle with the bluecoats, and as much as he'd be proud to die as a warrior, the opportunity to continue to strike fear in the palefaces that were continuing to pour into Arapahoe land outweighed that desire.

He conferred with his warriors, and they hastily began to pack their critical items, like ammunition and a little food into bags, hung them over their shoulders, then grabbed their rifles, hung them across their backs and began to climb the two-hundred-foot high canyon walls, leaving their horses behind.

None had gone even a hundred feet up the wall when they heard the pounding hooves of the advancing cavalry.

———

Lieutenant Grafton saw the Arapahoe renegades trying to make their escape when his columns were still trotting and shouted for the columns to move at a canter to close the gap quickly before they reached the top of the canyon. They might lose them for another two weeks before being able to catch up with them, if at all.

Black Eagle hung onto a dwarf pine as he glanced behind him and saw the four columns of soldiers speeding closer, getting close to firing range.

"Move faster! They approach!" he shouted needlessly as the others already were scrambling as fast as they could up the steep wall.

———

The columns were only two hundred yards from the Arapahoe when Lieutenant Grafton shouted, "Fire at will!"

Seconds later, the canyon echoed with the eruption of sixty-eight Spencer carbines unleashing their .56 caliber lead missiles at the escaping Indians.

Black Eagle watched and felt the massive rounds explode the ground all around him and his warriors as he continued to crab up the wall, the safety of the plateau only thirty feet away now. But he heard the screams of some of his men as they took hits. Even a wound that normally wouldn't be fatal, became deadly when coupled with the long fall to the rocks below.

He had gone another fifteen feet and was so close when another round was fired by the bluecoats and he felt one of the bullets graze his right calf before smashing into the dirt of the canyon wall. He ignored the blood and the pain as he continued to crawl and then, he reached the live-saving flat ground and quickly rolled over the top onto his stomach.

The first thing Black Eagle did was to scan the wall to see how many of his men had made it to the top as he did. He was stunned when he saw that only Dark Cloud had reached the top with him.

"Dark Cloud!" he shouted, "has anyone else completed the climb?"

Dark Cloud replied, "No. I watched Gray Hawk fall, and he was the last."

Black Eagle stood and released an ear-piercing banshee scream and then pointed his Winchester down at the bluecoats two hundred yards down in the canyon and began to fire as rapidly as he could.

Dark Cloud then followed with his war cry and began doing the same.

———

Lieutenant Grafton shouted, "Keep firing, men!" as he wielded his saber, "Don't let them..."

His shout of encouragement died suddenly as one of Dark Cloud's .44s struck him in the upper part of his shoulder, right where his shoulder boards would be if he'd been wearing them. The bullet penetrated into his right upper lung and stayed there. He slumped forward in his saddle and dropped his saber onto the ground.

Sergeant Tucker shouted for Private Worthy to grab the lieutenant's sword and then took the young officer's horse's reins and led it out of range of the Arapahoe Winchesters.

Knowing that the renegades were no longer viable targets, the sergeant called for a cease fire, then formed the men back into columns, and executed a retreat out of the canyon.

As far as he and the army were concerned, Black Eagle was no longer a threat. He needed to get his officer to a doctor.

———

After their fusillade of gunfire into the bluecoats that had caused death to their leader, Black Eagle was mollified and with his smoking Winchester in his hand, he shouted insults at the fleeing bluecoats. Then, he remembered his wound and sat down.

As he did, he made the mistake of setting the butt of his rifle on the ground and reached for the barrel to lower it to the ground. As soon as he grabbed the barrel, he was reminded just how hot a rifle barrel can get after firing fifteen shots in just fifty seconds.

He cursed as the rifle dropped and he examined his burned right hand while Dark Cloud approached to look at his leg wound.

"It is not bad, Black Eagle. I will burn it with my knife."

"Do it now. We must travel soon before the bluecoats make it around to the plateau."

Dark Cloud nodded and began gathering brush for a small fire to heat his knife's blade to cauterize the wound.

———

The heavily laden wagon trundled up the incline with its huge load of hay. Tom was riding Copper alongside.

"I think this is the biggest load I've ever asked the team to bring back to the cabin," Mac said as they passed the halfway point.

"They seem to be handling it well," Molly said over the noise of the wagon's progress.

"I'll owe them more oats when we get back, though."

"At least Tom's not on board," Molly said, "he's getting bigger too. Have you noticed?"

Mac replied, "I have noticed, and so are you."

Molly rubbed her belly and said, "I'm not even showing yet."

"No, I meant in other places. The interesting ones."

Molly laughed and swatted Mac on the shoulder and said, "Oh, I am well aware that you noticed that change."

After they reached the barn, Molly went in to cook dinner while Tom and Mac began loading the hay into the loft. It was a long, hard job that took over an hour, and when it was done, and the horses taken care of, Mac and Tom washed in the creek before heading into the cabin.

———

Black Eagle hadn't made a sound when Dark Cloud had pressed the glowing steel blade to his wound but knew it would be difficult to walk on the leg, so for the rest of the day, the two warriors had stayed put.

"Where do we go, Black Eagle?" asked Dark Cloud as he chewed on some jerky.

"North. We must go north. Back to the campsite we used before. No bluecoats go there. There is game and fish, and after I heal, we will begin our attacks again."

Dark Cloud nodded and asked, "When will you be able to travel?"

"Soon. We'll leave soon."

———

Black Eagle and Dark Cloud began walking north as Molly was setting dinner on the table.

The walking was causing Black Eagle continuous pain in his leg, but they continued to step along at a fairly rapid pace. The only thing that troubled him, other than the loss of his warriors, was how much of their precious ammunition they had expended while firing down at the bluecoats. He was angry with himself for letting his rage cause him to lose control like that. Now, he and Dark Cloud were in dire need of more ammunition.

———

It was getting darker a lot earlier, and much cooler, too, but Mac and Molly were still on the front porch in their rockers talking. They were both wearing jackets now and Molly wore heavy socks to keep her feet and legs warm.

"It's a beautiful night, Mac. It's so peaceful."

"It is, and it's even more special because you're here, Molly."

Molly smiled at Mac. He said things like that often, but she never tired of hearing them because she knew that he meant every word.

"Tom is doing so very well with his lessons, Mac. Do you think he'll really go to college?"

"I do. You're not going to believe what he told me yesterday when we were studying history."

She asked, "What did he say?"

"We had just read about John Paul Jones, and he said he'd like to go to the U.S. Naval Academy, so he could command a ship."

Molly's eyebrows shot up and she exclaimed, "The navy? He's never even seen an ocean."

Mac shrugged and said, "He's not even twelve yet, Molly. He has a few years to change his mind. If he still wants to go when he's eligible, we should do all we can to help him."

"You're right, Mac, but it was such an odd thing to hear."

"It was to me when he first mentioned it, too."

After another twenty minutes, Mac and Molly returned to the cabin and then their bedroom, turning out all of the lamps after setting the fires in the fireplace and the heat stove.

———

"Do you smell the smoke?" Dark Cloud asked in a low voice.

"Yes. It is too much smoke for a campfire. White eyes live here now. They cannot be allowed to stay."

Dark Cloud said, "I only have two more cartridges for my gun. How many do you have?"

"One. But we do not need guns or bullets. We have other weapons. First, we need to find out how many are there and the best way to kill them. We will honor our lost brothers by taking some of their lives."

They continued to press forward following the smoke that seemed to grow stronger with each step.

———

Molly kissed Mac and said, "I swear, Mr. Jones, you get better at this every single time, and I thought I was going to lose my mind the first time."

Mac kissed her back, and ran his hand through her hair before saying, "That's only because you are an inspiration, Mrs. Jones. You are a beautiful, desirable woman."

Molly laid her head on Mac's chest and sighed. Life could never get any better than this.

———

"Why would the white man build a cabin on top of a creek?" asked Dark Cloud as he and Black Eagle stared at the odd construction.

"Who knows why any white man does anything. They are all crazy, but I think our best weapon for this place is fire. He has two entrances, if we start the fire, he will run outside. We will be ready with our knives. I will take the front, and you will take the back."

Dark Cloud asked, "Where will we start the fire? It must be away from the water."

"We start it on this end. We need to collect kindling and wood."

He didn't have to add 'quietly'.

After leaning their rifles against a nearby tree, the two renegades began gathering and piling dry twigs and then branches until it was three feet high.

Once it was ready, Dark Cloud started the fire using white man's matches that he kept in a pouch. The blaze quickly grew as they separated and pulled their knives as Black Eagle stepped quietly in a crouch around to the front of the cabin while Dark Cloud snuck around the back.

Black Eagle had no difficulties in stepping onto the front porch, but Dark Cloud had to cross the creek to get to the back porch, and that did create a very serious problem.

It was dark, the current was swift, and the rocks slippery. Like Tom when he believed he could cross the river in his waders. Dark Cloud thought he'd have no trouble with the nine-foot wide creek.

But when he just passed the halfway point, his right foot slipped off the top of a round rock and with the help of the rushing water, he suddenly lost his balance.

He plunged into the icy water, emitting a short shriek that he couldn't prevent from escaping his lungs as the shock of the frigid liquid struck his chest.

MAC'S CABIN

Mac and Molly were just drifting off to sleep when they heard the sudden cry, and both jerked to full alertness immediately.

Still naked, both quickly slid from under the covers, Mac grabbing his pistol that hung from the bedpost, while Molly threw on her nightdress then trotted out of the bedroom to get her rifle.

Tom was still sound asleep as the two adults ran into the living room.

———

Black Eagle, as soon as he heard Dark Cloud's shriek, knew what had happened, and took almost a minute while he debated going around to check on his friend, or to enter the cabin and kill the white man. By the time he made his decision to kill rather than assist, it was too late, but he didn't know it yet.

———

Because they had heard the sound from the back of the cabin, both Mac and Molly quietly approached the back door and Mac was just preparing to open it when they heard the front door to the mud room open.

Mac quickly whipped his pistol in that direction, cocked the hammer and not a second later, saw an Indian throw open the front door with his knife gleaming in the light from the fireplace.

He spotted Mac, screamed and brought his knife up, but that was as far as he would ever get as Mac pulled the trigger to his Smith & Wesson, sending the .44 though Black Eagle's sternum, knocking him backwards into the front door. He slumped to the floor, his knife dropping to the floor.

Tom came racing out of his bedroom, stared at a naked Mac, then at a dead Indian on the floor.

"Mac! What happened?" he shouted.

Mac quickly said, "I want you both armed and prepared. There's at least one more out there, and maybe as many as eight. Go!"

Mac didn't bother getting dressed, he just stepped out onto the back porch into the cold September air and waited for his night vision to arrive.

Meanwhile the fire on the side of the house was growing and none of them knew of the danger.

Dark Cloud, after slipping into the water, had been swept another fifty yards downstream, but had finally regained his footing and stepped onto the other side of the creek. To make matters worse, he no longer had his knife which was somewhere on the creek's bed.

He had heard the gunshot and assumed that Black Eagle was dead. Now, he must avenge his leader. He decided to retrieve his rifle, which meant crossing the creek again. This time, he was much more careful and made it to the other side in a minute, just as Mac reached the back porch and was standing, waiting for his eyes to adjust to the darkness.

Dark Cloud saw the white man appear, outlined against the light from the cabin's doorway. He had a pistol, so Dark Cloud began using the trees as cover to hide his path to his rifle, just fifty yards away.

Molly had stepped past the dead Indian and into the mud room. Tom walked behind his mother with his Winchester.

The door to the mudroom was already open, so they both slowly stepped out to the front porch and that was when Tom spotted the flickering light from the fire on the side of the house. He couldn't see the flames, but something was burning.

"Mama! There's a fire over there!" he shouted as he pointed.

Molly had been looking to her right, toward the creek when Tom shouted. She quickly turned back, saw the light and rushed down the steps with her Winchester in her hands.

MAC'S CABIN

Tom followed his mother as they raced to the other side of the house.

When they saw the tall blaze that was just beginning to lick at the green-painted wood, she shouted, "Tom, go into the house and get two pails. Quickly!"

Tom didn't hesitate, but ran back to the porch, climbed the steps and dashed inside, leaping over Black Eagle's body. He set down his rifle, grabbed two pails and then raced back to help his mother put out the fire that was threatening to consume their home.

———

Mac had heard that dreaded word 'fire' from Tom's shout, but when he heard Molly tell him to get the pails, he knew that he'd have to find the ones who set it to protect Molly and Tom.

He was about to return to the house when he caught a flash of a shadow moving toward the other side of the house where the fire was.

He turned and ran through the house, reached the front porch as Molly and Tom each staggered past with a pail of water.

"Stay behind me," he said as he leapt down before them.

"But the fire!" Molly shouted.

It was Molly's shout that alerted Dark Cloud to their presence as he reached the tree and grabbed a rifle. He had intended to shoot the man with the gun, but the voice was too close to ignore. He cocked the rifle's hammer and then saw Mac standing near a woman and a boy framed by the flames.

Mac then spotted Dark Cloud as he was bathed in the fire of his own creation and was bringing his Winchester to bear.

Mac couldn't waste time to aim but fired from the hip as soon as he spotted the Indian preparing to shoot. Then, he did something he always had thought to be wasteful. He fanned the remaining four shots at Dark Cloud.

Dark Cloud had his finger on the trigger when Mac's second shot struck his right knee. He screamed, his Winchester was jerked back as it fired, and the round disappeared into the night.

Before he fell, Mac's third round drilled into his chest on the left side, but only a half an inch from the edge. The slug shattered his seventh rib which punched into his lung.

He might have survived both of those wounds had he not taken Mac's last shot in the neck, finishing him off.

Mac was empty, and useless against any more Arapahoe, so he shouted to Molly, "Get your rifle, Molly I'll handle the fire!"

Mac grabbed the first pail and threw it onto the fire, hearing the satisfying hiss as steam blew away from the fire. He then took Tom's pail and did the same. He didn't wait to see how much effect they had, but trotted down to the creek, filled both pails and lugged them back to the fire, his bare feet feeling every pebble and pine needle as he stepped along.

The two full buckets did the trick, reducing the small inferno to a smoldering mass of black charred branches. He then took another nearby branch and used it to pull the mess away from the cabin.

His job done, he walked over quickly to Dark Cloud's body, picked up the Winchester, and then took the second one from where it had been leaning on the tree.

Molly walked up to him, ignoring his nakedness, and said, "Are there more, Mac?"

Mac shook his head and replied, "I don't think so. These two left their Winchesters against that tree. I'm sure they must have been with Black Eagle, but I don't know where the rest of his warriors are."

"You'd better get back inside and get some clothes on," Molly said, "I can only ignore that for so long."

"I'll do that and move that other one out of our house and drag him out to be with his partner. I'll bury them nearby. This used to be their land once."

"Okay. Now, please come in, husband."

Mac nodded and when they got near Tom, Mac just nodded as he saw the boy with his Winchester in his hands.

Tom nodded back, knowing he had done what was needed.

———

Thirty minutes later, a fully clothed Mac Jones was sitting with Molly and Tom at the kitchen table with a cup of coffee in his hands. Black Eagle's body had been moved outside and the blood scrubbed from the floor.

"That was close, Mac," Molly said.

"Too close, Molly. But I believe that with the coming cold and snow, it'll be the last problem of that sort unless the rest of Black Eagle's band comes seeking revenge. I think the one that broke into the house was Black Eagle himself. He was wearing an eagle feather that had been dyed black. I have no idea who the second one was. I'll take any ornamentation they wore and telegraph the army and let them figure it out."

"So, we'll be riding to LaPorte tomorrow?"

"Yes, but we won't be taking the wagon. We'll ride, so it will be faster. We send the telegram to the army, have lunch, and wait for a reply. I don't want to come riding back here not knowing how many more are left."

"Now, can we get some sleep?" Molly asked with a sigh.

———

The next morning, after breakfast, Mac took a pickaxe and a spade, harnessed one of the draft horses and just laid the bodies on a tarp and looped a rope through the tarp's grommets, then he mounted Pete and led the draft horse away from the cabin.

He took the two bodies to where he had found the campfire. It wasn't an easy place to dig, but an hour later, he had a hole dug and before he set the two bodies into the ground, he took whatever he could that might identify them to the army before sliding them into the ground and folding the tarp over the top. After covering the bodies with dirt and rock he mounted Pete and led the draft horse back to the corral. He left Pete saddled for the ride into LaPorte but unharnessed the draft horse before saddling Copper and Molly's black gelding that she had named Harry just because she thought it suited him.

When they arrived in LaPorte, they naturally stopped at Armstrong's first, because Mac thought he'd get the word out about the proximity of Black Eagle's band.

"Morning, Z.T. I have some news that you need to pass around," Mac said as he walked in the door.

"Mornin', Mac. I'll swap you news for news then. What's yours?"

"We had a couple of Arapahoe try to burn us out last night and I shot them both and buried them north of my place. I know one was Black Eagle, but I don't know who the second one was. I wanted everyone to know they were around, though."

Z.T. scratched his head and grinned, "Well, don't that beat all. We got a telegram yesterday that the army killed all of Black Eagle's bunch about fifteen miles south of here in a box canyon."

Mac opened his saddlebag and pulled out the black eagle feather and said, "I think they're exaggerating a bit, Z.T. I'm going to send a telegram down to Fort Supton and let them know. At least I don't have to worry about the rest unless the army really told a tall tale to impress the boss back east."

"I wouldn't put it past 'em, Mac."

"I wouldn't either, Z.T. Thanks for the information."

After they left the store, Mac sent his telegram, then they went to lunch.

After they finished, they walked to the Western Union office to see if there had been a reply and Mac was a bit surprised that there had been one. He read the message, thanked the operator, then they left the office.

Once outside, Mac handed Molly the telegram and said, "The army said that they got all but two and thanked us for eliminating Black Eagle and Dark Cloud."

"You don't sound pleased about it, Mac," she said as she hooked her arm through his and they began walking back to their horses.

"Oh, I know that they both deserved to die for their crimes. They weren't fighting armed soldiers unless they had to. They were killing innocent men, women and children because they were angry at us for taking their lands. But they took those lands from other tribes, too, so that's just the way of the world. Maybe it's just that I'm getting tired of handling so many dead bodies."

Molly pulled his hand down to her belly and said, "In a few months, you'll be handling one very live, new body that will be with us for a long time."

Mac smiled at his wife, then leaned over and kissed her just before they reached their horses, mounted and turned north to ride out of LaPorte.

———

Two hours later, their horses returned to the barn, Mac and Molly stood looking at the wall of the cabin where black soot and bubbled paint marked the height of the previous night's flames.

227

"I'll clean that off and cover it with paint. You won't even notice it by next week."

"Good. Let's go inside," Molly said.

Mac put his right arm around Molly's shoulder, and she hugged his waist with his left as they walked away from the damage, up the steps and into the house.

———

Later that night, Mac and Molly shifted their talk indoors as a cold rain fell. They were seated together on the couch as a warm fire crackled and popped eight feet away.

Molly was tucked under Mac's arm with her legs tucked under her skirt as they talked.

Molly had Mac's right hand in both of hers and was studying it when she asked, "Mac, when I was looking at that fire damage, I wondered what would happen if it had continued and burned down the cabin? This was your sanctuary. Would you rebuild by yourself the same way you built this one?"

Mac kissed the top of her head and replied, "I'd rebuild our cabin, Molly, but not in the same way, and not for the same reason. Remember when I told you that story and how I thought I'd never find peace until I had done enough penance? After I left you on the porch and walked to my tent, I laid awake for hours just thinking about what had just happened. Why did I tell you and no one else? As I was telling you the story, even though I couldn't see you, I sensed your compassion. I could almost feel it. Then I finally realized that it wasn't penance that I sought. It wasn't even forgiveness. After telling you what I had never told another person, I knew what it was. I needed to have someone to fill the emptiness in my soul from what I had lost. This cabin isn't my sanctuary, Molly. You are."

EPILOGUE

It was a long winter that year, stretching into early April. Mac was getting worried because Molly was due any day and there was still snow blocking the way to LaPorte. Molly assured him that it would be okay, because she had been through this once before and had written out the instructions for him if it came to that.

Tom's twelfth birthday was coming up on April third, and they were planning a small party.

Molly had baked a sort of a cake that was really a large, sweet biscuit. But with plenty of strawberry preserves and honey, it would be a tasty treat.

Molly was preparing lunch on that day, with Mac practically hovering over her by the cookstove when her water broke and the two males in the house launched into frenzied panic.

Molly just calmed them both down and Mac helped her to their bedroom and laid her down on a new sheet and put three pillows behind her head while Tom pumped water into a pot and put it on the cookstove.

Then came the waiting. For six hours, Molly labored while Mac fretted, but stayed with her while Tom waited in the kitchen, worrying about his mother.

Finally, Molly knew it was time for Mac to welcome their new daughter, according to Molly.

Twenty minutes later, Mac held their precious little girl in his hands as she cried to protest her entry into the cold. As she wailed, Mac smiled, cut the umbilical cord and set her in Molly's welcoming arms.

After cleaning up the mess, Mac covered his wife with blankets and wrapped their daughter in a small blanket they had bought in October along with all of the other necessities or just niceties for newborns. He brought his wife some water and food as she held their daughter.

"Are you okay, Molly?" he asked.

"This was so easy, Mac. And she's so perfect, as I knew she would be," Mollie replied as she held their daughter.

"It didn't seem easy to me, Molly. I was scared to death for you."

"You should have been around when I had Tom. That was scary, even for me. I was in labor for almost a full day with him. Our little Eva was very kind to her mama."

Mac finally was able to relax as he looked at his perfect wife and their perfect daughter.

―――

When Molly became pregnant again, Mac and Tom, now already taller than Molly at thirteen, stretched the cabin on the side where Black Eagle and Dark Cloud had tried to set fire to the place. Molly wasn't surprised that the cabin grew by four more bedrooms, either. It seemed to be Mac's way.

That same year, when they were in Fort Collins, Molly overheard the name 'Bob Phillips' at the new emporium looking for more baby things and had asked the woman how she knew the name. Matilda Richard, now Johnson, after Molly had explained how she knew that name, told her story. The two women empathized with each other and became good friends.

―――

By the time Tom took his entrance examination for the Naval Academy, he had two more sisters after Eva. Little Madeline arriving barely a year later, and then Jennie. Jennie was only three years old when he left Colorado to take the train to Annapolis, and Eva and

Madeline were heartbroken to see their big brother leave. Jennie cried along with them just because they seemed so sad. Molly, who hadn't spent a day away from Tom her entire life, was almost empty of tears as he stepped onto the train platform. The only dry eyes in the house belonged to his very proud father.

But four years later, when the Jones family all took the train to Maryland to see Midshipman Tom Saunders receive his commission as an ensign in the United States Navy, even those masculine eyes were misty when Tom took the oath as a commissioned officer.

After he was commissioned, Mac and Molly, like so many other parents, were present as Tom married his sweetheart he had met in Baltimore. They had met Elizabeth Lawrence before and knew that Tom had found the right woman for him. They both knew how difficult it would be being the wife of a naval officer and told her she could visit them in their expanded cabin whenever he was at sea.

They stayed with Tom for a few days until he received his orders and then Mac, Molly and the girls all returned to their home in Colorado.

As it turned out, there were quite a few more gold nuggets in the creek and the north fork of the Cache La Poudre. The girls all behaved like it was an Easter egg hunt during the summer months, but Mac and Molly simply dropped the nuggets into more Mason jars, filling a total of three of the quart-sized containers; one for each daughter should they ever want them. Most of their income over the years came from the interest on the almost ten thousand dollars that they eventually wound up in their bank account after Mac withdrew his balance from the rock.

With their very low costs of living, and additional income from their extensive strawberry fields, Mac and Molly were able to set aside more than they were using.

Tom and Elizabeth provided six grandchildren for Mac and Molly; four boys and two girls. Tom did well in the Navy and in 1898, at the age of thirty-five, he was captain of the U.S.S. Concord, a gunboat that was part of the flotilla under Admiral Dewey that fought the Battle of Manila Bay.

With all the girls happily married and Tom still somewhere on the open sea, Mac and Molly spent their time together doing what they had done since they married. They worked the fields, kept the buildings in condition and cared for the animals, and every night, when the weather allowed them, they sat on their front porch held hands and talked.

In July of 1899, Mac and Molly were doing just that. Soon, Tom, Elizabeth and their six children, Eva, Madeline and Jennie, along with their husbands and children would be arriving on the train for a twenty-fifth anniversary party.

But tonight, to them, it was much more special than the anniversary of their marriage.

The marriage was just a formality to put on paper what they already knew in their hearts. What mattered much more was that day twenty-five years ago when a new Molly was born, and they began their new life together.

So, that evening before they returned to the cabin, Mac smiled at his wife, then rose, and stood in front of her, looking down to those beautiful brown eyes that were already filling with tears.

He slowly extended his right hand, and Molly placed her hand in his as he said, "Ma'am, my name is Mac Jones. How do you do?"

Molly's hand was trembling as she remembered that night as she replied, "It's a pleasure meeting you, Mr. Jones. My name is Molly Bradford. Please call me Molly."

MAC'S CABIN

1	Rock Creek	12/26/2016
2	North of Denton	01/02/2017
3	Fort Selden	01/07/2017
4	Scotts Bluff	01/14/2017
5	South of Denver	01/22/2017
6	Miles City	01/28/2017
7	Hopewell	02/04/2017
8	Nueva Luz	02/12/2017
9	The Witch of Dakota	02/19/2017
10	Baker City	03/13/2017
11	The Gun Smith	03/21/2017
12	Gus	03/24/2017
13	Wilmore	04/06/2017
14	Mister Thor	04/20/2017
15	Nora	04/26/2017
16	Max	05/09/2017
17	Hunting Pearl	05/14/2017
18	Bessie	05/25/2017
19	The Last Four	05/29/2017
20	Zack	06/12/2017
21	Finding Bucky	06/21/2017
22	The Debt	06/30/2017
23	The Scalawags	07/11/2017
24	The Stampede	07/20/2017
25	The Wake of the Bertrand	07/31/2017
26	Cole	08/09/2017
27	Luke	09/05/2017
28	The Eclipse	09/21/2017
29	A.J. Smith	10/03/2017
30	Slow John	11/05/2017
31	The Second Star	11/15/2017
32	Tate	12/03/2017
33	Virgil's Herd	12/14/2017
34	Marsh's Valley	01/01/2018
35	Alex Paine	01/18/2018
36	Ben Gray	02/05/2018
37	War Adams	03/05/2018